**More praise for Edie Claire
and the Leigh Koslow mystery series**

Never Buried

"Funny, fast-paced, clever. . . . Edie Claire writes
with style and dash, creating characters with
real pains, aches, fears, and foibles."
—Carolyn Hart,
author of *The Death on Demand*
and *Henrie O Mysteries*

"A thoroughly delightful debut. Bright, breezy,
and witty. I couldn't put it down."
—Tamar Myers,
author of *The Crepes of Wrath*

"*Never Buried* kept me up until 2 A.M. Leigh
Koslow is a great addition to the ranks of
amateur detectives. The setting was a welcome
change." Sandstrom,
of *The Smoking Gun*

ength of the story is
haracters."
—*Pittsburgh Magazine*

D1359947

Never Sorry

"A provocative puzzler with a real grabber of an ending. You'll never look at a zoo the same way again." —Selma Eichler, author of
Murder Can Upset Your Mother

"Along with appealing characters and a blessedly lucid writing style, Edie Claire delivers a solid plot that keeps the pages turning. *Never Sorry* is ever entertaining." —Margaret Maron,
author of *Home Fires*

"Leigh Koslow makes for an engaging heroine who is believable enough for any reader to identify with. *Never Sorry* is a fun mystery with unexpected twists and turns."
—Jessica Speart,
author of *Bird Brained*

"A witty tale peopled with very amusing characters. Claire does a fine job in plotting and the solution to the mystery is bound to surprise you."
—*Romantic Times*

Never Preach Past Noon

ALSO BY EDIE CLAIRE

Never Buried
Never Sorry
Never Preach Past Noon

NEVER KISSED GOODNIGHT

A Leigh Koslow Mystery

Edie Claire

A SIGNET BOOK

SIGNET
Published by New American Library, a division of
Penguin Putnam Inc., 375 Hudson Street,
New York, New York 10014, U.S.A.
Penguin Books Ltd, 27 Wrights Lane,
London W8 5TZ, England
Penguin Books Australia Ltd, Ringwood,
Victoria, Australia
Penguin Books Canada Ltd, 10 Alcorn Avenue,
Toronto, Ontario, Canada M4V 3B2
Penguin Books (N.Z.) Ltd, 182–190 Wairau Road,
Auckland 10, New Zealand

Penguin Books Ltd, Registered Offices:
Harmondsworth, Middlesex, England

First Published by Signet, an imprint of New American Library,
a division of Penguin Putnam Inc.

First Signet Printing, October 2001
10 9 8 7 6 5 4 3 2 1

PUBLISHER'S NOTE
This is a work of fiction. Names, characters, places, and incidents either
are the product of the author's imagination or are used fictitiously,
and any resemblance to actual persons, living or dead, business
establishments, events, or locales is entirely coincidental.

ACKNOWLEDGMENTS

As always, thanks are gratefully extended to those who have answered my endless questions about police procedure and the law, including Siri and Joe Jeffrey and Scott Robinette. I would also like to mention that I have totally forgiven Ellen Bowermaster for beating me out of that Erin Walton role in 1979. Really.

Chapter 1

It was cold, there was an annoying sound coming from somewhere, and Leigh wanted both things to go away. It had been frigid the last few days—unfairly so for early November, even in Pittsburgh. And though her first few months of marriage had, for the most part, been delightedly blissful, the war over the thermostat remained contentious. Case in point: it was 5:00 a.m., her warm-blooded husband was sound asleep, and she was freezing to death. Evidently her covert 11:00 p.m. adjustment had not been the last.

She pulled the covers up tight under her chin and muttered into her pillow. She could get out of bed and turn up the heat, of course, but that would mean getting colder before she got warmer. It would also require rousing herself to full consciousness, which was even less appealing. Instead she snuggled closer to Warren J. Harmon III, who wrapped his arm around her obligingly, despite the elbow that jabbed absently into his ribs. She was just getting comfortably warm again when the sound—long since forgotten—repeated itself.

Reluctantly, she disengaged the warm arm and sat up. Someone was knocking on the apartment door.

She shook her head to clear the cobwebs. A knock on the door in the predawn hours. No preceding buzzer. There were two choices. It was either a neighbor from the complex or a family member to whom she had foolishly entrusted the building key. The gentle rapping came again, this time in a uniquely modified rendition of "shave and a haircut."

Cara? Leigh swung her feet over the side of the bed with a shiver. Nobody but her cousin could recreate their childhood code so perfectly. And Cara did have a key to the building, though not to Warren's apartment. Only to Leigh's bachelorette pad cum storage unit upstairs, which she couldn't afford to part with until their house hunt was over.

So what was her cousin doing here?

Leigh grabbed a fuzzy bathrobe from her closet and went to open the door, adjusting the thermostat on the way. Cara March drifted in with an almost ethereal air, her long, strawberry-blond hair flowing unchecked around her china-doll face and shoulders. She looked at Leigh apologetically, then spoke in a whisper. "I'm sorry. I didn't wake Warren too, did I?"

"Not much does," Leigh answered groggily. Only after she had blinked a few more times did she notice her cousin's red-rimmed eyes and streaked cheeks. "Are you all right?" she asked quickly. She knew plenty of women who went half their lives with tear-stained faces, but her cousin wasn't one of them. She was more the type to blunder into a hornet's nest and insist she was having fun.

Cara nodded. "I'm fine, really. I know you must think I've lost my mind—coming here in the middle of the night like this, but I just wondered if . . . well, if we could talk."

Leigh gave her cousin a long, considered look, then made a beeline for the coffeemaker. Warren had given her a nice one with a timer for her thirty-first birthday, but since waiting three more hours for caffeine wasn't an option, she shut off the autopilot and hit BREW with a vengeance. "Sure," she said mildly. "What are cousins for? Just give me two swallows before I have to be coherent, okay?"

Cara laughed awkwardly and slipped into a kitchen chair. "It's the least I can do, isn't it? I am sorry. Barging in on newlyweds when they've barely had their six month anniversary—I should be shot." A smile spread over her face. "I still can't believe that whirlwind wedding of yours. No notice, no frills. If your mom didn't like Warren so much, she'd have had a cow."

Leigh grinned. "You know I hate a fuss. Besides, Warren refused to live in sin, and I'm not a patient person."

Her cousin grinned back, no doubt still amused by how long Leigh had insisted she and her old college buddy were just friends. Though Cara had been quite vocal in her suspicions otherwise at the time, she had so far managed to refrain from I-told-you-sos. Extreme niceness was just one of several traits that made Cara hard to hate, despite the fact that she was both smart and gorgeous.

The cover-girl face turned penitent again. "I don't intend to make a habit out of this again. Really, I don't."

Leigh waved a hand dismissively, remembering how, when growing up in brick row houses side by side, she and her cousin used to lean out over the alley in the middle of the night and tap on each other's second-story windows with fishing poles. They had shared all their dreams and nightmares, and in later years, detailed accounts of their dates. In the latter category, of course, only Cara had had much to talk about.

Their after-hours chats had eventually converted to phone calls, which Cara made first from the Rhode

Island School of Design, then later from Manhattan, where her career as a graphic artist had blossomed. Leigh had stayed in Pittsburgh, graduating from the city university and enjoying a considerably less flourishing career as an advertising copywriter. Despite their separation, however, Leigh had remained her cousin's chief confidant up until a few years ago, when Cara had returned to Pittsburgh a happily married woman. Then the nighttime conferences had ceased.

Until now.

Leigh looked at her cousin worriedly. Flawless bone structure aside, there were rather ghastly looking bags under Cara's eyes, and her peaches-and-cream complexion was unusually sallow. "Are you sure you're all right?" she asked again. "Where are Gil and Mathias?"

Cara's eyes glimmered heavily with mother guilt, then fixed on her hands. "They're home together. Mathias is sleeping like an angel, I'm sure." Her face hardened. "As for Gil, he's probably pacing the floor, wondering when I'll come home."

Leigh's own eyes widened. Such reckless disregard on Cara's part for the feelings of her sainted husband was definitely a red flag. The world's most obnoxiously happy couple having a lover's quarrel? She glanced desperately at the coffeemaker, which chugged along at a snail's pace, oblivious to her distress. Resisting the urge to position her mouth under the spigot, she instead stuck a soup spoon into the stream and brought a few precious drops to her lips. Time must be bought.

"It's just—" Cara began more weakly, her voice cracking. "It's just that—I can't talk to him anymore."

Leigh inhaled two more spoonfuls of coffee before

settling down at the table. So Gil was in the dog-house. What on earth could he have done? Granted, his primitive machismo and total lack of humor had never endeared him to Leigh, but aside from that, he was pretty near perfect. Rich, gorgeous, successful, generous—and absolutely crazy about his wife and son. "What do you mean, you can't talk to him?"

Cara shifted her gaze from her hands to the table-top. "He's hiding something from me."

Leigh sat still, her mind performing a little psycho-logical triage. Cara had always trusted Gil implicitly, and even Leigh had never doubted his integrity where his wife was concerned. Perhaps Cara was ov-erreacting to something? It was no secret that all the women in Leigh's family—excluding herself, of course—were prone to melodrama. This could all be about something as innocent as a surprise party.

"Gil loves you very much," she assured her cousin confidently. "You must have just misunderstood something."

Cara's watery, sea-green eyes turned on her cousin resentfully. "No, I didn't. He's been lying to me. You think I wouldn't know?"

Leigh didn't answer. Perhaps a simple misunder-standing couldn't explain it. That sort of thing hap-pened to couples who passed in the night, but Cara and Gil had a rare marriage—they actually talked to each other. If she had a suspicion, she would con-front him outright. And if he was still evasive . . .

She got up and quickly emptied the coffee pot into her cup, heedless of the thin stream of liquid that ran down onto the burner with a hiss. It would evaporate eventually. She sat back down and took a long swig.

"Tell me what happened," she said gently.

Cara rubbed her hands roughly over the corners of her eyes, resentful of the traitorous moisture. She cleared her throat. "It started a week or so ago. You know we have a post office box; since we bought Snow Creek Farm, he's been very careful—almost paranoid—about keeping our address private. He usually picks up the mail on his way home from work, but I have a key too, and if I'm out in the morning, I'll go ahead and get it. But when I went in last Friday, he'd already been there. And he did the same thing Monday and Tuesday."

Cara paused, and Leigh took a few more drags of coffee, hoping it would help the story make more sense.

"Don't you see?" Cara continued, frustrated. "He leaves for work long before the mail is put out. But he's been making a point of doubling back to pick it up before I get there. *Every day.*"

Leigh continued to stare at her dumbly. "So he was waiting for something he didn't want you to see. That could be anything. A present."

Cara shook her head. "Wednesday I planned to be there even *before* they put the mail out. I caught him in the act."

"And?"

"And I accused him point-blank of trying to hide something. I wasn't even upset then, I felt more like—well, you know, like I was playing detective."

Leigh did know, only too well. Her cousin had never seemed to grow out of the Nancy Drew phase, perhaps because both Cara and the fictional girl detective were pretty redheads.

"I really thought it *was* a present of some sort," Cara continued. "He gives me such wonderful surprises all the time, you know."

Leigh nodded quickly. She had heard already—as had anyone else with whom her cousin had a passing acquaintance.

"But his reaction—it shocked me. He looked almost scared at first, then he got angry. Like *I* was doing something wrong. Then just as quickly, he got all apologetic and said that I was right, that he was expecting a present for me. He told me not to check the box until he'd said it had come."

"Well then," Leigh said optimistically. "Problem solved, right?"

Cara looked at her sadly, but patiently. "He was lying. I could tell as soon as the words were out of his mouth. He was nervous and uncomfortable— there was no present. Whatever he was hiding, it was something big. And bad."

Leigh gave her cousin another long, considered look, then slowly let out a breath. She hated to admit it, but it did sound like trouble. "Maybe he's protecting you from some unpleasant news," she said sensibly.

"I thought that too," Cara continued, struggling to keep her voice from wavering. "And I questioned him about it. But if the IRS was after us, if his business was being sued, if we were suddenly broke, we could deal with it together. He knows perfectly well that I'm not breakable—I'm as good in a crisis as he is. But he wouldn't talk, no matter how hard I pressed him. And if it was just bad news, I'm telling you—he would have cracked."

Leigh looked away. It was clear to anyone else who breathed that Cara's husband, despite his professions of admiration for his wife's "independent streak," was overprotective as hell. But now wasn't the time to argue about it. "So what do you think he was doing?" she asked cautiously.

Cara's eyes fixed on the tabletop again. "I think it's something about him. He feels guilty about something he's done—or is doing. And he's afraid if I know, I'll hate him."

Leigh didn't care for the direction her cousin's thoughts were taking. Cara might be melodramatic, but paranoia was not in her nature. And even though the mail-snatching situation was disturbing, it hardly seemed drastic enough to justify a middle-of-the-night exodus. "There's more, isn't there?" she asked softly.

Cara swallowed, then nodded. "Wednesday night—after I confronted him—he was late getting home from work. He said he had important business to finish up, but I thought he was just avoiding me. So I packed up Matt and went to his office."

She paused a moment. "He wasn't there. No one was. It was locked up tight. He's never lied about where he was going before." Her eyes misted over again, and Leigh excused herself to get more coffee. She put on the tea kettle as well—a weepy guest had to be served something.

Cara blinked her eyes stubbornly and continued. "He didn't come home till almost eight o'clock. I should have asked him where he'd been, but I couldn't. I didn't want to admit I'd checked up on him. And he was so sweet that evening—he put Mathias to bed, then made popcorn and watched *Sleepless in Seattle* with me. He hates that movie. I just—I couldn't say anything."

Leigh couldn't help but think of all the cheating husbands she had seen or read about who did nice things for their wives to assuage a guilty conscience. She shook her head in denial. No way. She would never believe Gil was seeing another woman. Why on earth would he, when his own wife was such a knockout? And even if she wasn't, he really did love her. She was sure of it.

"Cara—" Leigh began, but her cousin cut her off with a head shake.

"You haven't heard the rest. Earlier today—I mean yesterday, Friday—he called again from work and said he'd be late. He apologized, but said that if I could wait till eight-thirty to eat, he'd bring home something special. I couldn't stand it, Leigh. I had to know where he was going. So I took Matt out again and waited for him to leave the office. Then I followed him."

Leigh began to get a sick feeling in her stomach, but she finished off her coffee anyway.

"He drove to an apartment complex in Shadyside. An upscale one. It didn't have any businesses in it, just residences. He parked and started toward the front door. That's when he saw me."

Leigh's eyebrows rose. Although anyone with an iota of feminine perception could tell Gil didn't have a violent bone in his body, he was hardly what you would call even-tempered. The fact that he was not above flexing his muscles for emphasis was something she could personally vouch for, and his righteous indignation routine was particularly tedious. "What happened?" she asked hesitantly.

"Nothing, really," Cara answered calmly. "He looked angry at first, but by the time he got to the car, he seemed more sad. He got in with me, and we talked for a long time. He was very understanding."

It sounded like a happy ending, but clearly it couldn't have been. "What did he say?"

"He said that he was having legal problems and was meeting with an old friend of his who was a lawyer. The last part at least was true—I've met the man, but I didn't know where he lived."

"Did he say what the problems were? Why he was hiding them from you?"

Cara grimaced. "He had a story prepared for me, yes. But it wasn't true. And don't ask me how I know—I just do. It was perfectly plausible in every way. But he was lying to me, Leigh. I'm sure of it."

The tea kettle whistled, and Leigh hastened to pour her cousin a cup of chamomile. Personally, she loathed the stuff, which was why she had a stockpile culled from variety packs. But it was supposed to be soothing, and that sounded appropriate. She brought the cup to the table and sat back down. "He must have a good reason for lying, then," she said helplessly.

"I'm sure he thinks he does. But that's not good enough. After our talk, he went into the apartment building anyway. I took Matt home and put him to bed. As soon as Gil got back, I told him I needed to think, and I left."

Leigh's eyes widened. "You've been out all night?"

Cara nodded. "I went to Mom's for a while. She's still on her trip, you know. I just sat on her couch, thinking. Gil called there right away—but I kept the phone off the hook until I was ready to leave. Then I came here."

The shrill sound of her own telephone ringing interrupted Leigh's next comment, and she rose quickly to answer it. Warren was a deep sleeper, but he wasn't dead. "Yes?" she said, knowing full well who she would be talking to.

A slightly shaky man's voice answered. "Leigh? It's Gil. Please tell me Cara is there." The heartfelt anxiety in the voice won Leigh's empathy, even if she wasn't entirely sure it was deserved. "She's here," she assured him quickly.

The sigh of relief on the other end of the line was audible. "Thank God. Can I talk to her?"

Leigh glanced at Cara, who shook her head firmly.

"Tell him I'll be home before Mathias wakes up," she said coolly.

"She's fine, Gil," Leigh answered, using a little license in translation. "She says for you not to worry and that she'll be home for Matt's breakfast. Okay?"

The pause on the other end of the line was long. "She still won't talk to me," he said miserably. "I see. Just tell her I love her then, okay?"

"Will do."

"And Leigh," he continued as she started to hang up, "thanks for looking out for her."

She digested the comment with curiosity. Despite Cara's self-reliant air, her oblivious good nature and almost compulsive impulsiveness had always made for trouble. So much so that Leigh had spent most of her childhood trying to shield her cousin—who was not quite two years younger—from everything from stubbed toes to mono. It was a role she hadn't relinquished lightly, even after they had both grown up. But it was a role Cara's white knight of a husband had never appreciated. In fact, he often accused Leigh of getting his wife *into* trouble, which, of course, was entirely unjustified. So why was he thanking her now?

Guilty conscience. "No problem," Leigh answered carefully. She said good-bye and hung up. "He sounded very worried about you," she told Cara honestly. "I really think you should go home now."

Cara shook her head and took a sip of chamomile. "I need to ask a favor. Will you do it?"

Leigh's stomach got heavier. It was just like her cousin to want a commitment before the explanation. And if the seriousness of Cara's tone was any indication, the "favor" sounded loaded. "Do what?" she asked hesitantly.

"Matt has a swimming class tomorrow—I mean,

later this morning—at the high school. Afterwards, some of the other moms and toddlers have arranged to eat lunch together up in Wexford. Gil knows I'll be gone a long time."

Leigh could see where the request was going. She could also see that it was a fool's errand, to say the least. But saying no to relatives in need had never been her forte.

"I want you to follow Gil. See where he goes, who he talks to. I can't do it myself; he'll be looking for me. But he won't be looking for you—I'll convince him everything's okay when I get home. Then you can find out what's really going on."

Leigh exhaled uncomfortably. "Are you sure you two can't just talk this out?"

Cara shook her head. "I told you—I tried that. He lied to me." She paused, and her lower lip quivered slightly. "I don't want to think it might be—" The calm, detached demeanor she had been fighting to keep finally crumbled, and her eyes teared up with a vengeance. "It can't be another woman, Leigh. It just can't. You've got to find out for me. Anything else, I can deal with. Anything."

Leigh reached out an arm and squeezed her cousin by the shoulders, her protective instincts coming on strong. It was as though she were ten again, and Leroy Budnick had just bent the wheel of Cara's brand new bicycle because she wouldn't let him pop wheelies with it. Leroy Budnick had regretted that move, she remembered with a smirk. *Nobody* made her little cousin cry.

"It's not another woman," she said soothingly. "It's not. Gil loves you, and he's just trying to protect you from something. I'm sure of it."

She *was* sure of it, she thought to herself determinedly. And she was going to prove it.

Chapter 2

Try as she might to rationalize her actions, when Leigh found herself drumming her fingers on the dashboard of her Cavalier later that morning, parked at an odd angle off the mouth of a side road near Cara's farm, she couldn't help feeling a little ridiculous. In the movies, stakeouts always managed to occur near convenient alleys, where one could be suitably inconspicuous. She just looked like some schmuck who had pulled off to fix her makeup and gotten stuck in the mud.

She wasn't certain, for that matter, that she *wasn't* stuck in the mud. It had rained for days, and the wet ground that had stiffened overnight was probably thawing as she sat. Trying to convince herself that she could not actually feel the car sinking, she mulled over her options.

She couldn't move anywhere else—there was no other place where she could keep an eye on the end of Cara's driveway without being plainly visible to Gil at some point on his way out. All but the last of the oaks had lost their leaves, leaving precious little coverage for a bright white car on a rainy day. As it was, if he turned toward her on Snow Creek Road, she'd have to backpedal fast to look as if she'd just come up on the intersection, and even then he could still notice her. He'd seen her car before, after all, and if he was the least bit suspicious . . .

She sighed. It was a risk she had to take. She would have liked to borrow another car, but Warren's neon-blue Beetle and her father's wreck of a station wagon were even more conspicuous, and her mother and aunts were off trekking through India to fulfill their lifelong shared fantasy of seeing the Taj Mahal. Leigh still had a hard time imagining her mother in a boat on the Ganges, but Lydie and Bess had somehow managed to talk her into it, minus the optional excursion to Katmandu, of course. Canoes, Frances drew the line at.

A shiny Lexus suddenly sidled up beside the Cavalier, and the middle-aged man inside threw Leigh a glare as he was forced to push his car's nose out onto the road in order to see around her. Looking sheepishly at her steering wheel, Leigh wondered how much longer her resolve would last. It had been twenty minutes since Cara left with Matt—surely if Gil had clandestine plans, he would have left the farm by now.

She jumped as an immense SUV rattled up noisily and took off from beside her after barely slowing down. The soccer mom inside wasn't the least bit fazed by the oddly parked car, which, after all, was well below her line of sight. But the distraction almost cost Leigh her cover, because while she sat choking on fumes, Gil's car was pulling up the farm's driveway. By the time she noticed the purple Saturn, it had already pulled out onto Snow Creek Road and was headed her way.

She threw the Cavalier into reverse and was gratified to find herself back on pavement with only a minimum of wheel spinning and mud splattering. But by the time she looked forward again, the Saturn was gone. Had he seen her as he passed? He certainly could have, but she chose to assume otherwise. The car must have been going pretty fast—and he probably had something important on his mind.

After a few seconds' pause, she pulled out on the road after him, doing a quick mental run-through of her plan. Unfortunately, what had seemed perfectly logical after her third cup of predawn coffee seemed considerably weaker now that her stomach was rumbling for lunch. The car-trailing business, she had come to realize, was not as simple as it looked on TV. Sure, she could try to stay a discreet distance behind him, but since he knew the Cavalier, she'd have to keep a few cars between them. And if traffic thinned, she'd have to drop way back, where she would stand a good chance of losing him.

Even if she could determine where he was going, there was no guarantee that his travels had anything to do with the secret he was keeping from Cara. And if she got caught, she would once again be at the mercy of his macho chest-beating routine. Not that she could blame him—she'd certainly be ticked if she found a purple Saturn trailing her around on a Saturday—but that wasn't the issue. Her mission was to help her cousin get some peace of mind, and she was going to give it a try, come what may.

The first intersections went well. A steady stream of traffic met them at Perry Highway, and she was able to stay behind him easily as they cruised south past the usual mix of new buildings and residences-turned-commercial that marked the suburban expansion of a once-sleepy corridor. Her heart leapt in her chest a little each time they approached a cross street. Was he going to someone's house? Northway Mall? Foodland?

She breathed a sigh of relief as they passed the

turnoff to the latter, since following someone else around on a grocery run would be even more humiliating than getting her Cavalier stuck in the mud. But Gil's trek down the well-worn suburban corridor continued unabated all the way into Perrysville, where the four-lane road abruptly narrowed to two. Too late, Leigh realized that she'd come out of the last intersection directly behind the Saturn. She slowed down worriedly, but they got a lucky break— a minivan trying to turn onto the road in front of her. She stopped and waved it ahead, regaining her cover.

As Gil trolled on down into West View, she followed more cautiously, and as he passed the bulk of the business district, her brow furrowed. Where on earth could he be going? He'd already passed two turnoffs to Interstate 279, which was the quickest way to get anywhere near Pittsburgh proper. Besides residences, there wasn't much else south of them that couldn't have been reached more easily by going another way.

It wasn't until she caught the back of the Saturn turning onto Ridgeview Avenue that Leigh began to get it. He *was* going to a residence. But not that of a paramour. Only the densest man would step out on the same street his mother-in-law lived on.

Leigh turned onto Ridgeview and slowed down to a crawl, careful not to get within sight of Gil's rearview mirror. Having grown up on the street was a definite advantage, she thought with a smile. She stopped just before the road took a sharp bend and parked alongside the curb. The Cavalier would be out of sight from her aunt Lydie's house, and she could approach on foot. It was perfect.

She watched from the corner with satisfaction as Gil, two thirds of a block away and none the wiser, sprinted up his mother-in-law's front steps, turned a key in the door, and disappeared inside. She was hurrying down the sidewalk after him when she was accosted by a rusty, aged voice.

"Leigh Koslow? That you, girl?"

She looked up at the familiar sight of one Dorothy Snodgrass, who despite the dismal weather was settled comfortably on her porch swing, swathed in cheap blankets and sipping tea from a Steelers coffee mug. Knowing Dorothy, an unusually resourceful widow in her seventies, the tea was probably spiked.

Leigh smiled. "Mrs. Snodgrass! Yes, it's me. But you shouldn't be out on a day like today. It's miserable out here."

The older woman smiled broadly, revealing dentures that had seen more tea than Boston Harbor. "Well, now, missy, seems like I'm the one with the blankets."

Leigh noted, without looking down, that she had indeed forgotten to put her jacket on. Thrill of the chase and all that. "Touché," she acknowledged. "How have you been?"

"Good as ever," the woman answered succinctly. Dorothy Snodgrass had never been a complainer, which made her one of the more popular Ridgeview retirees. That and her proclivity for baking cookies had won her the admiration of more than one generation of Ridgeview children. "I've got some M&Ms inside, don't you know," she said, cocking her head enticingly. "And this tea's mighty good for a grown-up."

Definitely spiked. "Thanks, Mrs. Snodgrass," Leigh said with honest regret, "but I'm afraid I can't stop, even for your M&M cookies. I'm on a mission."

The older woman's brow furrowed, and she leaned over to peer down the street in the direction Leigh had been walking. "That *is* Lydie's son-in-law just went in up there, isn't it?"

Mrs. Snodgrass's powers of observation came as no surprise. For the last forty years she'd been a one-woman neighborhood watch patrol, and she did a darned good job of it too—having thwarted more than one would-be burglar and rescued several children from abuse. But though Mrs. Snodgrass knew everyone and everything that happened on the street, no one considered her a snoop. Because in addition to having a good heart, she had the good sense to know when to keep her mouth shut.

"Yes, that's Cara's husband," Leigh answered. "Nothing to worry about."

Mrs. Snodgrass smiled knowingly and lifted her wrinkled hands in the air. "Fine enough, then. You have a nice mission, young lady. And next time," she added, tapping the mug with a smirk, "leave time for the good stuff."

Leigh smiled and promised she would, wishing some of the good stuff were in her belly already. She was cold and getting colder, but had no intention of backtracking to get her coat. She'd made her bed—she'd lie in it.

As she approached her aunt Lydie's house with chattering teeth, she made a point of noting two things in favor of her spy junket. One, the day was sufficiently dark and dismal that she would easily be able to see through the windows into any lighted rooms inside. Two, she had no fears of being spotted by her parents next door. Her father worked every Saturday morning at his veterinary practice in Avalon, and her mother—conveniently enough—was on the other side of the world.

She slunk up to the side of her aunt's house and positioned herself amidst the rhododendrons. The living room windows were fairly high above the ground, but she found that with her adult height, she could just peer over the ledge. Gil was inside all right, though why, she couldn't imagine.

His tall, GQ form was in the process of rooting through Lydie's prized antique secretary, opening drawers and peering into the myriad of tiny cubbies. She frowned. What could Lydie possibly have that he would look for without either her—or Cara's—knowledge?

Leigh continued to watch as Gil made short work of the secretary and moved on to some of the other pieces of furniture. Papers seemed to interest him, and when he ran into an old stack of yellowed newspapers in the bottom drawer of a china cabinet, he pored over them intently. But whatever he was searching for, he seemed unable to find it. Stack by stack he pulled out papers and loose pictures, sifted through them, then put them neatly back in place. Finally, the living room furniture having been exhausted, he headed up the staircase.

Feeling in her pocket for her keys, Leigh slipped across the narrow stretch of side yard and up onto her parents' back porch. Warren might make fun of her ten-ton key ring—all the contents of which she would be hard-pressed to identify—but it was certainly coming in handy now. She opened the door and walked into her parents' house, careful not to switch on any lights. She reached her old bedroom at a run, knowing she'd have a good view of Cara's former room as long as the blinds weren't down.

But a quick inspection of the dark room across the alley indicated that his wife's old bedroom was not on the top of Gil's search list. It was Lydie's bedroom that was lit. Leigh moved quickly to what was now her mother's sewing room and was pleased to find she had a straight shot at Gil through her aunt's open curtains. She couldn't see the whole room, but she could see enough to know that he was concentrating on the closet.

Looking frustrated and generally awkward, Gil pushed aside dresses and rooted through a variety of organizers, opening anything that didn't look as if it contained clothes. Leigh could only stare in puzzlement. What kind of papers could Gil possibly be looking for? And why would he think Lydie would keep them in her closet?

She thought about it for more than half an hour, as Gil restlessly filtered through Lydie's bureau and chest of drawers, then disappeared to search other places Leigh couldn't see. From the procession of lights, however, she could tell that he covered every room, including the attic and the basement, before finishing up in the kitchen. Back outside in the cold, she fervently wished that whatever it was, he would just find the thing and get it over with, but it wasn't to be. Looking utterly exhausted, Gil finally sank into a kitchen chair and laid his head on his hands.

She watched him curiously. As the hunt had wound down, his expression had grown increasingly distraught, but she didn't get the idea that he was surprised by the failure. The whole rampage had seemed more like an act of desperation—a shot in the dark. Did he even know himself what he was looking for?

After a long moment, he lifted his head and gazed idly at the pile of accumulated mail on the table that someone—undoubtedly Leigh's father—had been collecting for Lydie while she was on vacation. He was sifting slowly through the pile when his hands froze, his eyes locking on something in the stack. He hesitated only a moment before ripping it open.

Leigh watched anxiously, trying to see what had caught his attention, but she could tell only that he had pulled a sheet of paper from a hand-addressed, letter-sized envelope. Her heartbeat quickened as Gil's face paled and his hazel eyes widened.

He rose from the table in one furious motion, his arm swinging the letter in the air and bringing it down on the table with a vengeance. His words were muffled, but Leigh got the gist, even if she'd never heard anyone use that particular four-letter combination before. Whatever it was, it was bad.

He shoved the paper and envelope into his pocket and stormed out of the kitchen toward the front door, and Leigh took off like a shot. If he was ready to leave, she would have to make it to her car in double time in order not to be seen. And in order to keep following him.

She had made it only as far as Mrs. Snodgrass's house when he emerged, and catching a glimpse of him over her shoulder, she quickly dodged behind the generous girth of an old maple tree, breathing heavily. "Stay there, honey," Mrs. Snodgrass said quietly from her swing. "He didn't see you."

Leigh listened for the sound of the Saturn's engine starting up, but heard nothing. "Where did he go?" she asked breathlessly.

Mrs. Snodgrass rocked back and forth casually. "He's knocking over at your folks'," she answered. "Of course, we both know nobody's going to answer."

Leigh started to step out from behind the tree, but the older woman quickly waved her back. "Not yet— he's on his way back to his car now." After a moment, she continued. "All right, he's inside. You'd better start off now or you'll lose him."

Leigh opened her mouth in thanks, but Mrs. Snodgrass cut her off. "I'll expect you to come by another time and tell me all about it," she instructed with amusement, "but for now—off with you. Hurry!"

Gil's Saturn took off like a bat out of hell, and Leigh thought for sure she would lose him. But the traffic in West View was conveniently heavy, and as he was forced to slow down, she found she could trail him at a reasonable distance. They waited through a long succession of stoplights, during which she tried to make sense of her cousin-in-law's bizarre actions. He had clearly gone to Lydie's house looking for something, but whatever it was, she didn't think it was the letter. The mail was plainly visible on the table, and he hadn't seemed the least bit interested in it on his first pass through the kitchen. He'd been looking for something else—something he suspected would be hidden. Perhaps the letter was another problem altogether.

The Saturn kept weaving closer and closer to the north side of the Ohio River, and Leigh followed in surprise as she realized where he was going. They were in Avalon, approaching the Koslow Animal Clinic. First he had knocked on her parents' door; now he was here. He wanted to talk to her father. But why?

She pulled over to the side of the steep, cobblestone street, planning to let him park and go in first, but once again he surprised her. The Saturn cruised slowly past the back of the clinic as if surveying the crowded parking area, hesitated, then moved on. Leigh sighed and took off after it once more. Of course her father would be busy with clients on a Saturday morning. What did Gil expect? Surely if it was some sort of emergency . . .

Her thoughts were interrupted by panic as she lost her quarry at a stoplight on the borough's main drag, California Avenue. When the light flashed green, she pursued it as best she could, but speeding in Avalon was never a good idea. Pedestrians were out and about even in the lousiest weather, and the rough cobblestone streets could take years off a car's suspension. Figuring he'd probably headed back to I-279, she took that route herself, but the Saturn was nowhere to be seen.

Defeated and confused, she drove back up to Ross Township and parked in front of her apartment building. It was time for some food—and to wait for Cara's inevitable phone call. What she would report, however, she had no idea.

She was almost at the front door when she stopped cold. Gil's car was right before her eyes again, sitting placidly in one of the coveted visitor's spots.

Chapter 3

The Saturn wasn't empty. Gil sat with his head on the headrest, staring out into space. But when he caught sight of her, he got out quickly.

"Leigh!" he called pleasantly. "I almost missed you."

She watched in puzzlement as he came toward her. First he had been looking for her dad; now, oddity of oddities, he appeared to be looking for her. Ironic, that, but she wasn't knocking it. At least he seemed to have no clue she'd been behind him all morning.

"Gil," she answered, trying her best to sound casual. "What's up? Have you been waiting long?"

He shook his full head of sandy blond hair and smiled at her with perfect teeth. Years ago, his chiseled California-surfer look had wreaked havoc on her hormones, but their one and only date had mercifully diminished the effect. They had met through the ad agency she worked for, and she had been flabbergasted when he asked her out to dinner at Top of the Triangle, a downtown Pittsburgh eatery with a view to die for. Back when she was an idiot, his good looks and gladiator complex had seemed a dream come true. But they hadn't even made it to their entrees before she realized that the man who had everything had everything *but* a sense of humor, which was, of course, a fatal flaw. By dessert she had off-handedly referred him to Cara for design work, and the rest was history.

"I'm glad I caught you," he continued, accompanying her into the lobby and onto the elevator. His smooth tenor voice turned serious. "I was hoping you had a few minutes to talk."

Leigh assured him that she did, and the two were soon settled on the couch in her apartment, sipping Diet Cokes. He had refused any food, but she, unwilling to starve for the sake of politeness, dove hungrily into a canister of cheese puffs. She couldn't wait to hear what he had to say, but unfortunately, on reaching the apartment, he seemed to lose his nerve.

"So I guess Warren's not around much these days," he said idly.

She shook her head, her mouth being temporarily full of cheese puffs. "The election's only three days away," she said finally. "He's got a really good chance of winning the District 2 seat, but it'll be close. In the meantime, I'm lucky if he even comes home at night."

She meant the comment as an innocent exaggeration, but its relevance to Gil's predicament made him tense up immediately. He rose from the couch and began to pace. "Thanks for sending Cara home safely last night," he began. "I was worried about her."

"So was I," Leigh responded bluntly, deciding not to pull punches.

He ignored the comment and continued to pace, talking more to himself than to her. "I never expected she would react like this."

Leigh waited a minute for him to say more, then pressed. "What exactly did you expect?"

Gil stopped pacing and stared at her. "I don't

know how much Cara told you, but the fact is, she's upset because I've been keeping something from her. What she doesn't understand is that I have to, because I know what something like this could do to her. I thought I could handle the situation on my own, but now I'm not so sure." He dropped back down on the couch again, his voice sounding defeated. "Everything has suddenly gotten more complicated. And with Lydie out of town, I need your help."

Leigh's mind raced. For a moment she had feared a *Fatal Attraction* scenario, but since she doubted any cheating husband would seek help from his wife's family, she dismissed it. And judging from the look in Gil's eyes, his primary problem at the moment was fear rather than guilt. But how on earth could she or his mother-in-law help?

Eventually she found her voice. "What can I do?"

He exhaled loudly, then fixed her with an intense, hopeful stare. "It's about Mason Dublin."

She stared back, her heart beginning to pound. "Cara's father?"

He nodded. "I need to know everything you can tell me about him. His marriage to Lydie, when he left, why he left, whether he's ever been back, and most importantly—where he might be now."

Leigh sat dumbly for a moment, then found herself glancing furtively around the room, as if checking to make sure no one else had overheard. Mason Dublin had always been a taboo subject in the family, and old habits died hard. But they were all grown-ups now. They could talk about it, couldn't they? It just so happened that ever since Cara had become a grown-up, she hadn't wanted to.

It wasn't a topic to be taken lightly. "Why do you

want to know about Mason?" she asked quietly. "Can't Cara answer your questions?"

Gil let out a frustrated breath and turned away from her. "Come on, Leigh. You know what effect that man's abandonment has had on Cara. Now she's finally reached a point where she seems settled about it, and I don't want to mess that up."

Neither did Leigh. She could remember well the few times her cousin had been genuinely distraught, and the worst by far were directly attributable to Mason Dublin, the father she had never met.

The story had been the same as long as she could remember, neither Cara's mother nor anyone else in the family having ever chosen to sugarcoat it. Lydie had fallen madly in love with a charming young man who sold steak knives door-to-door and had foolishly eloped with him before they really knew each other. Lydie soon realized she had made a mistake, but by then she was pregnant. And though the couple planned to stay together, the marriage didn't last. Mason met someone else, and before his daughter was born he had left, never to be heard from again.

It was tough stuff for a kid, and Cara had done about as well with it as could be expected. But Gil was right; the sense of peace she had gradually developed with the issue was fragile at best. There were too many unresolved questions, too much pain for the subject ever to be buried completely, even by an otherwise emotionally healthy adult.

"Why do you need to bring it up?" Leigh questioned. "Why does it matter now?"

Gil rested his head in his hands for a moment, then took a deep breath and looked up at her. "He called me."

Her heart skipped a beat. Although she had no particular reason to think it, she had always assumed that Mason Dublin must be dead. Perhaps that was what she wanted to be true, for Cara's sake. No matter how lousy a person he might have been, a dead father seemed easier to deal with than a live one who was capable of redemption—but didn't give a damn.

When she said nothing, Gil continued. "The call came in at the office. I've had a fair number of crank calls, ever since that accursed television show aired. My secretary has been screening them, but when the caller said he was my father-in-law, she thought she'd better put him through, just in case."

The show. The connection occurred to Leigh with the force of a freight train, and a wave of fear shot through her as she realized Gil's claim could be true.

"The show" was, in her humble opinion, a debacle of monumental proportion. It was also entirely Cara's fault. When *Movers and Shakers* had approached Gil about devoting a segment to his meteoric rise to riches, he had turned them down flat. The show wasn't as cheesy as some, and it did take the moral high ground of profiling people who had worked their way to the top the good old-fashioned way, as opposed to those who happened to be born with a big bank account, a great body, or a knack at playing the lotto. But it was exploitation nevertheless, and Gil had no interest in it.

Cara, on the other hand, had thought the whole idea perfectly marvelous. The idea of national television exposure thrilled her to no end, and she had harassed her husband mercilessly until he had agreed to do the show. When it aired two weeks before, she had been giddy with delight, proud as punch of her entrepreneurial hubby. The rest of the family—particularly Gil himself—were less enthused, finding such large-scale notoriety unsettling at best.

Gil was adamant that no scenes be shot at the suburban farm where the Marches lived, but Cara herself did make the cut, along with little Matt. The show had mentioned Cara's success as a graphic artist and even delved into their marriage a bit—the latter intrusion, again, being no one's fault but Cara's own. The consummate optimist had merely shrugged off her husband's embarrassment as modesty and set about making multiple videotapes to preserve for perpetuity.

Leigh had never even considered that a live-and-kicking Mason Dublin might be among the millions who happened to tune in that night. Neither, evidently, had anyone else.

"What did he say?" she asked weakly.

Gil swallowed, looking distinctly uncomfortable. "Not what you might expect, I'm afraid. He started off by introducing himself and asking if I was surprised to hear from him. But then he cut right to the chase. He wanted to know how much I knew about my mother-in-law."

Leigh blinked. "He what?"

"He was intentionally vague," Gil continued soberly. "But he was hinting that Lydie had some deep dark secret, something that could ruin her—and possibly Cara's—life. And he was testing me out to see if I knew about it." His eyes slid up to Leigh's expectantly, but hers remained suitably blank.

"Are you kidding?" she asked defensively. "Of course I've never heard of anything. Lydie's an angel and an open book besides. What gives?"

Gil rose and groaned in frustration. "There must be *something*, Leigh," he said quietly, his voice turning grave. "Because whatever it is, he seemed very sure I'd be willing to pay to keep it quiet."

Blood rushed quickly up into Leigh's face, and her cheeks burned. For a moment, she was speechless.

She simply sat, listening to the beating of her own heart. "Cara's father called because—" she faltered. "Because he wanted to blackmail you?"

Gil's eyes bore into her own. "You got it."

Chapter 4

Leigh felt unable to process how bad Gil's news really was. Not only was Mason Dublin alive, he was even more of a scoundrel than she had imagined.

And if Cara knew, it would kill her.

"How did he leave it with you?" she asked finally, setting aside the cheese puffs. Not only was her appetite gone, but what she'd eaten earlier was threatening a reappearance.

"He said that if I didn't know what he was talking about, I should ask my mother-in-law," Gil answered tightly. "And he said he'd make contact again in a few days. He didn't say how, though, and I was worried that he might get to Cara first. We just had our unlisted number changed at home, so I wasn't concerned about that—but I did keep a watch on the post office box. I didn't think he could get the box number, but I didn't want to take any chances." He sat back down, heavily, on the couch beside Leigh. "I didn't want to believe him—about Lydie," he said more quietly. "I figured there was a good chance he was making the whole thing up. That he'd seen the TV piece and was just trying to figure out a way to cash in on a rich in-law."

"That could be it," she said hopefully.

"Maybe," he continued skeptically. "But if Lydie really doesn't have anything to hide, not only would

Mason get nothing, he'd risk prosecution for trying.
That scheme would only work if he *knew* that Lydie
was out of the country and that I might not be able
to get in touch with her before the payoff was due.
But I can't figure out any way that he could know
about her travel plans—and besides, he wasn't pushing me to deliver. He didn't call back for a week. It
was like he was trying to make me—and probably
Lydie—sweat for a while.

"After the first call, I hired a private investigator
to trace the number from the office's Caller ID records and to try to get a fix on Mason Dublin and
what he's been up to the last thirty years. The PI has
a solid reputation; I found him through an old friend
who's a corporate insurance attorney. I was meeting
him at my friend's place in Shadyside on Wednesday
when Cara followed me."

He paused a moment, obviously reliving the unpleasant marital encounter.

Leigh tried to spare him. "So what did you find
out?"

He exhaled with frustration. "Not enough. The
first call came from a pay phone at an outlet mall
in someplace called Boaz, Alabama. Which might be
helpful, except that the PI couldn't find any other
trace of Mason anywhere near there—at least not in
the last six months. He had managed to track Mason's comings and goings pretty well, all the way
from the sixties up to then, but as of last spring,
the trail simply ended. It's as though Mason Dublin
dropped off the face of the earth."

If only, Leigh thought ruefully. "So he did call
back?"

Gil nodded. "Yesterday. But I was ready for him.
The PI suggested I keep playing dumb, to get all the
information out of him that I could. I tried, but this

time Mason seemed in a hurry to get off the phone. All he said was that he wanted thirty thousand in cash in a McDonald's Happy Meal box in a particular trash can at the bus station downtown. If I didn't produce it, or if something happened and he didn't get home, a buddy would send a letter to the police—revealing everything.''

Leigh swallowed. "And where did that call come from?''

Gil's expression turned grim. "The Greyhound bus station.''

Leigh turned her gaze aside, not wishing him to see the fear in her eyes. Mason Dublin was in Pittsburgh. What Gil was telling her was nothing less than a nightmare—and it was becoming more real every minute. "Did the detective find out anything about Lydie?'' she asked weakly, trying to compose herself. "Any possible explanation?''

He shook his head with frustration. "No, nothing on record. And I was adamant that he not interview anyone in the family—at least not yet. I can't let this get back to Cara—not unless I've absolutely no other choice. You understand.''

She nodded. As much as she would have liked to condemn his covert maneuvering, she knew that, in his place, she would have done the same thing.

"I put off trying to contact Lydie as well,'' he continued, sounding regretful. "As I said, I thought at first it might be a hoax, and I was hoping that with the PI's help, I could handle it without anyone in the family having to know. I hated to ruin the only real vacation Lydie's ever taken. India's a tough place to track a tourist down, even with a good itinerary. I'd be leaving emergency messages with hotels, and we'd be playing phone tag, trying to get a good line through. First she'd have a heart attack thinking something terrible had happened to Cara or Mathias, and then she'd have to hear the real news." Guilt clouded his eyes. "I should have called her anyway, but I was too optimistic about what the PI could find out on his own. Now I've waited too long."

"What do you mean?" Leigh asked, distressed.

"Lydie's already in Nepal, on that wildlife excursion. She and Bess will be spending the next two nights in a jungle lodge—there's no way I can reach them there."

She exhaled slowly, then smiled with hope. "But my mother will be back tomorrow!" she exclaimed. "She decided against the optional extension, remember? And I guarantee Lydie won't have any secrets that her twin couldn't tell you."

Gil smiled politely, but shook his head. "I already tried to reach your mother, and she's en route as we speak, but she won't be back soon enough to help us. Mason was quite specific. The drop-off has to be tonight."

Leigh rose and began to pace in frustration. "So what are you going to do? I can't help you. I haven't a clue if this thing is for real."

"Wait a minute," Gil interrupted. "You haven't heard the whole story yet."

Leigh stopped pacing, but she was too uptight to sit down.

"As soon as Cara left the house this morning, I headed over to Lydie's. I didn't know what I was looking for, but I was desperate. I thought maybe I could find some clue what she was hiding. I didn't, of course."

She felt a small amount of guilt, but tried to ignore it. She could confess that she already knew where he had been today, but what would be the point?

"I did find something I wasn't expecting," he continued, not looking at her. He reached into a pocket and pulled out the crumpled letter he had taken from Lydie's mail stack in the kitchen. "Take a look at this."

Leigh pounced on the letter nervously, spreading it out in her hands. It was written on plain white copy paper, block letters of black ink scribbled in an uncertain—and decidedly unskilled—hand.

Dear Lydie,

Sorry to bug you but I need money and I no you got it now. Else I'll tell everyboddy whut you did. Send to Genrel Delivry in Panama City us name Ed Jones. Five grand for now or Im telling.

Mason

Leigh blinked at the letter for a moment before she could talk. "Us name Ed Jones?" she asked shakily.

"I think he means 'use the name Ed Jones,'" Gil responded. "Whoever 'he' is."

She tried to think, but the wheels in her brain didn't seem to be getting any traction. "It doesn't sound like Mason, does it?" she conjectured. "I mean, I don't know much about him, but whoever wrote this letter sounds borderline illiterate. And why would Mason put the squeeze on you and Lydie both? Surely he assumed you would compare notes."

Gil shook his head. "I don't think it is from Mason. I don't know who the hell it's from. But it was mailed the day after the show aired."

She flipped over the envelope and looked at the postmark. From Panama City, Florida. And the dates matched.

"Good God." She sank down on the couch again, her legs feeling distinctly unreliable. "Another blackmail threat from the deep South. Sounds like Mason's a blabbermouth."

They sat quietly for another moment while Gil extracted the letter from Leigh's hands and put it back in his pocket. "I've got to get this to the PI and see what he thinks," he said finally. "But before we make any plans about what to do tonight, there's one more person we can talk to." He glanced at his watch. "When does your father finish his appointments?"

Leigh looked reflexively at her own watch, but her brain didn't even register the time. She got up quickly and motioned for Gil to follow her.

"Right now."

Randall Koslow, DVM, peered at his daughter curiously over the stacks of backlogged veterinary journals and junk mail that were heaped high on the modest metal desk in his basement office. "Have a seat," he said calmly, directing Gil to a stepstool and her to a pile of twenty-pound bags of Science Diet. "What's up?"

Leigh slid onto the top bag of dog food with ease, but then looked from her father to Gil uncertainly. She wasn't sure where to begin. Her father was always a rock in a crisis, but the subject matter here was delicate, to say the least. She thought a moment, then reminded herself that with Randall, the direct approach was best rewarded.

"There's no easy way to ask this, Dad," she began. "Mason Dublin—and quite possibly someone else— is trying to blackmail Gil. They're threatening to expose something damaging about Lydie's past, and we don't know what it is. We were hoping you might."

Randall's pale eyes didn't blink. Gil jumped in. "I've been working with a private investigator," he explained. "He hasn't been able to find anything incriminating about Lydie, but he hasn't interviewed the principals yet, either. I can't imagine that Lydie would have any dark secrets in her past, but if she does, I'm afraid they are in danger of resurfacing. I can't reach her or her sisters, and I have to make a decision by tonight whether to meet Mason Dublin's demands—or call his bluff."

Randall looked from Gil back to his daughter and began to drum his fingers on his knee. His expression had barely changed, which, as always, Leigh found comforting. For the thousandth time, she wished she had inherited more of his cool and less of her mother's hysteria.

"Have you consulted the police?" he asked quietly.

Leigh threw a glance at Gil, who looked slightly defensive. "No," he answered. "I couldn't see any way to enlist their help without involving Cara." His voice turned serious. "This would kill her."

Randall studied Gil's face, then nodded solemnly. "I imagine that it would, yes."

An Akita in the oversized runs around the corner let loose with a long, undulating yowl. It was a mournful sound, and it frazzled Leigh's already frayed nerves. "Dad," she said impatiently, "you don't look all that surprised. Does this sound like something Mason would do? Is there anything to it?"

He took a deep breath, removed his glasses, and breathed on the lenses. Leigh prepared herself. Randall's cleaning of imaginary spots with the hem of his lab coat was one of his few distress signals.

"The only dark secret I know of in Lydie's past is her refusal to let anyone tell Cara the truth about

Mason," he said quietly. "But it sounds like that's not what you're looking for."

Gil studied him for a moment, then shook his head. "I got the distinct impression that this secret would put Lydie in some kind of trouble with the law."

Randall nodded. "Then I'm afraid I can't help you, except to say I think it's probably a bluff."

Leigh watched the exchange with confusion. She was definitely missing something. "What do you mean, 'the truth about Mason?' " she asked her father. "We already know he's a two-timing, child-abandoning louse, and now we know he's a black-mailer. How much worse can he be?"

Mason replaced his glasses and faced his daughter squarely. "Lydie had a lot of hard decisions to make when she had Cara," he began. "She picked the course she thought was best for the child."

Leigh's stomach knotted uncomfortably, but she tried not to look as panicked as she felt, or her father might not go on. Surely it couldn't be possible. Had everyone in the family been lying—both to her and Cara—all these years? About what?

The shrill yaps of a Maltese burst out suddenly from the kennel room, and Leigh jumped nervously. Randall appeared not to notice. "I suppose there's no point in keeping the secrets anymore," he explained soberly, "at least not from the two of you. But I think you should let Lydie decide when and how to tell Cara—if it comes to that."

Gil nodded, and Randall went on. Leigh held her breath.

"Lydie hated the thought of Cara growing up thinking she'd been abandoned—but she was even more concerned about the damage Mason could cause by staying in his daughter's life. So she kicked him out. Then she concocted a story about his leaving her for another woman while she was still pregnant."

Randall cleared his throat and rubbed his eyes before continuing. "She thought it would be easier on Cara to believe that her father had never laid eyes on her—so she wouldn't feel like she had been personally rejected. But she didn't want Cara to fabricate unrealistic ideas about Mason's character, either. If the child could imagine her father as decent, she might try to look for him someday. Lydie wanted to avoid that at all costs."

The words sank into Leigh's soul with a dull ache. What she had believed her whole life was all wrong. She tried to squelch the feelings of betrayal that brewed up inside her, but it was hard. And it would be a lot harder for Cara. "But Dad," she said determinedly, "if there was no other woman, why did Lydie kick Mason out? What did he do?"

Randall exhaled, long and hard. "There's no easy way to say this, honey. Cara's father was a wanted criminal."

Chapter 5

"Wanted?" Gil cried, rising from his stool. The Maltese yapped on mercilessly, driving virtual nails into Leigh's throbbing temples. "You mean he committed a crime before Cara was born? But the PI didn't find any convictions until 1974!"

Randall paused a moment, then nodded. "He wasn't wanted in the sense that the police were looking for him by name, no. He took off without ever having been fingered as a suspect—at least as far as we knew. But he was guilty all right."

Leigh looked helplessly from her father to Gil. "Guilty of what?"

Randall faced her squarely. "Armed robbery."

She slid back farther on the dog-food bags, her composure deflating. Cara's father—brandishing a gun. It couldn't be true.

Randall watched her reaction with concern. "I can't claim I knew Mason all that well, but if it helps, my impression was that he did not have a violent nature. I always believed the robbery was more a matter of his getting in over his head with a bad egg."

"I didn't know of any violent crimes," Gil responded, his voice troubled. "The PI found only white-collar stuff on his record—bookmaking, counterfeiting, fraud. He was in and out of prison all through the seventies and eighties, but the last ten years or so he seemed to have mellowed."

Randall absorbed the information, the wrinkles on his brow deepening. "Mason had smarts of a sort, but he was headstrong, greedy, and just plain foolish. The crimes don't surprise me."

A silence descended over the dim office, and Leigh realized that her head was continuing to pound even though the Maltese was no longer barking. Cara's father was a criminal. And everyone in the family had known—from the very beginning.

Irrational anger began to replace shock, and she rose quickly. "Would you give me a ride back home now, Gil?" she asked, already starting out. "I need to do some things."

It was obvious from the looks on Gil's and Randall's faces that they knew she had nothing in particular to do. But both seemed sympathetic. "We'll talk again when your mother gets home. All right, Leigh?" Randall said firmly. It wasn't really a question.

Leigh nodded and sprinted up the stairs toward daylight. The air in the basement of the Koslow Animal Clinic had never smelled great, but she couldn't remember when it had felt more oppressive.

Gil dropped her off in front of her apartment building, and she walked slowly inside and up the stairs. Her mind was in a complete muddle, and she wished desperately that she could talk to Warren, but he was out and would be out all day. She should have been surprised, therefore, to open her door and find someone sitting on the couch. But she wasn't.

"Leigh!" Cara said eagerly, jumping up and rushing to meet her cousin. "I thought you'd never get back! Where on earth have you been? I've been going nuts trying to reach you. I can't get Gil either—he didn't even take his cell phone. Just left some stupid note saying he'd be back later. You have to tell me what happened!"

Leigh hadn't progressed more than a foot inside the door, and it didn't look as if she was going to get any farther without using force. Needing at least three seconds to gather her thoughts, she pushed past Cara into the kitchen and extracted a Diet Coke from the refrigerator.

"Leigh!" Cara began again, her voice tinged with desperation. "Talk to me!" A high-pitched sound erupted from behind the couch, and Cara turned toward it immediately. "Mathias? Are you okay?"

A chubby, strawberry-blond toddler rounded the corner of the couch, grinning broadly. He pointed at the top shelf of the entertainment center and squealed with delight. "Kitty up!"

Both women turned to look at the black Persian cat that had taken refuge between a pewter fox and a portrait of Warren's parents. She looked tired.

"You mustn't chase the kitty, Mathias," Cara said gently, handing him a toy from a bag by the couch. She turned back to Leigh. "I'm sorry. Warren told us we could wait here for you. You don't mind?"

Leigh shook her head and took a long swig of her drink. So Warren had been here, at least for a little while. It figured that she would miss him. She went to say hello to her honorary nephew, then sank down onto the couch. Her cousin dogged her every move like a shadow, and she was glad that she and Gil had had the foresight to get their stories straight on the way over.

When she finally took a breath as if to speak, Cara tensed visibly. She halted and started again. *Please let this work.* "There isn't any other woman, Cara. I think you know that. Gil loves you very much. But you were right; he has been hiding something."

The tension in Cara's face relaxed only slightly. "Hiding what?"

Leigh took another breath. "He's been trying to protect you from an ugly situation. He's being blackmailed."

Cara's eyes widened. "Blackmailed? By who? Over what?"

"We don't know who," Leigh lied, hoping for dispensation on the grounds that she was serving a greater good. "But someone claims they know something about your mother. Something that could get her into trouble with the law. And they want Gil to pay to keep it quiet."

For several seconds, Cara said nothing. Then she exploded with a semi-hysterical laugh. "My *mother*?" she said incredulously, rising. "My mother in trouble with the law? That's the craziest thing I ever heard of! How could Gil ever believe something like that was true? He should have just told the moron to shove it!" She shook her head and plopped back down on the couch. "I can't believe this. Of all the—" She turned suddenly, her questioning eyes fixed on her cousin. "He called the police, didn't he?"

Leigh swallowed. This part would be tricky. "Well, no. He thought it would be better, under the circumstances, if he had a private detective handle it. That's where he was Wednesday night, and last night too."

"A private detective?" Cara repeated, her voice carrying a thin note of sarcasm. "That's ridiculous. He didn't need to hide all this from me. If he'd just told me, I could have assured him it was a hoax." She gave her cousin a shrewd stare. "He was determined to keep this from me, wasn't he? That's why he was afraid to involve the police—he couldn't guarantee they'd keep me out of it."

Leigh said nothing. They had both expected Cara to be upset with Gil. The secrecy thing was, after all, a little more difficult to explain with Mason Dublin omitted from the picture. But she appeared to be buying it. So far, so good.

"He was guarding the PO box because he didn't know how the blackmailer was going to make his next contact," Leigh explained. "The PI's job was to see if there could possibly be anything to the threat. Gil figured there wasn't, but he was just being careful. And with your mother out of town—"

"My mother's being out of town only gave him more reason to ask me about it," Cara insisted angrily. "All this running around, wasting money, over something so stupid!" She paused a moment and stewed.

Leigh was glad that steam didn't actually flow from a person's ears, or her apartment would be filling with it. "Don't go postal on me, Cara," she chastised, attempting playfulness. "You don't have a cheating husband. You have a knight in shining armor who's gone to great lengths to keep his lady from distress. He's a man—he doesn't know any better. Give the guy a break, OK?" A part of her couldn't believe she was pleading her cousin-in-law's case, but there it was.

Cara sat stiffly as her son toddled up to her with a cat toy. She took the plastic mouse into her lap on mommy autopilot, and a grinning Mathias took off immediately for more treasure. "I suppose you're right," she said finally, her voice calmer. "But I still don't understand why he hired a detective. Not unless he really did think my mother was an outlaw."

Leigh grinned. She knew her cousin well enough

to know that the PI thing rankled as much as Gil's overprotectiveness. Not ʼhat Cara had anything against private detectives—she just fancied she could do a better job herself.

"And how did you find all this out?" Cara asked. "Did you confront him?"

"Um, no," Leigh said honestly. "It was the other way around. I followed him all the way from the farm back to here. He was coming to look for me."

"For you?"

Leigh wasn't surprised at the touch of annoyance in her cousin's voice. Gil had wanted info on his mother-in-law, and he had gone to everyone in the world but his wife. Ouch. Best to leave Randall out of the equation as well, obviously. "He just wanted to make sure I didn't know any family secrets," she explained. "And he never did figure out that I was following him this morning, so if it's all the same to you, we can just forget that ever happened."

Cara came close to smiling, but not quite. "Fine. But I'm giving him hell about the rest of it." She rose and began to collect the toys Mathias had scattered. Cat toys on the coffee table, child toys in her bag. "Where is Gil now, anyway?" she asked pointedly. "And where did you go after you talked to him? Why didn't you call me?"

Leigh cursed her cousin's ability to spot fallacies. She probably would make a good PI. "You weren't home yet the first time I called," she lied again. "And I had some errands to run. Sorry it took so long. As for Gil, I believe he went to meet with the private detective again. I'm sure he'll be home soon."

The last part, at least, was true. Gil had wanted to show the detective the second blackmail letter, and they had to decide what to do about the drop-off tonight. Whether he leveled with Cara about those issues was up to him. She'd done her part of the lying.

Cara bundled up Mathias and his things, thanked Leigh for her efforts, and took off hastily. When the door had closed behind them, Leigh stretched out on the couch and was immediately pounced upon by a ball of black fur. The cat then jumped onto the coffee table, sniffing the disturbed toys with what little nose she had. She threw her master an indignant glare and meowed in protest. "Don't be so territorial, Mao Tse," Leigh answered, pulling the imperial beast back onto her stomach. "All nice children share. At least he stayed out of your litter box this time, didn't he?"

Unappeased, the cat jumped away, and Leigh sat reluctantly back up. She was tired, but this was no time for a nap, willing cat or no. Her father's words kept floating back into her mind, and try as she might, she couldn't shelve them.

Cara's father was a wanted criminal.

She tried to picture Mason Dublin in her mind, as she had done so many times as a child. He was Cara's father, not hers, but in a way they shared him—just as they had always shared Randall's attention. They had imagined him as a secret agent, or an international spy. Anything to explain why he had had to leave and why he had to stay away. Any reason other than that he didn't care.

There were no pictures of him—not one. Lydie claimed she had had only a few, and had thrown those away. So Leigh and Cara had pictured him as they chose—one day tall and dashing, the next sweet and dimpled. It was Cara's dream that he would come back for her some day, that he would settle the little misunderstanding with Lydie, and that they would all live happily ever after. It had been Leigh's dream too.

Foolishness.

Moisture welled up unexpectedly in the corners of her eyes, and she blinked it away, embarrassed. Who *was* Mason Dublin? Was he really nothing but a no-account, low-life criminal? A part of her refused to believe it, even with reality staring her in the face. She was a big believer in genetics, after all, and Lydie plus slimeball did not equal Cara. There must be more to the story.

She took a deep breath, which came in with a shudder. This was all affecting her a good deal more than she'd have liked. It wasn't about her, after all. And she needed to keep a straight head for Cara.

She paced about the apartment for a few minutes, looking for a mundane chore to take her mind off the obvious. But distraction didn't work. She had too many questions about Mason Dublin. Questions that couldn't be answered until her mother got home. Unless . . .

Suddenly inspired, she grabbed her coat and keys and headed for the door. She did have a degree in journalism, even if she'd only worked in advertising. Surely she could find out a few things on her own. Starting with an objective account of a thirty-year-old armed robbery.

Maybe things weren't as bad as they seemed. Either way, she had to know.

Leigh was in no mood to talk to her father again, but desperate situations called for desperate measures. She had been naïve to assume she could find out anything about the crime Mason had committed when she wasn't even sure of the date, much less the other details. So after fifteen fruitless minutes of

searching superficially through microfiche of the
Pittsburgh Post, she found a payphone and swallowed
her pride.

"I'm at the Carnegie Library in Oakland, Dad," she
began tonelessly. "I want to look up the newspaper
account of that armed robbery. Do you remember
when it was? What bank?"

Randall Koslow paused only a moment before giving his typical calm, no-nonsense manner of reply.
"It was in 1970, around Christmas. A bank in Butler—I'm not sure what it was called then. Bank
names change." He cleared his throat. "Are you sure
you want to pursue this? Your mother can answer
all of your questions tomorrow."

"I'm sure," Leigh said simply, knowing her father
wouldn't press the issue. He hadn't raised her from
an infant without knowing that once she got a mission in her head, tomorrow was never soon enough.
"I'll be over as soon as Mom gets home," she continued. "Thanks, Dad."

Armed with new and valuable knowledge, she
pulled out the December *Post* reels for 1970 and
started digging. A bank in Monroeville had been
robbed on the fourth; the lone gunman had managed
to obtain only a few hundred dollars from the fright-
ened teller before he had become spooked and fled.
The teller described the man as tall and thin, with a
dark toupee and false mustache.

Leigh read the account with a rapidly beating
heart. Could this have been Mason too? She had no
way of knowing. She scanned through several more
weeks of microfiche, her head beginning to throb
again as the tiny, slightly blurred print flashed by.
On the front page of the *Post* from December 21st,
1970, she halted.

Bank Manager Shot in Butler Robbery. It was in the

right hand column, prominently displayed. Her stomach did a quick flip-flop, and she swallowed uncomfortably. Her father hadn't said that anyone was hurt.

Richard M. Kirk, a manager at the First Liberty Bank on Main Street in downtown Butler, remains in critical condition today after receiving a gunshot wound to the chest during a robbery at that location late yesterday afternoon. According to several witnesses, two men wearing dark clothing and hairpieces entered the front door of the First Liberty Bank shortly before closing time and drew guns on the bank staff.

One of the men, whom witnesses describe as being in his mid to late twenties and around six feet tall, approached Millicent Knable, a teller, and demanded cash. The other man, described as 5 feet 9 or 10 inches tall and in his late teens or early twenties, remained by the door of the bank watching the front of the building.

Witnesses say that Knable was attempting to load cash into a bag when she became flustered and began to fumble the money, agitating the taller gunman. When Kirk stepped away from the other employees to assist her, the gunman fired. He took the bag from Knable, and both men fled.

State police currently have no comment on whether the robbery could be linked to the holdup of the East National Bank in Monroeville earlier this month. Anyone having seen men matching this description in the Butler area yesterday are encouraged to contact the State Police.

Leigh's hand trembled slightly as she scrolled through the microfiche to the next day's headlines.

Armed robbery was bad enough, but actually shooting someone?

In critical condition.

She took a deep breath. Had the man died? Surely not, or her father would have mentioned it. She was no scholar of criminal justice, but she did know that a death, intentional or otherwise, definitely raised the stakes on the average felony—for the accomplice as well as the perpetrator.

And Mason Dublin was the accomplice. It was all she was willing to accept. Her father had said that Mason had fallen in with a "bad egg", so it made sense. He had stood guard at the door, that was all. He had had no part in the shooting. He had probably felt terrible about it.

Leigh stopped scrolling for a moment and rubbed her aching eyes. She knew she was being silly. No one had ever told her that Mason Dublin was a decent person. In fact, her family had always tried to instill the opposite sentiment, however gently. But he was Cara's father, and that had to count for something. Was it so wrong of her to hope for the best?

Suspect in Butler Shooting Takes Own Life.

The headline jumped off the page the moment she opened her eyes, and she read it with a rapidly beating heart.

Facing apprehension by State Police at a motel in Bridgeville, Jerry Lem Donovan, formerly of Kilbuck County, fatally shot himself in the chest with his own handgun. An all-points bulletin had been issued for Donovan in conjunction with two recent bank robberies, one of which resulted in the shooting of an employee . . .

So Mason *was* the accomplice, she confirmed, breathing a little easier.

Descriptions of the two robberies followed, but her attention was drawn quickly to the end of the article.

> No suspects have as yet been identified in the search for the Donovan's accomplice in the Butler robbery. The shooting victim remains hospitalized in fair condition.

Fair condition. Her hopes rose. So, the bank manager had probably recovered. The State Police had failed to finger the accomplice, and Mason Dublin left town with his reputation—such as it was—intact, never to be seen again.

At least not until now.

She scanned through the next three weeks' worth of news, but could find no follow-up on either the bank manager's condition or the hunt for Jerry Donovan's accomplice. The lack of press was encouraging; if the victim had died of complications later, it would almost certainly have been reported. Whether any progress the police might have made identifying Mason would have made the papers, she wasn't sure, but she did know from the PI's research that Mason was never actually arrested.

At least not for armed robbery.

Stop trying to minimize this, she commanded herself in frustration. Mason was scum of the earth, and she would be better off to accept that and move on. He wasn't her father. He wasn't even a blood relative. And if she wanted to keep Cara from going through ten times the anguish she'd been feeling in the last few hours, she had to keep her own emotions out of it.

She rose, considered whether she should make

copies of the article, and decided against it. The last
thing she needed was to have a copy of the story
lying around for Cara to stumble onto someday. Besides, it was ancient history. She needed to concentrate on the present. And at that very moment, Gil
was probably back at the farm, trying desperately to
make Cara believe his part of their carefully edited
version of events. Gil wasn't inept, but Cara wasn't
gullible either. Pulling the wool over her eyes would
take serious finesse.

Leigh collected her things and headed out of the
library determinedly. She would go out to the farm
herself. She wanted to know what the private investigator had said about the ridiculous letter the second
blackmailer had sent to Lydie, and she wanted to
know what Gil's plan was for the drop-off tonight.
He might need her help, after all.

Chapter 6

It wasn't easy to sneak up on someone at Snow Creek Farm; the gravel drive wound all the way down the side of the property and around the back of the farmhouse, and the Cavalier's tires crunched noisily as Leigh progressed. Gil's Saturn was parked in the drive, the official garage being large enough to hold only Cara's van and a few boxes of Christmas decorations. The farmhouse was small, much smaller than the stately Avalon Victorian the couple had lived in before Mathias was born. But it was an antique, and Cara loved it. And whatever Cara loved, Gil managed to tolerate.

Leigh parked her car next to Gil's and walked up to the back door. She hadn't been particularly successful on the trip over at planning what she was going to say, but winging it often served her well. She had just raised her hand to knock when her cousin opened the door, took hold of her wrist, and propelled her forcefully into the family room.

"You need to get on the phone to your friend Maura right now," Cara instructed, her blue-green eyes blazing. "My husband will not listen to reason. The police have to be contacted, or else we'll never find out who's really behind this. And I want whoever plans on slandering my mother's good name to

get what's coming to them. You agree with me, don't
you, Leigh?"

The lump that rose in Leigh's throat seemed far
too big to swallow. She turned her eyes from her
cousin's fierce gaze to Gil, who stood mutely on the
opposite side of the room. His eyes, which were radi-
ating husband-on-the-spot misery, sent her a clear
plea. *Stand firm.*

"Well?" Cara demanded as she hesitated. "Don't
you?"

Leigh somehow managed to swallow the lump.
"I—" she began uncertainly. Then she stopped.
Winging it, indeed. Blasted overconfidence!

"What is it with you two?" Cara said with frustration, knowing full well when her cousin was stalling.
"What can it possibly hurt to get the police involved
now? I'm telling you, my mother has nothing to
hide. Nothing!"

Inspiration suddenly dawned, and Leigh spoke up.
"No one believes your mother is a criminal," she said
gently. "There's no way. But maybe there's something in her past that's likely to be misunderstood,
or maybe it's just something silly and embarrassing.
Either way, going to the police would open up a
whole bag of worms, and you know how your
mother values her privacy. Don't you think—if she
were here—she would want to keep all this nonsense
as quiet as possible?"

Cara's determined face faltered for a moment, and
Leigh was heartened. Gil cast her an appreciative
glance, and she went on. "I know you're angry, and
you want to see this person punished, but I doubt
your mother would feel that way. You know how
she hates a fuss. Can you imagine her having to fill
out police reports, being worried that the whole
crazy story might get out to the press somehow?

Wouldn't she rather we just deal with this person privately? Call their bluff and be done with it?"

Red flared over Cara's high cheekbones, but the storm in her eyes calmed. She lowered her chin and sank down on the couch. "Maybe so," she said with resignation.

Gil crossed over quickly and sat down next to his wife, wrapping an arm comfortingly around her shoulders. "I'm sorry I didn't confide in you about this earlier," he said softly. "But I really do think we're handling this the way Lydie would want us to. What the PI suggested makes sense. Please—let's just see if the plan works before we get the police involved. All right?"

The plan?

An unhappy, high-pitched wail erupted from upstairs, and Cara rose instantly. "Matt must have had a bad dream," she said sadly. "I'll take care of it. Excuse me."

Leigh wasted no time. "What plan?" she whispered, accosting her cousin-in-law as soon as Cara was out of sight. "What did the PI say?"

Gil looked at her, his eyes not concealing a slight reservation in answering the question. "He thinks our best bet is to play dumb," he said finally. "We should make the drop-off minus the money, leaving a note instead. It will explain that we don't believe Mason really has anything on Lydie, that she's unreachable, and that we're not ponying up any cash unless he can provide some solid proof for his claim."

Leigh considered. "I suppose that might work. But what if he gets mad and carries through with his threat?"

"It's a risk," Gil answered soberly. "But it's unlikely. If he has something real, he won't want to squander it and gain nothing. He'll give us more information, then put the screws to us again. If he doesn't have anything real—which I hope to God is the case—there's a good chance he'll just disappear."

If only, Leigh thought. Mason could disappear as quickly as he had reappeared. Of course, then they would never know what the threats were all about. "So when does all this happen?" she asked.

"Midnight," Gil answered quickly, as Cara's footsteps began to descend the farmhouse's wooden stairs. "The PI's going to handle everything personally. I think it will work."

"And what about the letter to Lydie?" Leigh asked quickly. "What did he think about that?"

Gil cut her off with a head shake as Cara's footsteps approached the room. "Later," he mouthed.

A much calmer Cara strode through the doorway with an angelic-looking Mathias cuddled sleepily into her shoulder. She glanced at the grandfather clock in the corner, then looked at Leigh quizzically. "No offense, but what are you doing here? I forgot to mention it this afternoon, but when I saw Warren, he asked me to remind you about some dinner party you'd promised to go to tonight. Shouldn't you be getting ready?"

Leigh's eyes widened. She ran through a long string of mental curses, but being mindful of the toddler in the room, uttered only a single "shoot."

"Thanks so much," she said hastily, jumping up to leave. "Warren hardly ever asks me to play Mrs. Politician, but this event is really important for some reason. If I don't make it, he'll have my head on a platter."

Cara and Gil waved polite good-byes, and she scooted out the door. They all knew Warren wouldn't really get angry if she missed the party. He probably wouldn't even chew her out; he was too tenderhearted. He'd just tell her that it was all right—and then look really sad. She jumped into the Cavalier and revved up the engine. Being yelled at she could handle, but not that sad look.

The look that met her from across the crowded reception hall was worth the curling-iron burns on her neck and the still-damp feel of the blouse she had wrested prematurely from the dryer. Warren covered the distance between them in a few short strides and hugged her soundly.

"I hope you didn't worry," she said quickly, "I promised I'd be here, didn't I?"

Warren looked at his watch with a sly smile. "Worry? Me? You're only forty minutes late. I don't start worrying until at least fifty-five."

She smiled back. "Good plan." The room was so packed with people that many were standing shoulder to shoulder, and the servers were having trouble getting through with the hors d'oeuvres. None of the food, of course, was anywhere near her. But at least, she thought optimistically, being late meant she wouldn't have to wait nearly as long for the real dinner.

He took her hand. "Are you ready for this?"

She managed what she hoped was a brave look. There was nothing she hated more than making chit-chat with shallow political types dressed to the nines, but a commitment was a commitment. She was always willing to brainstorm for her husband's campaign in the PR department—in fact, she was darned good at it—but the social scene was another matter. "The little woman" was a role she despised, but if she had to choose between being an arm ornament and getting involved in politics herself, an arm ornament she would be. Warren never insisted she play the role, even though her absence at functions normally attended by couples had become rather conspicuous. But the County Council election was only days away, and whatever this function was—and she was trying hard to remember—it had seemed unusually important to Warren.

"Of course I'm ready," she said with a smile. "Successful politician's wife: take one. Let's go." His brown eyes twinkled at her, and she took a deep breath as he began to lead her toward a cluster of strangers. She could fake it with the best of them. Really, she could.

Four hours and half a migraine later, Leigh's spirits rose as she noted that some of the guests were starting to leave. If nothing else, their absence would allow a little more oxygen into the stuffy reception hall. She had done her best, but her blouse never had dried out, and the dull ache over her right temple was portending certain doom in the near future. Perhaps it wouldn't be too much longer before Warren was ready to leave.

"You're excused."

She turned hopefully toward her husband. "I'm what?"

He laughed and squeezed her hand. "Go ahead and go home if you want to—I don't mind. You've certainly done your part for the evening, and I'll be staying another hour or two at least."

Leigh tried to conceal her enthusiasm. "Are you sure? Will it look OK?"

"We came in separate cars, didn't we? Off with you."

She smiled and gave him a quick kiss good-bye. "Donuts for breakfast," she promised as she fled. "My treat."

The cold night air felt good in her lungs as she made her way through the well-lit parking lot and out to her car. *Freedom.* The throbbing in her head had ceased, and she felt an unexpected surge of energy. What time was it, anyway? She glanced down at her watch and discovered that her ordeal inside hadn't been quite as long as it had seemed. Gil's voice flashed suddenly through her mind.

Midnight.

She mentally calculated the distance to the top edge of Pittsburgh's Golden Triangle. Yes, she could make it. And why not? Bus stations were perfectly public places. No one ever had to know she was there. The PI wouldn't know her from Adam, and neither would Mason, of course. She could just sit and watch. And she would finally have a real picture to replace the made-up images that had haunted her since childhood.

She started up the Cavalier and pulled out of the lot. The time had come. She was going to see Cara's father with her own eyes.

Warren's jacket was just long enough to cover her knees, and she was glad of that. Her hastily concocted plan had omitted the whole concept of being inconspicuous, which she soon learned did not come easy when sitting in a plastic chair in the lobby of a bus station in formal evening attire.

Idiot.

But it was too late to turn back now. Thanks to her husband's tall frame, penchant for loose clothing, and habit of leaving a coat in both of their cars at all times, at least her suit was covered. The hose and pumps didn't fit in, but she was doing her best to tuck her feet under the chair. As long as no one mistook her for a female flasher, she thought grimly, she should be OK.

She had positioned herself in the row of chairs nearest the ticket booth, the only place where she had a clear view of the trash can in question. At least, she hoped it was the right can. There were three in the terminal, but the one near the vending machines was covered, as was the one outside the bathrooms. The waiting area had several of the short, cylindrical ashtray cans, but they weren't big enough to hold the prize. The open wire basket-style drum in front of her was the obvious choice, even if she hadn't been pretty sure she saw a Barbie-themed Happy Meal box already in place near the top.

But it was five after midnight, and so far nothing had happened.

She squirmed on the hard plastic seat and looked around the waiting room, feigning boredom. The other occupants seemed to have the bored look down pat. Elderly busgoers either snoozed or stared at the walls, while a few teens lounged in the corner, playing their boom box at a surprisingly considerate volume. The new mother who sat next to Leigh gazed off lazily into space, seemingly unaware of either the infant she was nursing or the two preschoolers who were fighting over possession of her purse. The few other singles in the room were almost all men. And then of course there was her. The proverbial sore thumb.

She sighed and checked her watch again. Surely Mason wouldn't wait too much longer. There was nothing to stop someone else from accidentally happening on his "money," not to mention the fact that the trash can could be emptied at any time.

So where was Mason, anyway? She had looked for him as soon as she had arrived, but was certain he wasn't among the crowd. The man she was looking for would be in his mid-fifties, five-feet, nine- or ten-inches tall, and most likely a natural redhead gone gray. Her cousin's peculiar shade of strawberry-blond hair had certainly not been inherited from her mother's side of the family, whose varied rosy hues Leigh knew to come exclusively from bottles.

There was only one man visible who could possibly fit the bill. He was white and about the right age, but that was all. He had swarthy Italian good looks, with jet-black hair streaked with gray at the temples and dark, piercing eyes. Outwardly he looked bored, like everyone else, but his eyes periodically swept the room, and twice she had had to avert her own gaze to dodge them.

He wasn't Mason Dublin. But—she thought with a devious smile—he could be the PI. The PI would be here too, of course, keeping watch on the very same can. She scanned the room again, following the gazes of anyone who seemed a likely suspect. What did PIs look like, anyway? She'd never seen one outside of the Hollywood rendition, and Hollywood was usually wrong about such things. Anyone Gil would hire would be a seasoned professional, and undoubtedly high-priced. But then, he would probably dress down for the occasion, to look like a traveler.

Would he come alone? Probably. The swarthy man had wrapped his arm around the much younger woman at his side and suddenly seemed less of a candidate. Leigh's eyes scanned over a thin, nicely dressed black man reading *Forbes* magazine (too smart) and an overweight, thirty-something white man with a comic book (not smart enough) to a short, pale, twenty-something man with a bushy, unkempt mustache.

A disguise? The idea of a private detective going

to a stakeout with a false mustache seemed juvenile, even to her, but what did she know? Almost all the other working-age men in the room had obvious traveling companions, and she couldn't believe male PIs regularly brought women on the job just for appearances. It had to be Mr. Mustache.

She began to watch him carefully and was disturbed to note how infrequently he glanced toward the can. Being inconspicuous was fine, but unless the detective had peripheral vision like an owl, he was going to miss the whole shebang. She was about to decide the quack wasn't worth his salt when she realized that she wasn't either.

A man was standing over the trash can, rummaging like mad.

Chapter 7

Leigh's spine straightened; her eyes fixed on the man at the trash can. *Curses.* His back was to her, and he was bent over too far for her to see his face. She wiggled to the edge of her chair, but the view was no better. Should she get up and walk where she could see him clearly? Would that be too obvious? If he saw her watching him, he might think she was a PI. Or more likely, a cop. Then what would he do?

Afraid to find out, she stayed rooted to her seat, feeling helpless. But after what was really only a few seconds, the man walked briskly away—Happy Meal box in hand.

Thinking no further, she rose and followed him.

The night was cold, and she knew that Warren's jacket would bring little comfort for her bare calves, but she walked on anyway. She wouldn't follow him far—just far enough to get a good, hard look at him. And if she was careful, he would never suspect a thing.

Her quarry made a beeline for the exit of the bus terminal, and she hung back as much as she dared. He might not be looking for a younger woman in a dress and floppy jacket, but he would certainly be worried that someone might follow him. Sure enough, he whirled around just as he reached the door, and Leigh dove into the alcove by the vending machines just in time.

Her heart beat madly as she stood there, counting the seconds. She still hadn't gotten a good look at him. But she did now know that he was of medium height and that what little hair remained in a ring around his bald head was an indeterminate mousy gray. He was neither heavy nor thin, but had an ageless aura that would probably allow him to pass for anything between fifty and seventy.

Having no intention of letting him slip away, she finished her countdown and stepped out, then sprang toward the door and walked into the cold.

Having worked in downtown Pittsburgh for years, she knew it to be a relatively safe place for a stroll, even if Saturday at midnight was not an optimal time. The streets were largely deserted after hours even during the week, and though most of the business district was well lit and patrolled, the very emptiness of it held the power to spook.

She quickly scoured 11th Street in both directions, and was relieved to see that the man was still in plain view, heading down Liberty Avenue at a brisk pace. What was more, a group of twenty-somethings were walking in the same direction a few paces ahead of her, making for excellent cover. She fell into step behind them, and after one of the girls gave her an initial wary glance, they simply ignored her.

Their progress was slower than his, however, and after the better part of a block she was certain she would lose him. But luck was with her again, and just as she was debating whether to leave her cover and catch up, she saw him duck into the entrance of the Amtrak station.

Eureka.

Breaking loose from the twenty-somethings without apology, she made for the train station as fast as her pumps would carry her. Her legs were shaky, but it wasn't the cold that was making her shiver. If anything, she was sweating up a major dry-cleaning bill. But the enormity of what she was doing was wreaking havoc with her nerves. At long last, she was about to put a real face on the name Mason Dublin.

The Amtrak station wasn't nearly as populated as the bus station, and she had no trouble locating him. He had stopped not ten feet from the door and was standing against the wall by a payphone, the Happy Meal box at his feet.

Leigh pivoted sideways and pretended to be studying a string of empty newspaper boxes. But he wasn't looking at her. He was staring at a piece of paper.

She jumped as he uttered an expletive and dashed the paper to the floor. He was close to her, maybe a little too close. She could see his face clearly now, and she stared with fascination as beads of sweat broke out across his reddened forehead, a look of desperation entering his clear, light-blue eyes.

Mason Dublin—in the flesh. All those years she and Cara had spent dreaming about him—a dashing, mysterious prince. And here he was. A ruddy-complected, tired-looking man with worry lines beyond his years. A poster child for Rogaine, and perhaps Arrid Extra Dry. She thought she had no expectations, but given the sinking feeling that was now overwhelming her, she knew she'd overestimated herself. The sad fact hit her square in the face. Mason Dublin was an ordinary schmuck.

And he was not pleased with the note in the Happy Meal box. He turned and leaned into the wall, pressing his forehead against a raised arm. The expletives continued to flow as he struck the wall repeatedly with the opposite fist. Leigh stood frozen. She wasn't sure how he would react to the note, but this wasn't it. Anger, yes. Definitely irritation. But what she was seeing was that and more. It was closer to despair.

He turned around again and slammed his back into the wall with a thump. Leigh watched as the anger seemed to drain out of him. His pale eyes had turned glassy, and she could swear that his rapid blinks were holding back tears.

But why? She started forward without thinking, and the peripheral motion seemed to stir him to action. He bounced immediately off the wall and strode purposefully toward the ticket booth.

Leigh walked to where he had been standing and picked up the pay phone receiver. It was lame cover, since she wasn't even bothering to punch the buttons, but he wasn't watching anyway. He was talking to the worker in the ticket booth.

What now? She had seen him, and that was all that she had wanted, right? Her knees continued to knock, and she struggled to get a grip on herself. It was ridiculous that she should feel so disappointed . . . and so cheated. But there it was.

An ordinary schmuck.

She began walking toward him with no particular plan. She had thought that seeing him would produce some sort of closure, but that wasn't happening. If anything, she felt more of a hole in her gut than ever. Who was Mason Dublin, really? Why was he so desperate to get money from his son-in-law? And what was he going to do now?

Pretending to be next in line, she stepped close enough to overhear some of his conversation with the ticket clerk. "Could I change it again later if I want?" he asked with a strained tone. "Or will the price go up?"

She couldn't hear the ticket seller's response, but Mason grunted in consent and wheeled around. Leigh ducked her head and pushed quickly up to the booth as he stomped past her.

"What you need, ma'am?" the man in the window asked expectantly.

Leigh looked up at him as if he were dense, then realized that that honor belonged to her. "Um, nothing," she said sheepishly. "Sorry. I changed my mind."

The man offered a nonjudgmental shrug, and Leigh wheeled around quickly. But Mason Dublin was nowhere in sight. She strode to the exit, clutching the jacket around her tightly.

Let it go, Leigh, the little voice of reason in the back of her head droned. But she paid no attention. Clearly, just seeing Mason Dublin wasn't really all she had wanted. She wanted to understand him. She wanted to know how any man decent enough for her aunt Lydie to love—and decent enough to share fifty percent of Cara's gene pool—could possibly give up a wife and child, only to blackmail them three decades later. It didn't make sense. *He* didn't make sense. And unfortunately for Leigh's little voice of reason, things she didn't understand always bugged the hell out of her.

She stepped back out onto Liberty Avenue and looked both ways. Nothing. How could he possibly have gotten out of sight so fast? She walked a little way up and down the street, but no nearby alleys looked particularly promising, and even if they had, she wasn't stupid enough to go tromping down one alone at this hour. Not quite, anyway.

A chill wind swept up her coat, and she shivered

again. He was gone; end of story. Admitting defeat, she bowed her face out of the gust and headed toward the parking garage. She had just reached 11th Street when a rapid movement caught her eye.

It was him again—jaywalking across the empty street with a duffel bag slung over his shoulder. He jogged toward the DoubleTree Hotel and the obvious object of his intentions—a lone cab. Leigh stood still and watched as he leaned down to converse with the driver, then jumped into the backseat. As the cab drove off, a string of curse words filtered through her foggy brain. It took a few seconds for her to realize it wasn't her mouth they were coming out of.

"And *who the hell*, I might add, are you?" the voice continued.

She turned to note that another man had somehow advanced on her from behind and was now planted firmly at her left elbow. Worse yet, he was glaring at her.

"Excuse me?" she said defensively, taking a quick step back. Logically, perhaps, she should have run screaming, but something about the man's manner marked him as a gentleman, despite his sharp words. Furthermore, she recognized him.

"Why were you following that man just now?" he demanded, struggling to control his tone.

Leigh didn't answer, but surveyed his tasteful business-casual outfit and intellectual-looking wire-rimmed spectacles with respect. *Forbes* magazine, indeed. The man looked more like a professor than a gumshoe. Perhaps that was his intent. "You don't look like a private investigator," she said mildly, annoyed with herself for dismissing him so easily before. "But you do swear like one."

His eyes narrowed briefly; then his face relaxed

somewhat. "The important thing is that I don't look like a cop. And I repeat, who the hell are you?"

She smiled a little. She knew she needed to be careful, since she had no proof this man really was Gil's PI, but her intuition was quite certain, and it had only rarely steered her wrong. "I'm Leigh. Perhaps your employer has mentioned me?"

The man surveyed her critically. "You're the sister-in-law, then," he said sullenly, turning to look in the direction of the departed cab. "Though why you felt you had to be here is beyond me. I've never seen anyone do a more obvious trail job."

Leigh bristled, but found her ego quickly deflating. Once she'd laid eyes on Mason, she'd forgotten all about the detective—and the whole point of his being there. He was supposed to be following the black-mailer, but evidently he'd been following her as well. Not too hard, since she'd made no attempt at all to look inconspicuous to anyone behind her. He must think she was a nutcase.

It was a common mistake.

"Sorry," she said sheepishly. "And I'm the cousin-in-law, actually. I just wanted to see him for myself. I didn't mean to get in the way."

The detective's dark eyes softened a bit. "Trent Walker here, Walker Investigations. And I don't think he noticed you. He wasn't looking for a woman. He wasn't being very careful at all, as a matter of fact. Just got damn lucky with that cab, or I'd still have him."

He gave her another long, studying look, his manner now all business. "Did you overhear the conversation at the ticket booth?"

Leigh repeated what little she had heard, and he nodded in understanding. She wanted to ask him some questions of her own, but she knew he wouldn't answer them. He had only her word that she was the cousin-in-law of his employer; and in any event, he wasn't on her payroll. But she could piece most of it together for herself.

Mason had probably planned on leaving with the money as soon as possible—perhaps the very next train. But when the deal fell through, he had changed his plans. He had switched his ticket for a later departure, retrieved his duffel bag from a locker somewhere in the terminal—undoubtedly while she was out looking for him on the street—and hailed a cab. But a cab to where?

One thing seemed evident. He wasn't leaving Pittsburgh immediately. And if he wasn't leaving, it must be because he had something worth staying for. Like Plan B.

Producing real evidence against her aunt Lydie.

Chapter 8

Leigh paced restlessly in her apartment the next morning, far more antsy than usual after only two cups of coffee. She had tossed and turned all night, and her mind was still racing. Warren was asleep, and though she sorely needed a sympathetic ear, she didn't want him to face the election any more sleep deprived than he already was. Nor was she particularly eager to explain the last twenty-four hours.

She would have unburdened her soul last night, but she had slipped into the apartment only minutes before he had, and feeling chicken, she had decided to play possum. Though her husband wasn't in the same Me-Tarzan league as Gil, had he arrived to find their apartment empty two hours after she had left the party, he might have worried just a tad. Not that he was overprotective per se, but he did have a thing about wanting to know where she was and whether or not a felony had been committed.

She wished she really had been asleep, since two nights without a full seven hours was more than her thirty-something constitution could take. But sleep hadn't come. What had come was an endless replay of Mason Dublin's face as he read the note in the Happy Meal box, furious, dispirited, and completely alien. A blackmailer. A bank robber. A wonderful woman's biological father.

The images conflicted in a big way. In fact, the whole puzzle seemed more disturbing—and lacking crucial pieces—than it had been before she had seen the man. So what had happened after she left? The PI's car had been parked too far away for him to give chase personally, but he had jotted down the cab's number. When would he report to Gil? She had tried calling the farm and Cara's cell phone, but her cousin had the annoying habit of ignoring both, and though Gil undoubtedly had a cell phone of his own, Leigh hadn't previously had any burning desire to get the number.

She glanced at her watch. Her mother's plane was due in this morning, and for once, she couldn't wait to talk to her. There would be no more pussyfooting about Mason and Lydie's stormy past. Her mother knew the whole truth, and Leigh intended to drag every bit of it out of her as soon as she stepped off the gangway.

"Your mother will be jet-lagged," her father had said succinctly when she had called him at dawn to suggest she make the airport run herself. He hadn't bothered recommending that she let Frances unpack and get settled before the onslaught; they both knew it wasn't going to happen.

After one last attempt to get through to Cara and Gil, Leigh scrawled a note to Warren and attached it to the coffeemaker with a sigh. They usually enjoyed Sunday "muffin" mornings together, but this week it wasn't to be. She'd even forgotten the donuts she'd promised him. But maybe if she was lucky, he'd still be home at lunchtime.

Traffic on her trek west of town was light, and she arrived at the airport right on schedule. But as her mother's plane was delayed, she was forced to burn off her anxiety by pacing the Airmall. Pittsburgh was blessed with a nice one, and after finding some comfort in an oversized bakery muffin and chocolate sampler, she headed back to the gate.

The weary passengers lumbered out the tunnel doorway like rejects from a sleep experiment, and Leigh's heart beat fast as she waited for her mother to appear. Getting information out of Frances wasn't all that easy under the best of circumstances, and this information was particularly sensitive. She was in the midst of deciding to change her plan of attack—again—when her mother finally appeared.

At least she thought it was her mother. The normally impeccably groomed, pearl-decked Barbara Bush impersonator she called Mom appeared to have been replaced by a much more hip woman in a wrinkled sweatsuit and—Leigh blinked just to make sure—*sneakers*.

She approached the strange woman with apprehension. "Mom?" she asked tentatively.

"Leigh?" Frances answered with equal suspicion. "Where's your father? Is he all right?"

"He's fine," she replied with what she hoped was a reassuring smile. "I just offered to come get you myself, that's all."

Frances's eyebrows rose instantly. "Are *you* all right?"

Grinning sheepishly, Leigh took her mother's travel bag off her arm and started walking toward the baggage claim. "Of course I am. But I wasn't doing anything else, and I thought we could talk."

The look of anxiety brewing in Frances's bloodshot eyes flared into open alarm. "Good Lord," she said, halting in her tracks. "The election. You aren't giving Warren a hard time about not being home, are you? You know the man has responsibilities! Please tell me the two of you aren't having problems already.

You are, aren't you? You've been nagging him—I knew it."

Leigh stopped, took a deep breath, and did a quick about-face. Though her mother had a stellar track record of not approving of anything she'd ever done—particularly in the employment and love-life areas—her marriage to Warren Harmon had been one point on which they'd been in perfect agreement. In Frances's eyes, in fact, that decision had been the only thing standing between her daughter and certain doom. Frances worshipped the ground her new son-in-law walked on, and Leigh had no illusions about who her mother would testify for in divorce court.

"Warren and I are fine," she answered with her best attempt at patience. "The campaign's going splendidly. But he's at home sound asleep, and I needed to get out. So tell me, how was India?"

Frances's piercing, bird-like eyes surveyed her critically, and Leigh did her best to look innocent. Though she had always been proud of her talent for distorting the truth without actually lying, she knew her mother was wise to the concept. This time, thankfully, Frances's analysis went in her favor. The worry lines around her brow relaxed slightly—an indication that whatever she perceived her daughter was hiding, at least it had nothing to do with her sainted son-in-law.

"The architecture was lovely," Frances answered tiredly, "but India is an incredibly filthy country. You wouldn't believe the poverty—"

They walked through the hub and rode the escalators down to the transit area with Frances running through a long list of things in India that should be cleaned, and Leigh trying to figure out how to segue onto the topic of Mason Dublin without seeming un-interested in third-world hygiene.

She was watching through the large round win-dow at the end of the transit tunnel when the next train roared up quickly, and inspiration dawned. "So I guess the transportation system there isn't the best," she began casually. "Evidently the phone sys-tem isn't either, because Gil had a question he wanted to ask Lydie, and he couldn't get through."

Frances dropped the cleanliness tirade immediately and turned to Leigh with a look of intense curiosity, but thankfully not panic.

So far, so good. Thirty-one years as Frances Koslow's daughter had taught her nothing if not how to extract sensitive information in the most efficient way. She knew, for instance, that once Frances swung into full mother-worry mode, the only things she'd be forth-coming with would be nervous hand-rubbing and murmured predictions of doom. Getting Frances to squeal about whether or not her twin sister really did have something to hide would require the element of surprise, a careful setup, and a careful watch of the eyes.

Of course, she could choose to level with her mother from the beginning, but that method had its risks—namely that Frances would spill only to Gil and the PI and staunchly refuse to admit the truth to her own daughter. *That* she couldn't tolerate. She was up to her eyeballs in this mess of secrets, and she bloody well wanted out of the pit.

"Gil tried to call Lydie in India?" Frances asked, making no move to board the waiting train. "What on earth for?"

Leigh faced her mother squarely. The moment was now. "Someone told him she'd once committed a criminal act, and he wanted to know if it was true."

The words had no sooner left Leigh's mouth than she regretted both her plan and her choice of location. The color drained out of Frances's face instantly, and she stood stock still, her pupils expanding to alarming dimensions. The other travelers began brushing around them to board, and with one particularly ill-timed jostle, Frances's limp body began to sway. Leigh jumped forward quickly, seeing horrifying visions of her mother collapsing into the path of the closing train doors. "Mom!" she exclaimed, steadying her with hands on both arms. "Are you OK?"

"What did you say?" Frances asked weakly, her voice barely above a whisper. "Someone told Gil *what*?"

Leigh looked around for a place to sit, but saw nothing promising. Instead, she pulled her mother away from the train doors and leaned her up against the round window around the corner. Frances offered no resistance. "Tell me right now," she insisted, her face still deathly pale. "Who said what to Gil?"

Leigh took a deep breath and realized she didn't feel too steady on her own feet. She'd wanted to catch her mother off guard, but she hadn't wanted to give her a stroke. That Frances might react this severely hadn't even occurred to her—undoubtedly because she had never really believed Lydie had something to hide.

Had she been wrong? The look on her mother's face chilled her to the bone.

"Leigh Eleanor," Frances repeated, her eyes brimming with an emotion that was just short of terror. "Tell me!"

Leigh stepped unsteadily sideways and let the glass window support both of them. "It's Mason Dublin, Mom," she said in a whisper. "He's back."

* * *

Never in Leigh's life had she known her mother to order a drink as scandalous as a rum-and-Coke, particularly not on a Sunday morning. The fact that she was guzzling it without apology was even more disturbing.

The college-aged waiter surveyed his first patrons of the day with a raised eyebrow and an amused smile. "Rough flight, eh? Can I get you ladies anything else?"

Leigh—who had ordered nothing to begin with—shook her head, but Frances nodded, swallowing quickly. "Some crackers, please."

The waiter smiled again and departed.

"Mom," Leigh began again. "You've hardly said a word. Don't you dare get sloshed before you tell me what's going on."

Frances threw her daughter a disapproving glare. It was a familiar one, but with the added element of the bloodshot eyes, it was particularly scary. "I am not getting 'sloshed,'" she said resentfully. "I'm steadying my nerves."

Leigh sighed and waited while her mother took a few more swallows. She knew she had to be patient. Pushing Frances never accomplished anything, and besides, the story she'd just divulged—which was reasonably complete, although it failed to cover either trailing incident—had to come as quite a shock. Still, she had finished talking almost five minutes ago, and so far all Frances had had to say was "Look—the TGI Friday's is open. How convenient."

When the rum-and-Coke was two thirds gone, Leigh tried again. "Mom—"

"All right. All right," Frances said irritably. "I suppose there's no point in trying to hide the past from you, not anymore. As for Cara, that has to be Lydie's decision. You're not to pass on one word of this yourself. Is that understood?''

Her tone brooked no dissent, and Leigh nodded mutely.

Frances began with a sigh. "Lydie was very much in love with Mason Dublin when she married him, there's no denying that. He was a door-to-door salesman, and he could charm the pants off a snake. And you have to understand, Lydie was going through a rough period back then. The older sister she worshiped had been off the deep end ever since she'd lost her husband in Korea—you know how wild Bess was back in those days; we hardly ever saw her. As for me, I was living the life we had both always dreamed of. I was happily married and living in my own home, with a beautiful baby girl. Then there was Lydie—making a pittance as a waitress with no hope of being able to afford college. She had to live with your grandma and grandpa, and the rules of the house hadn't changed much since we were children. The situation would be tough on any sister, but with identical twins, it was especially difficult. We had always done everything together before. Lydie never resented me, and she adored you and your father, but she was very unhappy nonetheless. You might even say she was getting desperate—desperate for anything even remotely exciting to happen in her life. Unfortunately, that's when she met Mason Dublin, and she latched onto him like a life preserver.''

The waiter reappeared and set a basket of crackers down on the table in front of Frances. He hovered for a second, awaiting further instructions, then slipped quietly away, undoubtedly sensing this was no time to pitch an early lunch.

"Mason was charming and clever, and he had big dreams," Frances continued. "He talked of all the money he was going to make and the places he'd travel to. Your aunt is a very practical person, as you know, but she was young, bored, and lovestruck to boot. He swept her off her feet in a matter of days, and before anyone in the family even knew what was happening, they had eloped."

Leigh digested the information. She had never known her aunt Lydie to be anything but sensible, hard-working, and honest. Still, she had always had a fun-loving streak just below the surface, and it wasn't that hard to imagine such an emotion dominating her youth. Leigh couldn't blame her for eloping with a salesman. She just wished the tale had had a happier ending.

"So what went wrong?" she asked quietly.

Frances breathed out in a huff. "Everything, of course. Neither of them had any money saved up. Mason didn't own a car. More importantly, they had nowhere to live." She picked up her glass to take another drink, but finding it empty, opened a package of crackers instead. "Your grandma and grandpa were quite reasonable, under the circumstances. They offered to let Mason live with them, in exchange for a small amount of rent and some handy work."

The gloom in Frances's voice dragged down any hopes Leigh had of hearing about early marital good times. "I take it that didn't work out too well."

Frances waved her hand in dismissal. "Mason was a drifter, a free spirit. He hated living in that house. He wanted to go on the road full-time until he had saved enough money to get the two of them their own place. But Lydie didn't want him to leave. She was scared to death he wouldn't come back. So your grandpa got him a job at Heinz—low-level factory work. Mason hated that too, of course. He was miserable, and he started talking to Lydie about running off together and living on the road. I don't know if she would ever have agreed to that—I rather doubt it—but before she had a chance to decide, she found out she was pregnant."

The waiter returned, and this time Leigh did have a request. She wanted something sweet to counteract the quickly developing bad taste in her mouth. When the waiter had left, Frances continued.

"It was very distressing for all concerned, I'm afraid. Mason started talking about taking Lydie to New York City or Chicago and looking for work there, and your grandpa had a fit—and rightly so. He told Mason that if he didn't tough it out at Heinz, they'd throw him out for good, which sent Lydie into hysterics." She paused a moment, as if reliving a few more bad memories she didn't want to share. Then she cleared her throat and went on.

"So you can see the situation was rather desperate. I do believe Mason loved Lydie, but he was too young and too self-centered to give up his dreams of the good life. Getting rich was all he ever talked about—he was always cooking up some scheme or other that would be *the big one*, the one that would change his luck forever and give Lydie everything she'd ever wanted. He made up stories about the life they'd have—Lydie and he and the baby—traveling around the world making more and more money. The worse reality got, the more determined he became not to give in to it. That's why it happened."

It? Oddly, the thought of Mason as a criminal had somehow fled Leigh's mind. Now it was back. "So he decided to rob a bank?" she asked weakly.

Frances nodded sadly. "We never knew how he got linked up with the man who actually planned the heist. That man—something Donovan, I believe his name was—was a career criminal, and dangerous.

Lydie had never seen him before that night. Apparently, Mason had agreed to be an accomplice for a share of the take. It was supposed to be enough for he and Lydie to get a place of their own, to set them up for a while while Mason could look for a job he liked better."

The waiter appeared with Leigh's sweet roll and coffee, but she barely even noticed him. A horrifying thought was starting to brew in her insides. "Lydie didn't—" she began uncertainly. "I mean, they didn't plan—"

"Of course not!" Frances said indignantly. "Lydie had no idea what Mason was planning. He told her that he had a new idea and that they'd have a lot of money soon, but he was always saying that. After the robbery, when he told her what had really happened, she was absolutely devastated."

Leigh tried to imagine the horror of having the man she loved tell her that he'd just robbed a bank, but even her fertile imagination fell short. If her own squeaky-clean husband ever so much as kept the wrong change, she would be dumbfounded. "Then what happened?" she prompted.

"Lydie came and told me, of course," Frances answered tonelessly, her eyes once again seeming many years away, in a very grim place. "She made me swear never to tell anyone, not even Randall. And you know, I never did." She sounded proud of herself, in a sad sort of way. "The whole thing would have put your father in a very awkward position."

Leigh's brow furrowed. Her father was a straight-arrow all right, but Frances's story had ceased to make sense. She had to have told her husband about the robbery at some point, because he had been the one to tell Leigh about it. She was about to point that fact out when Frances began talking again, her mind still three decades in the past.

"The days after were the worst of both our lives. We listened to the news reports and read every paper, praying every minute that that poor bank employee who'd been shot would be all right. Lydie was beside herself. She wouldn't even talk to Mason—much less let him come back to the house. She told your grandma and grandpa that he had the flu and was staying with friends because he didn't want to give it to her when she was pregnant. In truth, neither of us knew where he was, and Lydie didn't seem to care. It was like a giant switch in her heart had suddenly turned off."

Except that love didn't work that way, Leigh thought. And Lydie was carrying his baby, besides. "But the man lived, didn't he?" she asked tenuously.

Frances nodded. "Thank the Lord for that. If he had died, Mason could have been charged with murder, even though he didn't do any of the shooting."

Leigh took a deep breath. "He said that?"

Frances nodded again. "He told Lydie that his role in the whole affair was just to watch the doors—that Donovan had assured him no one would get hurt. Mason swore to Lydie that the gun he was carrying was Donovan's, and that it wasn't even loaded. He did seem genuinely distressed about the man getting shot, I'll give him credit for that. But Lydie was having none of his excuses. She just shut him out. Slam. That was it. She told him to leave and that she never wanted to see him again."

They sat in silence for a moment, Leigh looking down at her untouched sweet roll while Frances compulsively wiped the table with a tiny cocktail napkin.

"It was a very difficult decision for Lydie to make," Frances said finally. "She must have still loved Mason, though she certainly didn't act like it. But her only concern was for her child. She refused to let Cara be brought up as the daughter of a bank robber. To grow up with an indignity like that . . . She paused another moment, shaking her head. "It may be hard for you to understand now, since nobody is held responsible for their own actions these days, much less their parents'. But back when you girls were little, who and what your parents were was very important. Cara would have been stigmatized, and Lydie couldn't bear that.

"That's why she told Mason to leave and never come back. She figured the sooner he got away from Pittsburgh, the less likely he was to get caught. And if he never got caught, she could make up whatever story she wanted to explain his disappearance. And that's exactly what she did."

Leigh felt her eyes growing moist, and she quickly took a sip of coffee. "What did Lydie tell Grandma and Grandpa?" she asked quietly.

"Oh, they knew about the robbery," Frances said matter-of-factly. "They weren't stupid. After a few days, when Mason didn't return, they started grilling Lydie, and eventually she told them."

"What did they do?" Leigh had a hard time imagining her stable, conservative grandparents dealing with such a tragedy, but then, she was having a hard time imagining most of Frances's story.

"What could they do?" her mother responded. "They supported Lydie's decision. Told her they'd do whatever they could to help her raise the child on her own. Randall and I promised too, of course."

The inconsistency that had bothered Leigh earlier popped back into her head. "But you said you never told Dad about the robbery," she said, confused.

Frances gave her daughter a hard stare, then pursed

her lips and sighed deeply. "That wasn't what I said," she answered softly, but firmly. "What I never told your father about—what I've never told anyone about . . ." She paused, maddeningly, and took a deep breath before looking her daughter straight in the eyes again. "What we never told anyone was how Mason and Donovan managed to escape from the police that night."

Leigh looked back at her mother's stony face and steeled herself for the worst.

"Your aunt Lydie drove the getaway car."

Chapter 9

Leigh stared blankly at her mother. "Lydie did what?" she croaked, her voice sounding like someone else's.

"You heard me," Frances replied brusquely. "She had no idea what she was doing, of course. Mason simply introduced her to a new friend of his one afternoon—Donovan—and they went out joyriding. Then Donovan said he and Mason had an errand to run, and he told Lydie she could take the car for a spin while they were out. She just had to be sure to be back at a certain corner by a certain time, because he had somewhere he had to go right afterwards.

"In retrospect, I know it sounds like an obvious setup, but it seemed like a harmless enough request at the time. Lydie could drive, but she didn't get the chance very often, and the car was a nice one. Not all girls back then even had the occasion to learn, you know. So she was happy to comply. It wasn't until Mason and Donovan returned to the car, sweaty and panicked, that she had any idea something was wrong. They just told her to drive back to West View, which she did. It wasn't until they ducked down in the seats that she suspected they were running away from something, and then she could hardly stop to argue about it. She thought that Mason was in danger, so of course she wanted to help."

"Of course," Leigh agreed sadly, looking at the sweet roll on her plate with no trace of appetite. The thought of what her aunt must have gone through made her nauseated. First there would have been the slow realization that the man she loved was a criminal, and then the horror of facing motherhood alone—with her baby's father rotting in jail. But there was even more to be afraid of. Lydie could have been charged as an accessory herself, in which case she might actually give birth in jail. . . . Leigh shuddered.

"I don't need to tell you how impossibly painful the whole incident was for Lydie," Frances continued soberly. "It changed her whole personality. She became almost mechanical—completely dedicated to giving Cara as close to a normal life as she possibly could. I've never seen any woman push herself harder, before or since. She worked two waitressing jobs while I babysat Cara along with you, and then she did some seamstress work on the side. She refused to take a dime from Mason, of course—she didn't want her daughter raised on dirty money. But between your grandparents and Randall and myself, we managed to set her up in the house next door to ours, and that was a real godsend. It was cheap because it needed a lot of work, but Lydie did most of it herself—she taught herself as she went. I think hard work simply became therapeutic for her. It helped her to forget."

Frances paused long enough to emit a deep sigh. "I know you think your aunt Lydie is a fun-loving soul, and she still is. But I often wonder how different she might have turned out if—" She cut herself off. "But I suppose that doesn't matter now." She took a deep breath and turned piercing eyes back on her daughter. "So you see, we have to take these blackmail threats very seriously."

Leigh nodded dumbly. There were too many concerns spiraling around in her head to make sense of, but she voiced the most obvious one first. "Do you think—" She paused. The words were hard to say for some reason. "Do you know if the statute of limitations has run out? I mean, Lydie's not really in any legal danger anymore, right?"

Frances shook her head. "I'm sure she's not. Mason always said—I mean, our understanding was that the statute of limitations for armed robbery was only about five years, so that hasn't been an issue for a while. Plus, I'm sure Lydie would stand a good chance of acquittal, with a decent lawyer. That lady lawyer of yours certainly did wonders."

Leigh chose to ignore the reference to her own nefarious past. Something else her mother had said was bothering her, but she couldn't quite put her finger on it.

"Prosecution isn't the issue," Frances continued. "The issue is Lydie's feelings. If this story ever became public knowledge, she'd be absolutely devastated. It's taken her a lifetime to get over the nightmare, and if the story were to suddenly become public—" She stopped with a shudder. "I just don't know what it would do to her. It can't happen, and that's that."

Leigh nodded in agreement, and the two sat quietly for a moment. Finally, Frances said in an exasperated tone, "I'm very surprised Mason has done this, frankly. It doesn't sound like him."

Leigh threw her mother a baffled look. "You're surprised that a man who would rob a bank would stoop to blackmail?"

Frances shook her head. "It's the timing. Mason could have blackmailed Lydie anytime he wanted. Why torture the poor woman now?"

The conversation she'd had with Gil popped back into Leigh's mind. "*Movers and Shakers,*" she said authoritatively. "Mason's blackmailing Gil, not Lydie—she wouldn't have enough money to bother. As for the timing, we figure he must have seen Gil and Cara on the television show and only then realized he had a rich son-in-law."

Frances's eyes clouded over with confusion, and with something else that could have been guilt—or maybe just empathy. "But you said that a letter came addressed to Lydie, at her house," she questioned.

Leigh backed up her thoughts and supposed she hadn't been too clear on that point. Probably because the second blackmail attempt never had made any sense, and as befuddled as the whole situation already was, her brain had chosen not to dwell on it. "We don't think the second letter was from Mason," she explained feebly. "It was written really poorly—grammar and spelling, I mean. It didn't sound like the same man Gil was talking to on the phone; it really seemed as though the threats were independent of each other. That's why we think that the second letter was just a half-hearted bluff. Like Mason shot off his mouth to a buddy about what he was going to do, and the buddy tried to capitalize on it himself. I'm not sure what the PI advised Gil to do about that one."

Frances continued to stare at her daughter with a puckered brow.

"What?" Leigh asked.

"Nothing," Frances said quickly. "I can't quite picture Mason doing this, that's all. I suppose he could be particularly desperate for money, but given the lifestyle he's undoubtedly led for the last thirty years, this can't possibly be the first time."

The image of Mason beating his fist on the wall of

the train station came back to Leigh with a rush. "He looked desperate to me, all right," she said grimly.

Frances cast a searching look on her daughter. "What exactly did you see him do? What did he look like?"

Leigh tried to come up with a colorful description of the man she had perceived as an ordinary schmuck—but she didn't think it was too helpful. "I bet he had red hair when he was younger, didn't he?" she asked when she had finished.

Frances nodded, her eyes far away. "Beautiful golden-red hair, a nice thick crop of it." She continued to stare into the distance for a moment, then quickly retrieved her purse from the chair back and stood up. "I'd like to discuss this with Gil before Lydie gets back. Perhaps you can distract Cara for a while this afternoon?"

Leigh nodded and rose. "I'll think of something." She started to pull some money from her wallet, but Frances waved her off.

"Put that away," she said, laying several bills on the check tray.

Leigh looked at her mother gratefully. All told, she had handled this much better than expected. For a pathological worrier, her mother did have a knack for coming through in the major crises. Leigh started to thank her, but got cut off.

"Just remember next time, dear," Frances said patronizingly, crooking one finger in the direction of the untouched sweet roll. "It's wasteful to order food when you don't plan on eating it."

By the time Leigh had helped locate Frances's luggage—which during their conversation had been summarily labeled as "unclaimed" and carted off to the airport's nether regions—and driven her home, it was well past noon. She was therefore disappointed, but not surprised, to find her apartment empty.

Empty of other people, that is. Its feline occupant proved delighted to see her, as evidenced by the fact that she bothered to rise from the verboten kitchen tabletop in greeting. "Hi, Mao," Leigh said affectionately, not up to scolding at the moment. "Whatcha lying on?"

Mao Tse had the habit of appropriating any new flat surface as a day bed, so notes left on the kitchen table qualified. Leigh scooped the Persian off a piece of yellow legal paper and read the familiar, overly neat handwriting that had been obscured beneath her.

> Got your note—and don't think I don't know you're up to something. This has to do with Cara's moonlight visit, doesn't it? I'll be back around five, but then I have a late dinner. We'll talk before. I'll even make you quesadillas. Be here. Love, W

Leigh smiled. She couldn't remember the last time she'd had quesadillas, but she knew it was before Warren's first campaign signs had gone up. She'd be here, all right. There were just a few more little issues she needed to settle. . . .

Keeping a purring Mao Tse under one arm, she grabbed the portable phone, plopped down on the couch, and dialed. A husky female voice picked up on the second ring.

"Yep?"

"Hey, Maura," Leigh answered, with as much cheer as she could muster. Thinking of the quesadillas definitely helped. "It's me."

"Koslow!" the voice replied, booming. "How the

hell are you guys? I guess it's getting down to the wire for the future prez, huh?"

Leigh smiled, feeling a little guilty. She, Warren, and Maura Polanski had been the three musketeers back in their college days at the University of Pittsburgh. The Creative Genius, the future President of the United States, and the Wondercop. It was only in the past year that their harmoniously platonic three-way friendship had been complicated by a marriage. Maura had seemed to take it all in stride, but then you never knew with Maura. The six-foot, two-inch, 210-pound detective seemed to take everything in stride.

"Just two more days now," Leigh answered. "I can't wait till it's all over, frankly. I hardly see the man. How are things with you?"

She listened while Maura gave her a brief update on the health of her mother and aunts, then an even briefer summary of her recent activities with Allegheny County's General Investigations squad. Maura was never one to gush. "So, what's up?"

"Nothing life threatening," Leigh answered, twiddling Mao Tse's tail nervously around her forefinger. It was the truth, literally, but at some level it still felt like a lie. Gil's reluctance to involve the police in his problems with Mason Dublin put her in a rather awkward position, seeing as how blackmail was right up Maura's alley. She understood his desire to keep Cara out of the fray, but her sixth sense knew good and well that one way or another, Detective Polanski would eventually end up right in the middle of it. That being the case, Leigh didn't intend to burn any bridges.

"I'm just doing some research for a friend," she began. She could call her cousin-in-law her friend, couldn't she? "And I've run up against a technical question I thought you might be able to answer for me."

There was a short pause, after which Maura uttered a distinctly suspicious-sounding, "Shoot."

Leigh took a breath. "My friend is looking into a bank robbery that happened back in the seventies. An employee was shot, but not killed. There were three perpetrators, none of whom were ever caught. He wants to know what the statute of limitations is on that sort of thing. You know, whether these people could still get into trouble with the law if their names came out as suspects."

She paused, her heart thumping as she counted the seconds before Maura's response. The longer the wait, the less likely that the policewoman was buying her story.

"Koslow," the husky voice replied sadly, a full five seconds later, "I thought marriage had mellowed you."

Drat. "What do you mean?" Leigh asked as innocently as possible. "It's just a technical question."

The detective sighed. "Nothing with you is ever technical. Now who the hell do you know that's mixed up with recovering bank robbers?"

Leigh exhaled in exasperation. "Please, Maura. Can't you just tell me? Marriage *has* mellowed me, I swear. Constant contentment. Continual bliss. Why would I go looking for trouble? Besides, do you really think Warren would just stand by and let me get involved with criminals?" The word "again" tried to tack itself onto the end of her sentence, but she squelched it just in time.

Two more seconds passed. "Warren's preoccupied," Maura said simply. "Now tell me the truth."

Leigh groaned. "I did. I have a friend who needs the information. He's trying to protect a relative. He doesn't want to involve the police, and I've got to respect that for obvious reasons."

The next pause seemed endless, but it was fruitful. "I believe the statute on armed robbery is five years," Maura said with resignation. "But that's for the state. If the bank was insured, you're dealing with federal law too. That I'd have to check on."

Leigh brightened. "Could you? Pretty please? My friend will be so relieved."

"I'll bet," Maura said, her voice dripping with sarcasm. "I'll get back to you. In the meantime—"

"I know, I know," Leigh said playfully, smiling to herself, "If you see my name on one more police report, you're going to put me under house arrest and sentence me to watch *Martha Stewart Living* 24/7."

The policewoman chuckled ever so slightly. "I like that."

An hour later the Cavalier pulled into Cara's gravel driveway, which the faint autumn sun was doing its best to dry out. Leigh grumbled as she parked and walked toward the farmhouse, then chastised herself for grumbling. She loved babysitting Mathias—really she did. But on this particular instance, she would much rather be at the private investigator's office, going over everything with her parents and Gil. Her presence, however, had not been considered necessary, and since Cara would be at a professional meeting most of the afternoon, it made sense for her to free up Gil while he had the chance to get away.

But still.

She knocked on the back door, and Gil's voice answered from somewhere within. "Come on in," he called, "I'm in the middle of a serious diaper here. Just a minute."

A strong aroma wafted past Leigh's nostrils as she entered, and she couldn't help but grin. Gil the Adonis, buried in toddler poop. It was a satisfying image.

She made her way into the kitchen and was stopped at once by the file that was neatly laid out on the table next to Gil's wallet and car keys. A quick, innocent flip of the front cover told her what she wanted to know. It was the PI's file on Mason Dublin. Throwing any possible guilt to the wind, she immediately sat down and dove right in.

The letterhead said Trent Walker, Walker Investigations. She tried again to picture the man she'd seen outside the bus station as a private detective, but he just didn't fit the mold. He had looked more like a history professor, or better yet, an accountant.

She scanned through some legal mumbo jumbo about services and fees, then happened on what was evidently Mason's rap sheet. Insurance fraud in Ohio, tax evasion in Illinois, and several check kiting convictions in California. It appeared Mason had been in and out of jail at least as often as he had changed states. His sins were relatively petty, however, and his sentences short. The one exception was also the last on the list—a counterfeiting conviction, for which he had served some respectable time. He had been released early for good behavior back in 1994 and apparently had not been in trouble since.

Until now, of course.

Leigh started to dig deeper into the file, but was stopped by the corner of a familiar-looking, worn flowered binder that poked out from the back. She turned to it quickly, the sight of it flooding her with a sudden, inexplicable sadness. She ran her finger gently over the cover, whose title had been lovingly embossed with yellow yarn by a pre-adolescent Cara. The last time she had seen this folder had been one of the worst days of Cara's life. It was also the last time, Leigh realized, that her cousin had openly mentioned the name of Mason Dublin.

The memory came back to Leigh in a painful wave as she traced the yarn letters with her eyes closed. *My Father*. There had been a time in Cara's early teens when she would stop at nothing to find the man who had abandoned her. And unbeknownst to anyone but Leigh, she had once come pretty close.

Chapter 10

Leigh opened the binder and realized she'd been holding her breath. She let it out in a sigh and began reading the childish cursive on the opening page.

My father's name is Mason Dublin. He was born sometime in the late 1940s, and in 1970, he married my mother, Lydie Morton Dublin. I was born a year later. My father had to leave before I was born, so we never got to meet each other. This is all that I know about Mason Dublin. The rest I'm working out on my own.

Pages of sketches followed—darn good ones for a girl so young. Cara had drawn Mason very similarly each time: tall and slender, with bushy strawberry-blond hair and blue-green eyes just like hers. Always, he was smiling. She drew him holding her as a baby and walking with her hand in hand as a child. She drew him flying airplanes, sailing ships, and blasting off to the moon. But it was the last picture that made Leigh's eyes well up with moisture. Mason and Lydie, standing outside a grand castle, with a grownup Princess Cara holding both their hands between them.

She flipped on ahead through endless stories of Mason and his exploits, many of which she had written herself, at Cara's request. They always ended the same way—with an explanation and a happy reunion. No matter how outlandish the explanations got, the reunions were always the same. *And they lived happily ever after*.

The book's scarcity of known facts about Mason Dublin struck Leigh now in a way that it hadn't as a child. She had always been instructed by her mother never to ask Lydie anything about Cara's father, not to bring the subject up at all. "It's too hurtful for your aunt to talk about," Frances would say. "Just leave the past in the past." Cara got little more from her own mother, who would tear up at the mere mention of her past husband, teaching her daughter from a young age that conversation on the subject was off limits.

Though both girls had accepted this silence as the way things were, looking back now, Leigh found it rather extreme. The red-blond hair and ocean-colored eyes Cara had drawn on her father had come from her own imagination—neither had ever heard a description of his appearance, much less seen a picture of him. The little bit Frances had just told Leigh was the only information she and Cara had ever had about the courtship and breakup, other than Lydie's lie about Mason going off with another woman, to which Cara had very gently been exposed long before she could fully comprehend it.

Couldn't the family have shared just a little more? Perhaps not. Lydie's greatest fear had been that Cara would try to locate Mason when she was older, and even the tiniest bit of information could make or break that quest. But Lydie had been waging an unrealistic battle. Cara was intelligent and headstrong, and when she finally did make up her mind to find out more about her father, there was absolutely nothing Lydie could have done to stop her.

Leigh flipped through more sketches and stories about Mason, which became more elaborate as their creator grew up. At one point, she remembered, Cara had gone through a period of anger, and the entries had changed into stormy renderings of betrayal and revenge. But none of these had stayed in the book. Cara's passions on the subject had soon flip-flopped, and she had torn the uglier pieces out and thrown them away. The last entry, however, remained the same. Leigh had seen it only once, briefly. And that was the last time she had seen the book at all, until today.

I have an aunt named Trudy Dublin who lives in Jennerstown, Pennsylvania. She hasn't seen or heard from Mason Dublin in years. My grandparents are dead. Trudy is an alcoholic and none of her information can be trusted.

Leigh closed the book and exhaled slowly, remembering the first time she had read those words. It had been the summer before she had started college at the University of Pittsburgh. Cara had just gotten her driver's license and was feeling particularly independent. Unbeknownst to Lydie, she had been doing some research and had located a copy of her parents' marriage license. Knowing Mason's date and place of birth and his parents' names, she had doggedly tracked down his older sister, who still lived in the same small town in the Laurel Mountains, just a couple of hours east of Pittsburgh.

Leigh could picture her cousin quite clearly as she set off that day, her cheeks flushed with excitement and her voice nearly giddy. "I've been waiting so long for this, Leigh!" she had gushed. "A real aunt! And she's going to answer all the questions Mom never would." Cara had hugged her and jumped into Frances's car, which Leigh had acquired for the day at great personal risk. "I'll be careful, I promise," Cara had said with a wave. "Remember—I was with you all day at rehearsal. Bye!"

Leigh normally loved practicing with her youth theater group, but she would have enjoyed that afternoon's rehearsal of *The Miracle Worker* much more if Cara really had stayed to watch. She was so nervous about what might befall her cousin—and her mother's car—that she had forgotten to duck when the girl playing Helen Keller took a swing at her, giving Annie Sullivan a very realistic bruised cheek for the duration.

When Cara had finally returned for her that evening, the car was fine, but it was the only thing that was. They rode home in near silence, with Cara unable to say much of anything without choking on the words. Her cheeks were stained with tears and her eyes were puffy—a rare state for her even at that tender age. Only after they were safely cloistered in Leigh's room did she seem to recover her voice.

"She was awful," Cara had begun without preamble. "I've never met anyone like her. The house was a dump—absolutely filthy. And I don't mean that she was poor," she interjected quickly. "I'm not being a snob about that. I mean that she didn't take care of anything. There was trash everywhere, crumbs, dust . . . and bottles. She was an alcoholic, I'm sure of it. She was either tipsy or had a hangover when I got there, I'm not sure. But she wasn't nice at all. I didn't even think she'd let me in at first, then when I told her who I was . . ."

Cara's voice had trailed off, and Leigh had waited

impatiently for more, her heart beating rapidly. "What did she do?"

"She invited me in," Cara had continued, her eyes far away. "She did tell me to sit down and everything. But all she said was, 'So Mason really did have a wife and kid. More's the pity.' I didn't know what to say to that, so I asked her if she had a picture of him. She laughed and pointed at a frame on the wall—it was her and Mason at his high school graduation."

Cara had gone on to insist that Mason had looked just like she'd always pictured him, but beyond that, her story had gotten dark again. "She said my grandparents are dead—that they died in a car accident a few months before the picture was taken. Mason graduated and took off; she didn't know where he was most of the time after that. He'd call once in a while—she knew he'd gotten married and that there was a baby—but then he'd go for years without contacting her. She claimed the last she heard from him was a postcard three Christmases ago, with no return address. And then she told me—"

At that point Cara had started to tear up again, and as Leigh recalled, she had joined her. "She told me that Mason was no good, and that I should turn around and go right back where I came from and forget all about him. She said no decent man would run off and leave his own baby and that I was better off without him."

The memory of those words stung Leigh even now, as she knew they had stung Cara for years afterward. The search had been abandoned, and Cara never again mentioned the aunt, or even her father, except in the most cursory manner. She seemed to have fallen into the same pit of denial that her mother inhabited—don't speak of it, and it will cease to exist.

As they grew older, Leigh had occasionally tried to broach the subject, but the rebuff was always the same. "I don't have a father," Cara would insist flippantly. "I had a sperm donor." Nevertheless, the pain in her eyes was always disturbingly deep, and Leigh couldn't help but worry what damage could be caused by a lifetime of suppressing such an emotion.

Her reverie was interrupted by a clean-washed masculine hand, which gently took the binder from her and returned it to the file. "You've seen that before, haven't you?" Gil asked quietly.

Leigh nodded, then looked up. Mathias was nestled in the crook of his father's other arm, looking quite pleased with himself. She smiled at him, then turned back to Gil. "Did Cara ever tell you about the visit to her aunt?" She suspected she knew the answer already—the fact that he had acquired Cara's book was pretty clear evidence that his wife had shared it with him at some point. Leigh was embarrassed to admit a twinge of jealousy. As far as she knew, Cara had never told anyone besides her about the disastrous visit, and it had always been an important secret between them. A part of her still assumed Cara would never discuss Mason with anyone else, but that was silly.

"She showed me the book shortly before we were married," Gil answered. "She almost never talks about her father, as you know. It still hurts too much. But if you're wondering if I know about Trudy Dublin, the answer's yes. The PI located her as well, and even attempted to question her."

Leigh's eyes widened. Of course. Why hadn't she thought of that? Mason could still be in contact with

his sister—she might even have a current address
for him.

But before she could get too optimistic, Gil shook
his head. "She's no help to us at the moment, I'm
afraid," he said grimly. "She's been living here in
Pittsburgh on the North Side for the last ten years,
but her apartment was burglarized last week, and
she was nearly beaten to death. She's been at Allegheny Central Hospital ever since, and she's been in
no condition to answer any questions about anything."

"How awful," Leigh said soberly, wondering at
the timing. Mason Dublin was back in town, and his
sister—admittedly an estranged one—was in the
same city, on death's door. It was coincidence she
didn't care to think about.

Pushing back a strong wave of anxiety, she held
her hands out for Mathias. The toddler leaned
toward them with a grin, and his father handed him
over, then tucked the file under his arm and picked
up his wallet and keys. "Cara may be home before
I am," he said, heading toward the family room. "If
so, just tell her I needed to meet with the PI again.
There's no need to explain your mother's involvement."

She looked after him skeptically. "I'm not sure
how much longer we can keep Cara out of it," she
said, following him to the back door. "Not since
there's really—I mean, not since we know the threat
from Mason is real."

Gil paused a moment and swung around to look
at her. He looked as if he was about to tell her something, but then he stopped. "There are some things
you don't know yet, Leigh," he explained quickly,
"that the PI found out. But I'm already running late.

Your parents or I can fill you in later, OK? Thanks for watching Matt."

It wasn't OK at all—the waiting-to-be-filled-in part—but Leigh didn't have much choice about it. Gil was out the door before she could reply, and Mathias was already clamoring to be put down. She set him on the floor with a pat, and he immediately toddled off toward a red plastic fire truck. *Things she didn't know yet. Like what?*

She stewed on the couch for several minutes before realizing that Mathias was trying to open the back door himself. "Go out," he said, as clearly as a precocious toddler could. "Out, Anlee!"

She looked through the picture windows at the sun shining over Mathias's customized play yard and decided it wasn't a bad idea. She put on the boy's jacket and took him out to the fenced-in enclosure, which was home to a sandbox, playhouse, and swings fit for a king. Given that the farm also featured a small pond and a creek that tended to flood, the fence seemed prudent. Leigh took the lid off the sandbox, watched Mathias step gleefully inside, then settled herself in Cara's gliding loveseat.

It was a cool day, but with the sun warm on her face and her recent lack of sleep catching up to her, she was afraid to close her eyes for fear of nodding off. She needn't have worried. Scarcely a minute of solitude had passed before four wet paws pounced jarringly into her lap.

"Aggie!" Mathias called enthusiastically. "Aggie dog!"

"Yes," Leigh answered, with considerably less enthusiasm, "so I noticed." The orange-and-white Brittany spaniel that had claimed her lap was now in the process of licking her face, as well as distributing a few more muddy paw prints on her chest. "Down,

Maggie. That's a girl," she said, attempting to round up the flailing paws and remove them from her person. She managed to shift the dog to the cushion beside her, and Maggie cooperated, though the licking continued.

"Aggie dog!" Matthias chanted, now in a singsong. Leigh grinned at the squirming beast that Gil had purchased for Cara as a watchdog. Showed what he knew. Like so many sporting dogs of her ilk, all Maggie ever wanted to do was run. The comings and goings of the farm's visitors were of little consequence—unless, of course, they wanted to run with her. Maggie tolerated the slow movement of the swing for another ten seconds or so, then took off again. She was heading toward the pond—which, if the state of Leigh's clothes was any indication, was probably where she had just come from—when she stopped short, ears perked. A millisecond's analysis later, she was bound hell-for-leather around the back of the barn.

"Aggie go," Mathias chanted.

Leigh watched as the little dog disappeared around the far corner of the old barn. She expected to see her bounding around the near edge any moment, but the dog didn't reappear.

Leigh's brow furrowed. Maggie had probably gotten waylaid by a chipmunk. Still, something about her long absence was disturbing. While just about anything could grab Maggie's attention, nothing ever managed to hold it for very long. Was there something behind the barn that she could be eating? A dead bird? A groundhog?

Mathias was intent with his work now, after having decided that all of his sandbox toys must be lined up along the fence with perfect precision. Leigh got up quietly and walked in the direction of the barn, watching the toddler over her shoulder as she went. "Maggie!" she called, knowing the effort was probably futile. She attempted a loud whistle, which she'd never been very good at. "Maggie? You still back there?"

She was only a few paces from the barn's back edge when a flash of orange and white shot out from around the corner and collided with her knees. "There you are!" Leigh said relieved, patting the ecstatic little spaniel. "What were you doing?"

The dog accepted only a few pats, then shot off to circle Matthias's play yard. This time he ignored her, having finished the alignment and moved on to the next phase of the project—filling each toy with sand one spoon-sized shovelful at a time. Maggie took the rebuff with good humor and dashed off toward the pond again.

Leigh smiled and began walking back to the loveseat. She had only gone a few steps when everything turned black.

Chapter 11

Leigh's face was cold, and she was lying on the damp ground. She lifted her head and looked up. She was at Cara's farm, outside by the barn, lying on the grass in a very uncomfortable position. She sat up a moment and looked around, unable to figure it out. What was she doing at Cara's, anyway?

Her eyes drifted toward the driveway, where the only vehicle visible was her Cavalier. She'd come out here for some reason, obviously. Now what was it?

Mason Dublin was trying to blackmail Gil, she recalled easily. And her mother had just told her that Lydie herself had been messed up in the bank robbery. She had come out here to baby-sit . . . Her mind began to clear as she struggled stiffly to her feet. But when her eyes landed on the open gate of Mathias's play yard, her brain, as well as her heart, stopped cold.

Mathias. The image of the toddler loomed up in her mind, overwhelming her with sheer terror. *Mathias!* Where was he? She began to run toward the play yard, stumbling a few times along the way. She tried to scream his name, but every time a sound escaped her throat, something in her skull seemed to crack, and her voice caught deep in her lungs.

The play yard was empty. She looked toward the house, where some rational part of her brain insisted he must be. She had taken him to the play yard, she remembered now. But then what happened? She tried to concentrate, but thinking sent sparks of pain shooting off behind her eyes and didn't produce any results besides. She couldn't remember what had happened next. Still, she had an overwhelming feeling that wherever Mathias was, it wasn't the house.

Led by some idea she couldn't quite put her finger on, she walked out into the center of the yard, and stood still. She might not be capable of yelling, but she could listen. Though the beating of her heart was so loud that she feared it would drown everything else out, she closed her eyes and thought of Mathias. If he was out there, he would be making noise. It was a cardinal rule of toddlerdom.

She waited only a few seconds before the blessed sound reached her ears. It was a high-pitched squeal, and it was coming from the woods by the road. Her feet moved instantly toward the sound, but after only a few paces, she stopped.

Something was wrong. The squeal wasn't a happy one, of that she was sure. It could be a cry of annoyance, or frustration, or fear. If she were Mathias's mother, she could probably have pinpointed it exactly, but since she wasn't, she'd have to do the best she could. But it wasn't just the squeal that bothered her. Had Mathias simply wandered away while she slept?

It only took an instant then for her brain to shake its cloudiness. She hadn't fallen asleep. She didn't know what had happened to her, but she knew one thing. Whatever had just happened wasn't an accident. She hadn't fallen asleep on the ground just because she was tired, and Mathias hadn't figured out how to undo a double child safety latch by himself.

He hadn't just wandered away. Someone must have taken him.

Kidnapped. The terror that shot through her then was so intense it burned. Mathias was screaming because someone was carrying him away. Away from his home, away from his mother—

An image of Cara floated up in Leigh's mind, her arms empty, her eyes dull. *My baby,* she was saying weakly. *Where is he?*

Leigh's eyes narrowed, and her whole body felt hot. *No.* This wasn't happening. And it wasn't going to happen. She cocked her ear toward the sound again, and determined that while it was indeed coming from the woods, it wasn't moving toward the driveway or the main road. Mathias seemed to be moving downstream along the creek.

The pain behind her eyes was forgotten as Leigh's mind began turning cartwheels, her fear replaced by sheer determination. She was sharp, she was on it, and she was *going* to get that baby. Her legs began to move, and after a few unsteady paces she broke into a run. But when the distant cry again met her ears, her steps slowed. Though her heart was still screaming for pursuit, her brain knew it was pointless. The abductor had too much of a head start. The best she could hope for would be to get a license plate number and description if they got into a car, but there was no guarantee she could reach them before they drove off, and even if she did, she would be a long way from a phone.

There had to be another way.

A *car*, she thought quickly. The abductor had to have one somewhere. He must have been staking out the farm, waiting for just the right, unguarded moment. The car couldn't be sitting in the driveway, or even on the shoulder of the side road where she had staked out Gil a few days before. There was too much traffic on that road and too many houses nearby for anyone to manhandle a screaming toddler without being noticed. So where else might a get-away car be hidden? If she couldn't beat them to it, she thought with a flash of hope, perhaps she could block their path out.

She turned and started back toward her own car, thinking about the layout of the farm and trying to visualize where Mathias's cries were headed. The creek flowed down from Wexford, and all along its far bank ran the Harmony Shortline, a wide, flat lane of grass that had once been a railroad bed. She and Cara had hiked up it soon after the farm had been purchased, with Cara spinning wild tales of how Mathias would ride it up to the high school some day, after it had been turned into a bike trail.

High school. The memory of Cara's carefree dreams for her son's future sent another wave of determined heat through Leigh's body. Where would the car be? *Think, woman—think.*

In a rush she remembered the hike and how the Shortline trail had been flanked on its other side by a winding residential road, first with a cluster of houses, then, as they had walked north, with more woods and a private road.

Of course. One could park a car on that road all day without rousing much suspicion. And odds were that no one would be close enough to see or hear anything. The only problem was—Mathias's cries hadn't been headed north. They'd been headed downstream, where there wasn't anywhere to park a car.

Leigh stopped in frustration. She didn't think the abductor would have left his car so near the road, but what if she was wrong? If so, she had no chance of catching them now, on foot or wheels. The best she could do would be to call the police immediately. But without a description of the vehicle . . .

She started back toward the house, but as the sound of rushing water struck a sudden, unexpected cord in her brain, she pivoted so sharply that she wiped out in the mud. The creek! The wet weather of late had swelled it significantly, and though it was hardly the stuff drownings are made of, traversing its north end with a toddler in tow would be tough. The water was waist high in the center, and the banks were steep. But at the south end of the farm by the main road, the creek widened out, and an adult—even one toting an unwilling load—could easily splash through it with no worse than wet pant legs.

She struggled to her feet with renewed optimism. That had to be it! He was headed downstream to get Mathias across the creek, then he would jog back up the Shortline to his car. But he wasn't as smart as he thought he was, because she was going to get there first.

She broke into another run, moving behind the barn and through the woods toward the north end of the farm. Though vaguely aware that there was something wrong with her head, she had no intention of wasting time dwelling on it. What she had to do now was find that bridge.

It took her only a few moments, since Cara's rummaging about all summer had cut a half-decent trail through the appropriate place in the brush. She slammed quickly through, heedlessly pushing branches and brambles out of her way. When she reached the creek, she halted only for a second, noting that the woods around her hadn't stopped moving at the same time she did. But she could worry about that later. Now she had to get across the bridge.

"I use the term 'bridge' loosely," Cara had said with a laugh the day she had first showed it to Leigh. "It's ancient. Built with two metal rails left over from the Shortline, and some kind of sheet metal. But it's stable enough. Come on!" Leigh had followed her insane cousin over the bridge that day, even though she'd thought better of it. Now would be no different.

She stepped out onto the contraption without hesitation, determined not to think how far the bank was below, or how much higher the creek was than it had been on her last passing. Once again she could hear occasional cries from Mathias, one or two of which she could swear had been muffled before they ended. *Go!* her heart screamed at her. *Go, go, go!*

But she could hurry only so much. The sheet metal was rusted through in various places, and several planks were missing entirely. At two points she had to rest a foot directly on the rails, and just as she neared the far bank, one of the planks loosened beneath her and slid. She lost her footing completely, but thanks to a low-lying branch, she was able to steady herself and land safely on the muddy slope.

She climbed up the far bank and pushed through the brush on the other side of the creek, thankful that it obscured any view of the bridge from the Shortline. Stepping carefully out onto the trail, she assured herself that her prey was not yet in sight, then ran headlong toward the private road.

When she saw the blue Escort ahead, she felt giddy with relief. Gotcha, you bastard, she thought without guilt, closing the distance between her and the car with a sprint her body hadn't attempted in years. When she reached it, she was breathless, but she kept moving. She'd found the car, but there was more she had to do. First off, identify it.

The Escort seemed new, and the inside was spotless. *A rental.* She tested the driver-side door and wasn't surprised to find it unlocked. Nothing to steal, after all—and perhaps no time to waste fumbling with keys later. She moved quickly around the back, staring hard at the license plate. Memorizing things had always come easily to her, but these numbers and letters were swimming a bit. She clenched her jaw to steady them, then committed the sequence to memory. NTZ-879. *Got it.*

Now what? Ideally, she would disable the car and then run for the nearest phone. But the only disabling thing she could think of was slashing the tires, and she had no knife. Beyond that, she was clueless. Perhaps she could just lift the hood and start unplugging things?

A shrill bark sounded from down the trail, and Leigh dodged quickly behind the rear fender. *Maggie,* she thought anxiously. Had the dog been following them all along? It wasn't unlikely. Maggie wasn't the type to molest strangers, particularly ones who patted her head, even if they were carrying crying toddlers. She was probably giving the abductor a wary escort, in which case he could be within sight of the car already.

Damn. Forgetting the car-disabling option, she quickly searched her brain for another plan. She would confront the kidnapper directly if she had to, but it would be difficult to pry Mathias from his arms, particularly if he was strong. The fact that he might very well be armed was not lost on her, but under the circumstances, it just wasn't relevant. He had Mathias, and that wouldn't do.

Another squeal from the toddler wafted to her

ears, closer this time. The cry penetrated her head and wove its way straight through to her bone marrow, making her quiver with anger. *Nobody messes with my nephew,* she reassured herself, fists clenched. *Not. Gonna. Happen.*

It occurred to her in a flash. He would approach the car on the driver's side, toss the toddler onto the passenger seat, and take off. That would be her chance. Perhaps it was a good thing that she hadn't been able to scream or call for Mathias earlier. Now she had an unlocked car and the element of surprise, and that might be just what she needed.

Positioning herself at the right end of the back bumper, she tried to calm her thumping heart and waited. She could hear footsteps now, and little interrupted grunts from Mathias.

"Quiet!" a man's voice said, low but with unmistakable irritation. "For God's sake, cool it. You're going to be fine."

Leigh tensed in horror as a soaking wet spaniel soared around the front corner of the car and ran headlong into her, almost knocking her over. Stifling her own cries, she sat up quickly and tried her best to ignore the dog. Maggie couldn't give her away now. She just couldn't. Leaning as far into and under the car as humanly possible, Leigh prayed the man wasn't paying any attention to the hyper dog and couldn't see her from where he was standing. Apparently her prayers were answered, because Maggie took off again as quickly as she had come, and the man's only response was to open the driver side door.

Now.

With a series of jerky and not at all seamless motions, Leigh shot out from behind the bumper, wrenched open the passenger door, reached inside, and found herself head to head with the man she had subconsciously expected to see. His pale blue eyes widened in shock as her arms circled the toddler he'd just let loose of—and started to pull.

Mason Dublin sat, stunned, for only a second, then reached over and grabbed after the moving child, catching one flailing ankle as the rest of the little body disappeared out the door. Mathias screamed, most certainly in pain this time as his tiny leg was stretched between the two of them. Leigh fought the urge to slacken her hold, choosing instead to lift her right foot and throw a vicious kick at Mason's outstretched elbow. He howled and dropped the ankle, and Leigh and Mathias bowled backward.

She kept to her feet, however, and as he struggled across the seat and out the passenger door, she scrambled around the Escort's front end, placing the car squarely between them. She was breathing like a freight train, and the toddler clamped tightly in her arms still hadn't stopped screaming in her ears, but such nuisances were only background. Her eyes were on Mason Dublin, and her brain was working just fine.

He stood up on the other side of the car and glared at her maliciously, then made a dive around the front fender. But Leigh was just as quick, and no matter which way he headed, she kept the car between them. Eventually his body slumped and he exhaled slowly. "Just give him to me," he said slowly, as if talking to a petulant child.

If her voice had been working, Leigh would have laughed.

"I said, give him to me," he repeated. "I don't know how you got here, but you're not going to mess this up. I can take him from you whenever I want, you know."

Her eyes narrowed, and a low gravelly voice erupted from what she assumed was her throat. "Not with your genitals intact."

Mason's pupils widened briefly, then his own eyes narrowed. "Why, you little—"

Suddenly aware of the tool that was now back at her disposal, Leigh pressed Mathias's head against her chest, covered his exposed ear with her forearm, and screamed her guts out.

Ignoring the occasional cries of a toddler was one thing, but ignoring the prolonged, panicked screaming of a grown woman was downright inhuman, and there simply had to be somebody within earshot. Mason stepped back, his brow furrowed with irritation as he looked wildly from side to side. Throwing her one more icy glare, he broke into a string of curses and dove back into the passenger seat.

Leigh quickly moved to the rear of the car, afraid that he was going to come straight through, but she needn't have worried. He merely scooted across into the driver's seat, fumbled with the keys, and started the engine.

She backed up quickly, not knowing if he planned to run her down for sport, and was relieved to see a deep drainage ditch just a few yards behind her. He couldn't pursue her there, not if he wanted to drive off afterwards. She watched the car carefully as she jumped down into the ditch, trying not to forget to keep screaming. Meanwhile her brain churned along steadily, trying to think of other scenarios he might try, and when the car started forward and drove away, she was temporarily flummoxed.

What was he up to now? She stood ankle deep in ditch water for several more seconds, with Mathias blubbering wildly in her face and an agitated Maggie pawing up and down her shins, before it occurred to her that he was gone. Really gone. As in, he wasn't coming back. He had given up and taken off. And Mathias, though not the happiest kid in the world, was perfectly safe and stashed firmly in her own arms.

Somehow, the revelation didn't seem to penetrate. "He's gone, sweetheart," she cooed to Mathias mechanically, her rusty voice almost blasé. "Let's go find Mommy."

She started walking slowly down the Shortline, having no delusions about her ability to maneuver the rickety bridge. Her body was tired—or something. She trod steadily to the wide part of the creek, splashed through with Mathias in tow, then walked back up through the woods and across the field toward the farmhouse. She had just reached the play yard when Cara's car pulled up into the driveway, and her smiling cousin got out.

"Well, hello!" she said cheerfully. "What are you doing here?" As she came closer, her eyes fixed on Leigh's wet pant legs, then Mathias's tear-stained cheeks. "What on earth happened?" she asked, alarmed. "Are you two OK?"

Leigh held the toddler out to his mother, and her arms—which had been locked into their clasping position a little more tightly than she had realized—complained with the effort. "He's just fine," she said calmly, watching as Mathias dove eagerly for Cara, nestling in rapidly and clinging to her neck. "Just fine."

It occurred to her that the words sounded as though someone else had said them. Then everything went black again.

Chapter 12

Cara was slapping Leigh's cheeks and screaming into her ear. It was very annoying.

"Stop it!" Leigh protested, lifting her head a little off whatever hard object it was lying on. A stab of pain shot through the back of her skull and down her neck, and she quickly let her head fall back down again. "Ouch," she said dully.

Cara let out a quick sigh of relief, but her eyes were still anxious. "Leigh, please. Talk to me. What happened? Did you hit your head?"

Leigh thought a moment, but she honestly had no idea. "Where are we?" she asked. She was lying out in the middle of her cousin's yard, which made no sense.

"Lie still, all right?" Cara said comfortingly. "Don't try to move. I'm going to run to the car and get my cell phone."

She was off like a shot, and Leigh was left alone with the cold November sun in her eyes and, in half a second, a frantic Brittany spaniel licking her face. "Maggie," she groaned, "please go away." Surprisingly, the dog complied, and in the moments before Cara reappeared, a brief glimpse of clarity returned to her painful brain.

"Mathias?" she called out suddenly, thinking she should get up, but before she managed to move, Cara had returned with a phone in one hand and Mathias on the opposite hip. He looked calm and content, and Leigh instantly relaxed, listening with detached indifference while Cara called for the paramedics. Then all at once, she remembered she had a mission.

"You have to call Gil!" she insisted, tugging on her cousin's arm. "He's at the PI's office. Hurry!"

Cara looked at her in confusion. "Don't you want me to call Warren? I don't know what happened, but you've obviously hit your head somehow. You've got a huge goose egg, and for all we know you've got a concussion to go along with it. Now what's his number? He has a cell phone, doesn't he?"

Leigh considered this information and realized that she had no idea what had happened to her head. But she did know that Mason had tried to take Mathias, and she knew that he had gotten away. "Did you call Gil yet?" she asked.

Cara's brow wrinkled with worry. "Leigh, please listen to me. Do you remember Warren's number? I'm afraid I don't have it."

Warren's cell phone number, Leigh thought wearily. She'd dialed it a million times. Whatever the heck it was. She started to shake her head, but another stab of pain quickly stopped her. "I can't remember," she said, frustrated.

"That's all right," Cara soothed. "I'll find him somehow. You just relax. The ambulance will be here any minute, and they'll give you something for that headache."

But Leigh wasn't to be soothed. She knew she should be doing something. She just wished she could remember what and then keep it in her head for more than five seconds. "Call the police," she blurted out.

Cara leaned down close to her in alarm. "The police? Why do you want the police?"

A part of Leigh still wanted to protect her younger cousin from the grim truth, but a larger part knew that wasn't feasible—or wise. Mason had tried to kidnap his grandson once, and he might try it again. Cara couldn't keep him safe if she didn't know.

"Leigh," Cara coaxed anxiously. "If it doesn't hurt too much, can you tell me what happened?"

"A man," she began, deciding a little vagueness would be all right, at least for now. "A man tried to take Mathias. Call Maura. I'll tell her."

Cara's face drained of color. She reached out an arm and clasped her son, who had wandered a few steps away, to her side. "What did you say?" she whispered.

"Call her, please," Leigh pleaded. "And call Gil at the PI's office and tell him to come home right away."

Cara sat rigidly for a moment, squeezing Mathias so tightly that he began to whimper. She loosened her hold on him only a little, glanced warily about the farm, then spun into action.

Leigh tried to relax and steady her thoughts as Cara fought her way through Directory Assistance and a long phone chain to reach Detective Maura Polanski. "Thank God it's you, Maura," she finally said with relief. She was attempting to explain what little she knew about the situation when Leigh motioned for the phone, and Cara held it down for her.

"It was a blue Escort," Leigh said, her voice little more than a croak. "A rental. The man was in his fifties, almost bald, gray hair, light blue eyes. Dingy clothes. He took off"—she thought a moment, realizing much to her chagrin that she had no idea how long ago he had departed—"Maybe twenty minutes ago? I don't know. I got the license number, though. It was—" She broke off again, panic overtaking her. She knew it. She *had* to know it.

"Take your time, Koslow," Maura said comfortingly.

Leigh tried to picture the plate in her mind, but the numbers and letters in the image were all swirling about, and no matter how hard she tried to reorganize them, they kept spelling out the same horrible words. MASON DUBLIN. She closed her eyes and winced. It was no use.

Cara pulled the phone away. "She's too fuzzy to remember now, Maura. I'm afraid she's going to pass out again." Cara responded to what were undoubtedly Maura's strict instructions with a few yeses and all-rights, then hung up the phone. "Leigh Koslow," she said softly, stroking her cousin's brow, "you're going to be just fine, you hear me? You have to be."

Leigh wanted to open her eyes and tell her cousin to stop worrying, but having her eyes closed felt too darned good. She was drowsy, and she just wanted to sleep. Even though she was sure that the wailing of the ambulance siren was physically drilling a hole in her skull, she refused to open her eyes. The drowsiness was nice, and she intended to hang on to it for a while.

"She's coming around, Warren."

Maura Polanski's deep voice somehow made its way through Leigh's brain without hurting, and she smiled with relief as the detective's chubby pink cheeks came into view, framed by her dark, short, forever-unstyled hair. There had been a lot of voices and a lot of faces clamoring around her, and she had been trying her darnedest to ignore them. But the pain in her head seemed finally to be gone, replaced with just a dull sense of pressure. She smiled as she noticed Warren's gorgeous brown eyes looking down at her too. Her two best buddies. How nice.

She knew she was in a hospital bed. The ambulance ride, the doctors, the big tunnel her head had been wheeled into, she'd been awake for all of it—sort of. She just hadn't been paying attention. But now everything seemed OK. Better than OK. It was probably some sort of narcotic-induced euphoria.

Excellent.

"Don't look at me like that," she protested. "I'm just peachy. Never been better. Turn up that opioid drip, man—I like it."

Warren sank down beside her and took her hand, and Maura laughed. "I don't think you're getting any of the heavy stuff, Koslow, but whatever it is, I'm glad it's working."

Leigh looked at her husband with a sudden sense of remorse. "Oh, shoot. I didn't miss the quesadillas, did I?"

Warren looked at her disbelievingly. His face was tight with worry, but his eyes smiled. "You know I'll make you quesadillas whenever you want," he said with attempted cheerfulness. "As long as you don't scare me to death like this ever again."

"No problem," Leigh answered cheerfully. Damn, those drugs were good. Maybe they had her on steroids.

"I don't want to hassle you too much too soon, Koslow," Maura began, pulling up a chair to the other side of the bed. "But the sooner you can tell me exactly what happened at Cara's place, the sooner we can get moving on it. We know that someone hit you on the head from behind, probably with a rock. We also know that a neighbor reported hearing a woman screaming a few minutes before Cara called me." She then repeated the information Leigh had given her over the phone, word for word. "Anything you can add to that now?"

Hit over the head with a rock? Leigh considered. She couldn't very well argue the fact, but she didn't remember it either. The last thing she remembered before blacking out was taking Mathias to the play yard. The next thing was waking up by the barn. She puzzled a moment. Then an image popped into her head, seemingly from nowhere. She looked up at Maura, smiling broadly. "NTZ-879," she said triumphantly. "It made me think of the name 'Nitzi,' and it's sort of like the phone number I had in college."

Maura pulled out a notebook and scribbled quickly. "The license plate on the Escort," she confirmed. "Good going. Anything else you can tell me?"

"He had his car parked on that private road on the other side of the Harmony Shortline," she explained. She then described as concisely as she could how she had managed to beat him back to his car and recapture Mathias, leaving out the crack about the genitals. Maura took everything down in her notebook, her facial expression unchanging.

"Had you ever seen this man before?" the detective asked when Leigh appeared to have finished.

She swallowed. "Yes. I saw him Saturday night at the Greyhound station. Have you talked to Gil about this yet? There's so much you need to know—"

Warren cut her off. "It couldn't have been Saturday night Leigh. You were with me at the dinner, remember?"

Leigh felt a stab of guilt. She still hadn't got around to confessing her meanderings. "It was after I left," she told him apologetically, before turning back to Maura. "You *have* talked to Gil, haven't you?"

Maura exhaled slowly, then nodded. "I have. Just now, as a matter of fact."

"So you know it was Mason," Leigh said, feeling more than a little relieved that the truth was out. "You know he tried to kidnap his own grandson. We've been wanting to keep Cara out of it—"

"I think," Maura said, rising, "that it's time you and Gil compared notes. He and Cara are waiting outside, along with your parents. I'm sure they're all anxious to see you. So if you'll excuse me, I've got work to do."

Maura saluted the other two musketeers and departed, leaving a pregnant pause hanging in the air.

Warren broke it. "Either you explain all of this now," he said a little too calmly, "or I'm going to explain corporate investment strategy."

Leigh winced. "You would torture a woman in a hospital bed?"

"Yes."

"I'll explain everything soon—I promise," she said earnestly. Although she was proud of the financial aptitude that was moving her husband along so well in politics, nothing—with the possible exception of Frances's friends' medical problems—could bore her more. "But right now I really need to talk to Gil, without Cara around. Do you think you could distract the rest of them for a while?"

Warren's eyebrows rose. "You want me to forgo asking why you were at a bus station in the middle of the night so that I can engineer a private meeting between you and a man who looks like a younger version of Robert Redford?"

She couldn't help smiling. "Well, yeah. But I promise to make it up to you."

"Darned right you will," he said suggestively, rising. "But I'm warning you, we *will* be back."

Leigh gave him an appreciative kiss, and he headed out the door. It was only a matter of seconds before Gil appeared alone, as she knew he would. Her politician husband could convince almost anybody of almost anything.

"So what did the PI say?" she asked her cousin-in-law anxiously, a million questions swirling in her head. "Was he able to track Mason after he left the bus station? Could he help the police find him now? And what about the situation with Lydie? Is she in any legal danger if we catch him and he squeals?"

"Hold on, there," Gil admonished with a tired smile, sitting down in the seat Maura had just vacated. "First things, first. Are you sure you're okay?"

"Of course I am, as long as Mathias is all right. I didn't hurt his leg, did I?"

He shook his head. "He's fine, thanks to you. We really can't tell you how—"

"Please don't," Leigh interrupted quickly, her face getting hot. Cara had gushed over her to excess already; she couldn't handle it from him too. "Just fill me in on what's happening."

He watched her with a puzzled expression, then sighed and rubbed a hand over a chin that hadn't been shaved in a while. "I'm guessing you didn't see the mug shots in the PI's file."

She stared at him dumbly. There were mug shots in the PI's file? She had only gotten as far as the rap sheet when Cara's notebook had distracted her. "No, I didn't see them," she answered. "But I did see Mason up close and personal at the bus station Saturday night. I hope I didn't get in the way or anything," she added quickly, wondering to what extent the PI had ratted on her. "But I got a perfectly good look at him. There's no doubt it was the same man who tried to kidnap Mathias."

At the word "kidnap," Gil's eyes assumed a haunted look. He had probably been blaming himself, she thought, wondering if the abduction attempt could have been prevented. But how could any of them have known that Mason was desperate enough for money to try something so heinous? And why, it occurred to her suddenly, would he be that desperate anyway, since he really did have information that could ruin Lydie's reputation, if not her life? After all, Gil hadn't refused to pay the blackmail. He'd only asked for the details of what Lydie had done. Mason could have provided those easily enough, couldn't he?

"Maybe he wasn't taking Mathias for ransom," she offered. "Maybe he—" she broke off. The theory sounded lame, but more bizarre things had happened. "Maybe he just wanted to see his grandson," she said softly.

He shook his head strongly, his eyes brimming with anger. "No. The police found a ransom note in the sandbox. It did ask for money, and it was signed Mason Dublin."

Leigh's hopes fell. "I see," she said soberly. There appeared to be no getting around it. Cara's biological father was as low as they came. And there was no hope of keeping that grim truth from her any longer. "So. Have you told Cara that her father is a blackmailer and a kidnapper too?" she asked miserably.

He looked back at her with equal misery. "In a way," he said heavily, "I wish he was."

She stared at him in confusion, and he continued. "It's what I didn't get a chance to tell you earlier. The PI had those mug shots of Mason Dublin all along, so he knew last night that the man who picked up the note at the bus station was *not* Cara's real father."

Leigh's mouth dropped open; then she snapped it shut. The ordinary schmuck . . . was an ordinary schmuck? "But if that guy wasn't Mason, then who—"

"That's just it," he explained tightly. "We haven't the faintest idea."

Chapter 13

"But why," Leigh questioned, her head starting to feel cloudy again. "Why would somebody else claim to be Mason?"

"The PI has two theories," Gil answered. "The first is that both this guy and the one who wrote the other letter somehow found out that Mason had both a rich son-in-law and a potential hold over his ex-wife. They decided to use the information at the same time—maybe because they'd just discovered it and maybe because they recognized my name and Cara's on *Movers and Shakers*, and it helped them figure out how to locate us."

Leigh looked back at him skeptically. As much as she would have liked to believe that Mason Dublin, miracle of miracles, really had nothing to do with any of this, she wasn't that much of an optimist. How could anyone possibly find out about Lydie's past unless Mason had told them? "Seems far-fetched," she responded.

He nodded in agreement. "There's the second theory."

Leigh waited.

"That Mason Dublin was really behind the whole thing, but sent a lackey or two to do his dirty work."

There was silence for a moment, and she wondered to herself which option was really better. In the first case, there was at least a glimmer of a chance that Cara's father was not a monster. On the other hand, if he *was* behind everything that had happened, they had a much better chance of tracking down the kidnapper.

"The second theory has its problems, too," Gil continued. "Both blackmailers were vague about the details of Lydie's crime, which Mason knew full well. And the fact that the man you saw resorted to kidnapping after we called his bluff . . ." He shook his head. "That's hard to figure with Mason in the picture."

An image of the kidnapper in the train station flashed through Leigh's mind. He had just read Gil's letter in the Happy Meal box, and she remembered the look in his eyes quite distinctly. It was sheer, total desperation. Not exactly the look an employee might sport when his boss's plans were foiled. Did he have something more personal at stake?

"So what did the PI find out?" she asked again. "Did he trace the cab the man got into last night?"

He nodded. "The cab took him to the airport, which we thought originally was good news. But now we suspect he was just trying to cover his tracks in case he was followed, because apparently all he did there was rent a car and drive back into town."

Leigh frowned. "Under Mason's name, I'm sure."

He threw her a determined, but slightly guilty look. "I don't know. Maura Polanski is taking over the investigation. But in light of what's happened, I'm keeping the PI on as a security consultant. We won't be caught off guard again."

An image flashed in her mind of Snow Creek Farm patrolled by armed guards and encircled by a twelve-foot-high electrified fence. Her cousin would be miserable. "So, how much have you explained to Cara?" she asked hesitantly.

Gil's eyes flickered with discomfort. "She saw the ransom note," he began. "So I admitted to her that the other threats had also come from men claiming to be Mason Dublin. Of course I knew then that they weren't from him, so I was able to reassure her. But she's not stupid. She's well aware that her father must have something to do with all this."

Leigh's stomach, which had been developing a nice pit of late, started churning again. "How did she take it? You didn't tell her about her mother's role in the robbery, did you?"

"Of course not," he said defensively. "Your parents and I agreed that that decision should be left to Lydie."

They heard Warren's voice loud in the hallway, and Leigh took it as a warning sign. Seconds later, Cara swung open the door. She looked pinched and pale, but she greeted Leigh with a broad smile.

"I had to fight your parents for the next visitor's spot," she said with feigned cheerfulness. "Your mom is champing at the bit to come fuss over you. How are you? Better?"

Leigh nodded and tried to smile back, but the emotion was just as fake on her end. Her cousin's method of dealing with pain had always been to suppress it, and Leigh wished, not for the first time, that her headstrong cousin would just break down and bawl like the rest of the world.

"Would you mind if we had a moment alone?" Cara asked her husband. Her voice was pleasant, but it brooked no dissent.

"Sure." Gil rose, hugged his wife's shoulders, and left, throwing Leigh a conspiratorial glance on his way. *You see how she is*, it said.

When the door had closed behind him, Cara turned her eyes toward Leigh. Despite her best efforts, the hurt that brimmed in them was obvious. "I know Gil was just trying to protect me," she said in a low, even voice. "You all were. But I can't help feeling like a fool because of it. And I want you to tell me the truth. Do you think my father is behind all of this?"

Leigh looked into her cousin's tortured face and felt like crying herself. "I don't know, Cara," she said weakly. "I really don't know. Nothing makes a whole lot of sense right now."

Cara's eyes searched hers for a moment; then she nodded and stood up. "I believe you," she said, her voice stronger, "but I do know that there's more Gil isn't telling me." She walked over to the hospital room window and stared out blankly. "The funny thing is, in a way I'm glad he won't. I'm not sure I want to hear it."

Leigh's heart sank a little. Her cousin's relentless—and often reckless—pursuit of real-life puzzles was legendary, but since her visit to Trudy Dublin, her father's disappearance was the one case she had had no interest in cracking. Evidently, the attempted kidnapping of her son fell into the same category. Too close to home.

"Cara," Leigh said helplessly. "Please try not to worry about Mathias. He's safe now. As for Mason Dublin—" She tried hard, but no comforting words came to mind. Was there nothing she could say?

Cara turned back from the window and sat down on Leigh's bedside again. "Never mind," she said distantly. "Mathias *will* be fine, and as for the rest— I've lived with a no-good father as long as I've been alive, so none of this should shock me. I've known ever since I met Trudy that all the childish wishing in the world wasn't going to turn the man into a hero. And I don't need him to be. I already have a father, a wonderful one."

Leigh smiled painfully. Randall had always gone out of his way to treat Cara as if she were his own, and Leigh had never minded sharing. The vet clinic, which her cousin had never had the stomach for, had always been Leigh's special place to be with her father. But when Randall wasn't working, he was always there for Cara. He never missed a father-daughter dinner or a dance recital, and he rearranged his whole schedule whenever the Indian Princesses had a camp-out. He had taught her how to pitch a ball overhand, interrogated her dates, and given her away at her wedding.

There was no doubt Cara did love Randall like a father. But that didn't mean anyone could heal the still-gaping hole in her heart.

"Why are you looking at me like that?" Cara admonished as Leigh's eyes grew moist. "I just said it doesn't matter to me how much of a loser Mason Dublin is. Now stop worrying about me, all right? I'm a big girl. You're the one with the concussion. Is there anything I can do for you?"

Leigh wiped her eyes and took a deep breath. "Yes," she said emphatically. "I want a Diet Coke and a Snickers. And I don't care what the damn chart says."

Cara grinned, for a moment looking more like her old self. "Done!"

"Good," the pudgy little neurologist said, pocketing his penlight. "Your neurologic examination is normal this morning, and the scan showed no signs of a skull fracture or bleeding."

"That means you're springing me, right?" Leigh

said hopefully. Dr. Varma was clearly of Indian descent, but his corpulent physique bespoke a distinctly American lifestyle. He hadn't even had a fit when he caught her with the chocolate, though he had been firm in his order that she stay overnight for observation.

"You're sprung," he quipped, "but you should rest at home at least a day. No work, no marathon jogging. Nothing strenuous for forty-eight hours, just to be safe."

Leigh smiled. She had already planned on taking off for the election, but an extra day away from Hook would be nice. She was bored stiff with the chemical company promotion she was spearheading, and though sitting at her desk staring at her computer screen probably wasn't considered strenuous, it did hurt her head at times.

She wanted some time off to think, to put the whole business with Mason Dublin in perspective. She was certain there was something they were all missing, and she was determined to figure out what it was. Particularly since an intriguing thought had occurred to her in the middle of the night last night, somewhere between the third and fourth time a nurse had interrupted her sleep to ask if she remembered her name and where she was. If her memory wasn't mistaken, someone of particular interest was also at Allegheny Central Hospital.

"The nurse will provide you with written instructions," the doctor continued. Then he smiled devilishly. "Of course, your mother requested her own set."

Leigh closed her eyes in embarrassment. Frances could be counted on to flip out over any minor injury, but a concussion was one of those classic catastrophes for which overzealous mothers spend their whole lifetimes preparing. Leigh had often wondered if her mother wasn't a little disappointed that despite all the times she had gone barefoot in the rain, she had never actually gotten pneumonia.

"Call if you experience any of the symptoms listed. OK?" The doctor pronounced the word "okee," and Leigh responded with a smile and a nod. He was no sooner out the door than she was on the phone.

"Yes," she said pleasantly to the receptionist at the hospital's main desk. "I was hoping to visit my aunt this morning—Trudy Dublin. Could you tell me her room number and when visiting hours are?" She committed the first piece of information to memory, ignoring the second. "Uh-huh. I know about her condition, but I really would like to see her, just for a minute. The doctor said OK. Right. Thanks."

She hung up the phone and proceeded to change from the hospital gown into the sweat suit Warren had brought her. He had promised to deliver donuts at nine, which meant she still had some time to kill. She wasn't a good liar, but the fibs she had just told were only white lies. She might not be Trudy Dublin's blood niece, but Cara was, and that was close enough. And the doctor did say *something* was OK, just not her visiting a trauma patient.

She dressed quickly and headed out, not certain whether she wanted to look like an inmate or a visitor. Visiting hours hadn't started yet, so street clothes might arouse suspicion. But she had no desire to go strolling around in a flimsy hospital gown either. Perhaps the sweat suit was a fair compromise. Any roving nurses would just assume she was an ambulatory patient out for a little exercise.

She slipped out her door and turned to look at the nameplate on the wall beside it. 912 KOSLOW, LEIGH. Excellent, she thought to herself. Trudy was only one floor up. Though physically she was feeling rather chipper, she couldn't deny there was still a certain fogginess clinging inside her head, and she had no desire to pass out in the middle of a long ride on a crowded elevator.

Walking slowly would suit her purposes better anyway, she reasoned. Most patients out for a stroll would take it easy. They also wouldn't be looking at all the room numbers as they walked by, she reminded herself, trying to get an idea of the layout with an occasional discreet glance. The halls were buzzing with uniformed people, but as could be expected, they all had more important things to do than notice her.

She found the elevators quickly enough, but a rather long walk awaited her on the tenth floor, and when she finally reached the door she sought, her head was throbbing a little. No matter, she assured herself. She would only stay a minute, then she would go straight back to bed and await her donuts.

DUBLIN, TRUDY. LAWHEAD, MARY ANNE, the nameplate announced. She looked both ways, then slowly opened the door. The room was still darkened by a partially closed shade, and both occupants appeared to be sleeping. The woman by the far window, who looked at least eighty years old, was snoring loudly, but it was the middle-aged woman in the near bed who immediately drew Leigh's attention.

What she had hoped to accomplish by seeing Mason's sister for herself, she hadn't fully worked out, but to deny a significant role for curiosity alone would be pointless. Cara's meeting with this woman had changed her whole mindset on her father drastically, and Leigh had always wondered exactly how that had happened. Had Cara told her everything about that horrible day? Maybe, maybe not. Somehow, in the back of her mind, it seemed that meeting Trudy Dublin herself would clarify things.

But gazing down at the limp figure, she immediately felt she had made a mistake. Mason's sister looked dreadful. She lay perfectly still in the bed, her ribs and left arm swathed in bulky padding. Her face was so badly bruised that only the waxy skin of her neck was left to betray her actual pallor, while swelling and an odd-looking brace on the right side of her mouth gave evidence to a broken and wired jaw. She breathed softly and quietly, her gaunt chest barely moving as the thin sheet rose and fell over ribs that were probably also broken. A morphine drip waited ready by the bed, good indication that sleep was probably all this woman had to look forward to for a while.

Saddened and more than a little horrified, she stepped closer to the woman and studied her face, trying to erase the bruises and imagine her awake and smiling. Was there a resemblance to Cara? Perhaps. They had the same high cheekbones, not to mention overall petite stature. But beyond that, it was impossible to tell. And even if the woman had been alert, one thing was certain. She was in no condition to answer questions from a self-serving passerby.

Feeling like a louse for even thinking of troubling her, Leigh touched the woman's hand lightly through the sheet. It was the most she could do in the way of an apology. The poor woman might have been an alcoholic, and she might have treated her niece badly once, but she didn't deserve this.

Leigh pulled her hand back and turned to leave, resolving to ask her cousin if she would be willing to visit. If what the woman had said all those years ago was true, Cara might be Trudy Dublin's only living relative. Except, of course, for her worthless jerk of a brother.

A motion in the doorway caught Leigh's eye, and she started. Someone had just been standing there, watching her. Security? Was she in trouble for being there? She moved to the doorway and looked both ways down the hall, but none of the uniformed employees bothered to look back at her.

She whispered an empathetic farewell to Trudy and scooted out. She wondered if the police had ever caught the man who beat her up, and resolved to ask Maura. Why Trudy Dublin's welfare was suddenly of such interest to her, she wasn't sure, but she couldn't shake the feeling that this woman and Cara needed each other.

Her head was back to hurting for real when she finally reached her own room, and she fell into the uncomfortable bed gratefully. A few minutes with her eyes closed, she reasoned, and she would be fine. She had to look one hundred percent healthy by the time her husband arrived, because he had promised her hysterical mother that he wouldn't take her home until she did, and Warren—despite his political inclinations—always kept his promises. She curled up on her side and smiled, thinking of how sweet and attentive he'd been the night before, even after she had confessed her midnight rendezvous. Fling all the ball-and-chain jokes you wish, she thought happily, burrowing into her pillow, marriage is where it's at.

She was in the middle of a somewhat more graphic memory when the unmistakable feeling of being watched assaulted her once again. Her eyes flew open, and her heart leapt as she saw the shadow of a figure standing above her. Flipping over in a flash, she found herself face to face with her silent visitor.

She drew in a breath as a familiar set of eyes met

hers. They weren't at all threatening, only curious. And perhaps a little concerned. She had looked into their sea-green depths a thousand times, and she knew their every twinkle and expression as well as she knew any eyes in the world.

They were Cara's eyes.

But the person standing beside her wasn't Cara.

Chapter 14

"Hello, Leigh," the man said casually, smiling.

Leigh stared back warily. Her medium height/medium build, late middle-aged visitor was wearing a plain blue scrub suit, unadorned with any particular laundry mark, much less a nametag. But she knew who he was.

She thought briefly of lunging for the call button, but her arm didn't move. His smile was disturbingly engaging. It reached right up into his eyes, which, besides being the same blue-green color as Cara's, twinkled with the same mischievous light. Windows to a restless, eternally optimistic soul.

"Didn't mean to scare you," he said kindly, still smiling. "You have a minute?"

Leigh surveyed his high cheekbones and thick crop of strawberry-blond hair, which was graying softly over the ears. If not for his square jawline and heavily weathered skin, he would almost be too pretty for a man. She took a deep breath and faced him squarely. The temptation to return his beguiling grin was strong, but she resisted it. "How did you know my name?"

He tossed his head in the direction of the hallway. "It's on the door," he said matter-of-factly. "Besides, you look like Francie."

She shifted uncomfortably on the bed, the last lingering doubts in her mind dispelled. The only people who ever called her mother "Francie" had been Frances's parents and siblings—i.e., people who could remember a time when she had deserved such a bouncy, frivolous-sounding nickname. Leigh herself was hard put to imagine her mother as anything but a Frances, even if the rumor were true that she had not always worn support hose and pearls. As for a physical resemblance between them, there was little evidence of it now, but she had to admit a certain likeness between herself and the twins' high school graduation pictures, when their naturally brown hair was still shoulder length. Today, with Lydie's dyed boy-cuts and Frances's curly white coif, Leigh was in little danger of being accused of resembling either.

Which made her all the more certain that the man in front of her was Mason Dublin.

"What do you want?" she blurted out. There were a million things she needed to ask him, not to mention the issue of tying his hands and feet and chaining him to the bed before he could slip away. But her reflexes seemed to be running slow this morning.

He paused a moment before answering with another question. "Do you know who I am?"

She nodded. Her heart was pounding in her chest, and a big part of her wanted to start asking him those million questions pronto. Why didn't you ever come back to see your daughter? How could you just abandon her—and why are you torturing her now? But she made herself try to concentrate. This was not some chummy, long-lost uncle she could invite home to dinner. He was a criminal. And he might very well be the reason her head hurt like hell again.

She crossed her arms defensively over her chest. "Tell me what you're doing here or I'm calling security."

Mason Dublin, who had the gall to look slightly amused, stepped back a few inches and raised his palms in a gesture of peace. "Didn't mean to upset you," he said softly. He was speaking in one of those husky-yet-gentle whispers that one normally heard only from actors in date movies, and it gave Leigh a clear revelation of what her poor, romance-starved aunt had been up against thirty years ago.

"I'm not upset," she said coolly. "I just get a little testy around men who try to kidnap my relatives."

The twinkle in the ocean-green eyes dulled. "I heard about that on the news," he said, his expression turning serious again. He stepped away and Leigh immediately leaned toward the call button, expecting him to flee. But instead, he began to pace at the foot of the bed. "The truth is, that's why I'm here. I want to help." He fixed her with a pleading look. "I need to know . . . This kidnapper. Did you get a good look at him?"

She stared at him for a long time, her brow wrinkled in concentration. She wished Warren or Maura were here. She wished anyone were here who could tell her this whole scene wasn't some kind of post-concussive hallucination. With the dull ache in the back of her skull pounding to new heights, she couldn't be sure she was thinking clearly. In fact, she was pretty sure she wasn't. "Why should I tell you?" she asked, more to stall for time than be impertinent.

Mason didn't seem offended. "Because it's important." His voice turned earnest. "Please. Was he in his mid-thirties, about six-foot-three, very skinny, with jet-black hair and Mick Jagger lips?"

Leigh's eyebrows rose at the description, which was comical at best. She would have thought he was teasing her, but the look on his face was solemn. "No," she answered promptly, not seeing how denying it could hurt anybody. "He didn't look anything like that."

Mason's five-star smile returned instantly, as did the twinkle in his eyes. "Wonderful." He watched her for a moment more, during which time she had the distinct and unsettling impression that he knew much more about her than her name. "Well," he said quickly, backing up. "It was nice talking with you, finally. Good-bye, Leigh."

"Hey!" She protested, sitting up and swinging her legs off the bed. "Not so fast!"

He turned back only halfway and looked at her regretfully. "I really can't hang around here anymore—it isn't safe for you. In fact, it would be best if you didn't tell anybody I was here at all. Could you do that?" He winked. "Appreciate it." His gaze showed clearly that he didn't expect her cooperation, but he headed toward the door anyway, not waiting for an answer.

Her heartbeat quickened, and she stood the rest of the way up. He couldn't leave now, he just couldn't. It wasn't fair. "Your name was on the ransom note!" she shrieked, hurting her own head.

To her relief, Mason Dublin stopped in his tracks. He wheeled around and stared at her, his pupils widening. "What did you say?"

"I said," she continued intently, "that whoever tried to kidnap your grandson signed *your* name to the ransom note. Now why would he do that? Tell me!"

Mason continued to stare at her for another moment, his eyes flashing with alarm. "What did he look like?" he asked evenly, not moving. He continued to stand quietly while she debated whether to answer, which seemed—at least to her—to take a very long time.

"He was your age, maybe a little older," she began unsteadily. "Medium height, medium build. Bald on top, with a little ring of gray hair on the sides."

She watched Mason carefully as she spoke, noting how his face gave away his emotions every bit as much as Cara's did. Clearly, he knew exactly who she was talking about. When she had finished the description, he turned his head away from her and swore under his breath. Then for a moment he simply stared at the wall beside her, looking alternately relieved and angry.

"Don't worry about him," he said finally, his eyes unwilling to meet hers. "I'll take care of him." He glanced down at his watch, then threw an anxious look toward the door. "I have to get out of here," he said distractedly. "Visiting hours are starting."

Ignoring the irony of the comment, she simply stood still and glared at him expectantly. If he thought he didn't owe any explanation, he had another think coming. But before she could protest, he spoke again.

"We'll have to talk more about this, Leigh. But not here. I can't be seen with you—or anyone in your family. Give me your phone number and I'll contact you later. All right?"

No, Leigh's rational mind insisted, it wasn't all right. The man was obviously involved in the kidnapping attempt somehow, and if she had any sense she would have called security as soon as he stepped into the room. But she hadn't. Why not?

Because she was a slave to her own foolish intuition, that was why. And for whatever undoubtedly idiotic reasons, she didn't believe the man in front of her would intentionally hurt anybody. She listened like a third party as her phone number came shooting out of her mouth.

Mason mumbled to himself when she finished, apparently committing the number to memory. Then he nodded, turned on his heel, and left.

Leigh sat numbly on the bed, watching the last spot where he'd stood. The whole scene had been surreal, her head was pounding, and all attempts she made at processing what had just happened were failing miserably. Finally, desperate to calm the throbbing, she simply lay back down and closed her eyes.

"Are you sure you don't want it yourself?" Maura asked politely, a vanilla-frosted donut already en route to her mouth.

Warren shook his head. "I had a few on the way over. You two eat up."

Leigh stared at the donut in her own hand with anguish. When she couldn't eat a chocolate-frosted cake, things were bad.

"Are you sure you feel well enough to go home today?" Warren asked, looking at her worriedly. "I can tell you're hiding something. What's up? Does your head still hurt?"

"A little," Leigh said quickly. It did hurt a little. It hurt a little several dozen times over. But what was really bugging her was the prospect of relating her recent Twilight-Zone experience without being looked at like a mental patient. She was a neurology patient. There was a difference.

"Maura," she began, forcing herself to take a small nibble of frosting, "did you know that Mason Dublin's sister was in this hospital?"

The detective nodded, speaking only after she had consumed another large bite. "Gil has got me up to date on everything the PI found out. But Trudy Dublin isn't well enough to be questioned right now."

"I know. I went to see her this morning."

They both looked at her in surprise. "Aren't you supposed to be staying in bed?" Warren asked accusingly.

Pride dictated that she ignore the reprimand, but secretly, she relished every moment of his husbandly concern. "Trudy was asleep," she began, "but when I was in the room, I felt like someone was watching me. And it turned out somebody was."

Maura and Warren both looked at her expectantly. She took a deep breath and started into her story, finishing without a pause. It sounded completely nuts. Add to that that she had been sound asleep when they arrived, and they were sure to think she was lost in la-la land.

"So what you're saying," Maura began flatly, jotting in her notebook, "is that Mason Dublin (1) was in this hospital, presumably visiting his sister incognito outside of visiting hours; (2) had some reason to believe a tall man with Mick Jagger lips had kidnapped Mathias; (3) was surprised to discover that his own name was on the ransom note; (4) recognized your description of the real kidnapper; and (5) thinks it's unsafe for him to be seen with anybody in your family."

Leigh nodded with surprise. Despite all odds, Maura not only seemed to believe her but had logically organized the facts to boot. Amazing. The detective tapped her pen on her notebook for a moment, then looked up at Warren. "This makes more sense than you might think," she said confidently. Then she turned back to Leigh. "You remember asking me to check out the statute of limitations on bank robbery?"

She nodded again. It had been only yesterday, but it seemed like ages ago.

"Robbery and aggravated assault carries a five-year statute—state and federal," Maura explained. "Your aunt could have been charged with robbery just for driving the getaway car, but more likely, she'd have been charged with something lesser, like hindering apprehension or prosecution. That only carries a two-year statute. Either way, she's in no danger now."

Leigh smiled in relief. "What about Mason?"

Maura's brow wrinkled slightly. "That's a bit trickier. The statute doesn't run if the suspect flees from justice and remains out of state—so if there had been a warrant out for him all this time, then technically he could still be prosecuted. But since it looks like he was never even named as a suspect, he's got nothing to worry about either."

Leigh digested the news slowly. "But then, why are two different people trying to blackmail Lydie and Gil? And why is Mason skulking around like a fugitive?"

"If what you just told us is true, then Mason knows the blackmailer who tried to kidnap Mathias. My guess is he dropped some information to his buddies about how he had this rich son-in-law he could put the squeeze on whenever he wanted to. Maybe they had all just watched the *Movers and Shakers* episode—who knows. Anyway, neither blackmailer seemed to know the whole story about the bank robbery. They were betting on a bluff, and when it didn't work, one got desperate and tried to kidnap Mathias instead."

Leigh remembered the look on Mason's face when she had described the kidnapper. Anger—perhaps at a buddy's betrayal—but also relief. He had seemed confident he could "handle" him. But what about the man he had *thought* might be the kidnapper? Was he hiding from that man—or the police?

Maura addressed her unspoken question. "Mason's not in any trouble with the law right now—I checked for outstanding warrants, and there aren't any. In fact, he's been squeaky clean ever since he was released from prison on the counterfeiting conviction. He'd been living in Alabama for years, working a steady job as a bartender. But six months ago he pulled up stakes and cleared out without a trace. The PI's convinced he's on the run, and I think he's right. The question is from what. And after hearing your story, I'm betting it's our new friend Jagger-lips."

Leigh and Warren were silent for a moment; then Warren exhaled with conviction. "Well, that does it," he announced. "No one in the family needs to have anything to do with this guy. If his friends are blackmailers and kidnappers, I have no desire to meet his enemies. Leigh—you're coming home. I don't like Mason knowing you're here. It could be dangerous just being around him."

"I agree," Maura said soberly. "But tracking him down may be our best bet for getting to the kidnapper." She turned to Leigh. "We found the Escort, thanks to your remembering the license number, but now we've hit a dead end. The car—rented under the name Mason Dublin, of course—was returned to the airport within an hour of the crime. We think the kidnapper took a cab back into town, but if he left on either a train or the bus, he used another alias. We need more info on this guy, and it sounds like Mason Dublin has it. We'll set up a tracer on your phone; maybe we'll get lucky and he'll call."

Warren's brow creased. "He could find out our address too, couldn't he? From the phone number?"

"Don't worry about that," Leigh interrupted, knowing what Maura's answer would be and feeling foolish for giving out her number at all. "If he wanted to drop in, he would have asked for my address in the first place, wouldn't he?"

She refrained from telling them that despite any good sense she might have to the contrary, she didn't think Cara's father posed any threat. Hadn't he been ready to walk out of her room after he established that Jagger-lips wasn't the kidnapper? But when he found out the kidnapper *was* someone he knew, he had stopped. Maybe he really did want to help.

"Besides," she continued, "all he could find out from the phone records would be what apartment complex we lived in. We've got decent security in the building now—I'm sure there's nothing to worry about. Can we just go home, please?"

Her husband eyed her skeptically and cast a questioning glance at the detective. "Don't look at me," Maura said, smiling slyly. "She's all yours, Harmon." She punctuated the statement by rising and delivering one of her signature back claps. Warren swayed, but only a little. Though Maura's back claps had felled many a heavier man, he had long since learned to brace himself.

"I don't think there's any need to clear out of your place," Maura continued. "But don't answer your phone at all till we get the tracer set up. And"—she threw Leigh a meaningful glare—"if he should try to contact you in person, just get away from him. Then let me know ASAP."

"Don't worry. Leigh will *not* be participating in any more clandestine rendezvous with criminals," Warren said firmly, eyeing her. He hadn't given her too much grief about her midnight excursion to the bus station, but then, she had confessed the whole thing while lying in a hospital bed. The next time could be touchier. She smiled at him innocently, but his warning glare didn't waver.

"I hope not," Maura answered, preparing to leave. There was a little note of amusement in her voice that made Leigh turn to look at her. The detective was taking all this seriously enough, but at the same time, she seemed to be in an unusually good mood. Curious.

"I'll check in with you guys in a few hours," Maura announced, still with a slight smile. "Right now, I have some hospital employees to question."

Chapter 15

"You are *not* going to stay here and baby-sit me all day," Leigh told her husband with conviction. "Not that I don't enjoy it, but the election is tomorrow, and I know you have a million things to do. So go. I'll be perfectly fine. You heard what the doctor said: a little rest for a few days and I'll be good as new. I'm just going to lie around and vegetate. Promise."

Warren didn't answer immediately. After getting her settled comfortably on the couch and confirming that the phone surveillance mechanisms were all in place, he had started rambling restlessly around the apartment. "How's your head?" he asked finally, ignoring her comment. "You can have another pain pill now if you want it."

"No thanks," she answered, wishing he would cut it out and stand still for a minute. Her headache had improved dramatically as soon as she was out of the hospital, but watching him pace around like an animal in a cage wasn't helping things. "Warren," she said heavily. "Get out of here. Please. I refuse to single-handedly wreck your campaign."

He stopped moving then and came and sat down next to her. "I do really need to go out for a while. But—"

"But what?"

"But we both know that the minute I'm out that

door, you're going to be up doing something you shouldn't."

She feigned innocence. "Like what, pray?"

"I shudder to think."

"Thanks for the vote of confidence, but I'll be fine."

"I know you will."

Her eyes narrowed in suspicion. "Does that mean you're staying or going?"

He flashed her an enigmatic smile and rose. "It means I've called in the A team."

A knock sounded on the apartment door, and horror dawned. "Oh, no," she exclaimed. "You didn't."

"I did," he said unapologetically. "And it seems she's right on schedule." He strode to the door and greeted Frances, who entered with a flourish—and a casserole dish.

"Hello, Leigh, dear," she said without smiling. "Have you been behaving yourself so far?"

Leigh didn't answer, but instead threw a panicked, irate glance at her husband, who was heading out the door with amazing speed. He paused only briefly to offer a good-bye wave. "I'll be back early this evening," he said with a grin. "Be good!"

His eyes twinkled evilly as he backed out, and Leigh returned her most ominous glare. Election or no election, retribution would be hers.

"Now," Frances announced, sitting down heavily on the armchair next to Leigh. "What shall we do this afternoon? You shouldn't be reading or watching any television, you know—it would be too hard on your eyes. But—" Her beady browns made a quick sweep of the room, and her lips pursed. "Oh, my. Poor Warren. I know you think you're busy, dear, but he really shouldn't have to do housework in the middle of an election."

Leigh groaned inwardly. Only Frances could simultaneously fuss at a person for overdoing and berate them for laziness. It was a gift.

In truth, Warren did do most of the cleaning, but only—as she had explained a thousand times—because his standards were higher than hers. Granted, he had let things slip a little in the pre-election fray, but not nearly enough to warrant her involvement. The heat kicked on, and Leigh began speaking quickly, hoping to distract her mother from the next performance of the dance of the cat-hair tumbleweeds. "The apartment is fine, Mom. Why don't we just sit and talk?" *You can tell me everything about Mason Dublin you left out the first time,* she thought optimistically. She cleared her throat and began, trying to sound conversational. "You never told me how much Cara looked like her father."

But Frances's hawk eyes were already fixed on a spot at the corner of the ceiling, and she hustled off to the kitchen without responding, returning a few moments later with a broom. "Mom," Leigh began again, "Did you hear what I said? I said I know that Cara looks just like her father."

Frances aimed the broom at the corner. "You've got a spider up here the size of Rhode Island."

Leigh gritted her teeth. "That's Harold," she growled. "Leave him alone."

A muffled whack issued from the corner. "Sorry," Frances said glibly. "He's at eternal rest."

Leigh kept a straight face and tried again. "What I'm trying to tell you is that I *saw Mason Dublin.* This morning. He came to my room at the hospital."

Frances said nothing for another moment as she strode about the room, running the broom along the edges of the ceiling. "Yes, I know," she responded flatly. "Warren told me all about it when he called."

Leigh's eyebrows rose. "So, aren't you surprised?

He came to Pittsburgh to visit his sister in the hospital. Or so he says. What do you think?"

Frances's expression remained stony as she turned her attention to a shaking out of the drapes. "I think that nothing that man could do would surprise me."

"He wasn't what I was expecting in a bank robber," Leigh continued, puzzling over her mother's reticence—and lack of curiosity. "I wonder if he could have changed over the years?"

"Possibly," Frances answered on an exhale. "But I doubt it. Bad judgment is bad judgment."

"Still," Leigh defended, wondering why she was doing so, "he was just a kid at the time, wasn't he? A lot younger than me."

Frances paused a moment and looked at her worriedly. "What does it matter now? What's done is done. Lydie doesn't want that man in her life or Cara's, and once this kidnapping business is straightened out, it would be better for everybody if you forgot you ever saw him. You haven't told Cara, have you?"

Leigh's brow furrowed. "Not yet, but why would I keep it from her? She knows everything else now."

Frances's eyes glittered with something Leigh vaguely recognized as guilt. "Perhaps," she said stiffly, turning away. "But I wish you'd wait until Lydie gets back. In the meantime, why don't you close your eyes for a few moments? Just tell me where you keep your carpet cleaner. There's a little spot right here . . ."

Leigh leaned her aching head back on the bench and gazed up into the gently swaying tree branches above.

Peace.

She might not be capable of eluding the Clean Ma-

chine completely, but her pleas for fresh air had been
a stroke of genius. The carpet cleaner did have an
annoying aroma, and since Frances couldn't possibly
be expected not to comply with the directions, which
said not to vacuum for fifteen minutes, Leigh knew
she could count on at least a temporary respite. She
gazed up from the bench, which sat in the apartment's marginal greenspace/playground, and could
just see Frances's snow-capped head peeping at her
from out their kitchen window.

She closed her eyes again. The Great Watchdog
never slept, but at least she could be ignored for a
while. The cool November sun felt good on her face,
and the throbbing in her head—which had recurred
shortly after her mother's arrival—began to lessen
again. Perhaps after this, a nap. Frances couldn't very
well deny her that.

She was just about to drift off somewhere when a
fallen leaf crackled near her feet, and the light left
her face.

Instinctively, her eyes flew open.

"Don't worry," a newly familiar voice said casually. "It's only me again."

She couldn't help jumping a bit, but quickly struggled to regain her cool. "Now you're following me?"
she asked with what she hoped was equal casualness.
"I thought you said you'd call."

"That was Plan B," Mason answered, tossing his
head toward the bench. "May I?"

Leigh hesitated only a second or two before scoot-
ing over. Maybe he was dangerous, and maybe he
wasn't. Either way, if she knew her mother, he would
soon be in the hands of the police. Frances wouldn't
let five minutes pass without checking on her, and
when she saw Mason, she'd dial 911 on the spot.
Leigh just needed to keep him here.

"So," she began, anxious to extract all the information she could in the meantime. "How is it that you're acquainted with a kidnapper, and how much of a kickback do you get for selling out your relatives?"

She watched his eyes, expecting to see either guilt or resentment, but neither appeared. Instead, his face softened into a smile—a sad, vulnerable smile that had probably served him well in his days as a knife salesman, not to mention his later life of fraudulent crime. "Like mother, like daughter," he said with admiration. "Always protecting the family. I like that. I'm trying to protect them too. That's why I had to talk to you again."

Leigh glared at him cynically. "Excuse me if I'm skeptical."

The smile only widened. "Apology accepted. But it's the truth." He scanned the courtyard and adjacent parking lot with a wary eye, then took a deep breath. "You can call off the fuzz; I'll tell you what happened with the kidnapping." His shoulders slumped a little, his cocky manner turning suddenly self-conscious. "It's like this. I'm an ex-con. Ex-cons tend to end up with other ex-cons—it's a law of nature. For the past couple of years I've been bartending, and I've met a lot of people you wouldn't want to meet. Normally I keep my business to myself, but occasionally I slip. A year or so ago my sister sent me a newspaper clipping about the baby, and I slipped."

She stared at him in confusion. "What do you mean, slipped?" she asked, getting angry. "You found out you had a grandson, so you asked somebody to kidnap him?"

This time his eyes did fill with resentment, but his response was mild. "Of course not. But I'd been drinking, and—" He paused and shook his head.

"There's no excuse. It just happened. Finding out that way, it got to me. I got angry and started drinking and talking crazy. So I told some buddies—" He sighed, looking thoroughly embarrassed. "Well, I mentioned that I had a rich son-in-law."

Leigh said nothing for a moment. "So you're telling me," she began skeptically, "that you had nothing to do with the blackmail, or the kidnapping? That these guys acted totally on their own?"

The aqua-green eyes turned on her curiously. "Blackmail? What blackmail?"

Leigh tore her eyes away from his and groaned. He had to be pulling her leg, and yet he looked so damn sincere. What was she supposed to believe? She told him about the phone calls and the letter and watched as his expression morphed from puzzlement to mortification—or an excellent imitation thereof. "So none of that was your fault either, right?" she finished with frustration.

He looked away and rubbed his hands over his face, which suddenly looked older. "Well, of course it was. If I hadn't opened my big mouth it wouldn't have happened."

She thought she got the picture now, but she wanted to clarify it. "So you weren't just bragging about how you had a son-in-law with a lot of money. You were bragging about how you could get some of that money by using dirt on your ex."

"Something like that," he said miserably. "But I would never—" He looked at her stony expression and stopped. "The letter from Panama City. How was it written? With misspellings?"

She nodded stiffly. "Out the wazoo." She was trying hard not to glance up at the window and look for her mother. Surely she had called the police by now?

Mason rose from the bench, swearing under his

breath. "That was Sammy. You don't have to worry about him either. He's just a kid. All he's good for is stealing cars, and he's not all that good at that. I doubt he could scrape together bus fare to get up here."

He cast another anxious glance around the court-yard and started talking quickly. "Look, Leigh. I can't be here any longer. I probably shouldn't have come in the first place. But when you told me it was Gordy . . . I'm sorry as hell about all of this. I want everyone to know that it was my fault, and I'm going to take care of it, OK? My—your cousin can stop worrying. Those guys are opportunists, but they're not bad men. Not really. Not like some I know."

Leigh looked into Mason's bewitching, Cara-like eyes and wished her urge to give in to them wasn't so strong. She took a deep breath. "So, how many other not-so-bad men have you been chatting with?"

He shook his head. "Those two were the only ones who knew enough to make trouble. And they didn't even know where you all lived—not until that stupid TV show."

Movers and Shakers, Leigh thought grimly. So, that *was* what had started it all. This Sammy and Gordy had recognized Cara as Mason's daughter. And why shouldn't they? She had given her maiden name be-cause she used it in her business, she was married to a rich entrepreneur, and furthermore, she looked just like her old man. Sammy had probably looked up the address of Mason's ex in the phone book; Gordy had taken a more direct approach and called Gil's business. Each probably had no idea what the other was up to. But only one had resorted to kid-napping when his blackmail bluff failed. At least, she thought apprehensively, she hoped that was the case. "You can't possibly expect us to call off the fuzz," she protested reasonably. "Not when Mathias could still be in danger."

"He's not," Mason insisted quickly. "I promise, I'll take care of both of them."

"How can you promise that?" Leigh asked, her voice rising. She had absolutely no reason to trust him. "What can you possibly do? This Gordy person could have killed your own grandson!"

He shook his head firmly. "No. He's not that kind. He has grandkids of his own."

"He snatched a toddler! Not to mention giving me a concussion."

Mason started to say something else, but after a glance at Leigh's irate face, he stopped. His eyes turned liquid. "Please listen to the rest. It's important. This kidnapping case has been on the TV news, and if you pursue it my name will be too. There's a good reason to avoid that, and it's got nothing to do with my sterling reputation." His voice dropped low. "I'm in trouble. Big trouble. And anyone linked to me is in trouble too. Those two men are the only ones who know about the family I left here, and it has to stay that way, for your own protection."

There was real fear in his eyes now, and the sight of it chilled Leigh to her bones. "Who are you running from?" she asked quietly.

Mason let out a breath and sank back down on the bench. But even before he reached it, a whizzing sound assaulted Leigh's ears, followed by a dull "whump." The next thing she knew she was on the concrete in front of the park bench—with Mason Dublin on top of her.

Tires squealed somewhere in the parking lot, and though she twisted to see what was going on, she found herself tightly pinned. Only when the sounds of a gunning engine had receded did Mason move

enough that she could breathe. "Stay down for another minute," he hissed into her ear. "Then run
back inside."

Not ordinarily one to follow directions without explanation, Leigh quickly decided to make an exception. She remained frozen to the spot, even as
Mason's footfalls indicated he would not be keeping
her company. Her scrambled brain tried to make
sense of what had just happened, but no matter how
she sliced it, her conclusion kept coming up the
same.

Somebody had just shot at them.

Chapter 16

Frances screamed. Repeatedly. And with every shrill "merciful heavens" and "oh, Lord, Lord, Lord," an electric drill pierced another part of Leigh's bruised skull. Otherwise, she was fine.

"Mom," she protested, "Mom! Stop it, will you? I'm perfectly all right." She glanced around the courtyard and surrounding parking lot, but saw nothing—and no one—else.

Besides her mother, of course, who was practically undressing her in her efforts to find a bullet hole. "I told you," Leigh insisted again, wiggling away. "I'm perfectly fine. Where's Mason?"

Her mother's dilated eyes stared daggers. "Who cares? That wretched bum could have gotten you killed! Now come inside, quickly!"

Leigh was about to comply when the flashing lights of an approaching police car stopped them both. "You did call the police," she mumbled.

"Well, of course!" Frances answered sharply. "I called the minute I saw him sitting with you. I wanted to come out myself, but I was afraid he'd take off if he saw me."

"It was really Mason, then, wasn't it?" Leigh asked in a low voice.

Frances's eyes blazed. "Who else would get my daughter shot at?" She cast an irate glance toward a corner of the building, around which Leigh presumed Mason had fled. "Lousy smiling con man. I never trusted him. Never." She was still muttering unkind things about her ex-brother-in-law when the police cruiser and an unmarked pulled up beside them. Detective Maura Polanski's large legs unfurled rapidly from the unmarked, followed by her hulking torso.

"What happened here?" she asked in her police voice, addressing Frances.

"Mason's gone," Frances answered bitterly. "He ran that way." She pointed, and one of the uniformed officers set off. "But more importantly," she continued, "a dark-haired man in a black Cadillac just shot at my daughter."

"A shooting?" Maura's eyes widened.

Leigh wished she'd gotten the chance to talk first. Shot at by a dark-haired man in a black Cadillac—it sounded like something from a low-budget gangster movie. "They weren't shooting at me," she clarified. "They were shooting at Mason. I think."

Another uniformed officer was dispatched into the parking lot, and Maura quickly barked some orders into her radio. She looked around the courtyard, which was devoid of other witnesses. "Didn't anyone else hear the shots?" she asked.

"He must have used a silencer," Leigh answered. "All I heard was a whooshing noise and a thump."

"I didn't hear anything," Frances interjected. "After the two of them hit the ground, I opened the door and saw a black car with a gun sticking out the window on the far side of the parking lot. Then the driver pulled the gun back in and peeled off."

Maura pushed a short lock of brown hair behind one ear. She was acting entirely businesslike, but the beads of sweat Leigh saw breaking out on her fore-

head betrayed a personal concern that was discon-
certing. Maura Polanski didn't get rattled over just
anything. "Did you get a good look at the man with
the gun?" she asked Frances.

"Not until he was driving out the exit—and then
he was going pretty fast. I can tell you that he was
tall," she said thoughtfully, "because his head was
way up near the car roof. His face was pale and
skinny and he had dark hair."

A chill crept up Leigh's spine. "Did he have Mick
Jagger lips?" she asked in a whisper.

Frances stared at her blankly. "Who?"

Never mind, Leigh thought. "Did he have big
lips?" she clarified.

Her mother still looked confused. "I couldn't possibly tell anything about his lips. He was too far
away."

Leigh threw an anxious look at Maura, whose
sharp eyes registered the same thoughts. But she
turned to Leigh with another question. "Where were
you when you heard the noise?"

Leigh pointed to the bench and Maura looked it
over carefully, then moved on to examine the tree
next to it. "Here," she said quietly, pointing to a
place on the trunk. "A bullet went in here."

Neither Leigh nor Frances had any desire to move
closer. Leigh shivered. "Mason was standing up,"
she began. "He had just started to sit down when I
heard the noise."

Maura nodded solemnly. "I see." She pulled out
her notebook and a pen, the beads of sweat on her
forehead increasing. "How about you two tell me the
whole story again—from the beginning?"

Leigh had finished her account, and Frances was
wrapping up hers, when the uniformed officer who
had left in pursuit of Mason reappeared around the

corner. He stared pointedly at the ground for a moment, then came toward them.

"Whatcha got?" Maura asked, closing her notebook.

"Nobody in sight," the officer reported. "But you should take a look at this." He walked back in the direction he had come, and Maura followed. Leigh stood still for a moment, then walked after them to the spot where the officer had paused a moment ago. The detective squatted down to examine something on the sidewalk, and Leigh moved in closer.

It was a series of red, comet-shaped stains.

She backed up, suddenly not feeling so well. Bullet sound effects were one thing. She had had no idea what was even happening until it was over. But blood on the pavement was something else. She retreated, knees knocking, and stumbled backward onto someone else's feet. She quickly sidestepped and mumbled an apology.

"No problem," answered Cara, her face nearly white. She looked from Leigh over to Frances, then down at the spots of blood. Mathias sat on her hip, sucking happily at the pacifier that was attached to his collar with a baseball clip. He issued a mild squawk of protest as his mother's grip tightened, then reached out his hands. "Anlee!" he cooed cheerfully.

Leigh smiled at the boy and offered him her own hand, but her gaze was stuck on her cousin, who didn't need to be there. "Cara," she said worriedly, "where did you come from?"

"I came to see how you were doing," her cousin answered thinly. "You want to tell me whose blood that is?"

*   *   *

"If you're sure there was only one shot, there's a good chance we're dealing with just a minor flesh wound," Maura said calmly. "The slug was in the tree; it didn't stop anywhere. And obviously he could still run."

Leigh wasn't at all sure that there had been only one shot, but with Cara sitting right across the table, she didn't want to make anything seem worse than it already was. For the last half hour, she, Frances, and Maura had been in her kitchen rehashing every detail of Mason's last two appearances, and her cousin had yet to say a word. She simply sat there, keeping one eye on Mathias and the other on a fixed spot of tabletop. She hadn't come alone; the body-guard who now stuck to her and Mathias like glue stood dutifully outside in the hall.

A knock sounded on the door, and Maura opened it to a uniformed officer who handed her an enve-lope. The two talked in hushed tones for a while; then the man left and Maura returned to the table. "The blood trail tapered, then stopped next to some on-street parking a few blocks away," she reported. "So it appears he was well enough to drive off. Might have just been grazed. We'll keep a lookout at the local ERs and clinics, just in case he goes in for treat-ment. As for the shooter, we'll keep up our efforts to locate the black Caddy, and we'll have a black-and-white keep an eye on this place, too."

Leigh threw another glance at her cousin, but saw only the same blank, washed-out expression. Her mother, whose initial hysteria had turned first into outrage, then into a burst of maternal proficiency, noticed it also. "Now, don't you worry, Cara, dear," Frances said, wrapping an arm around her niece's shoulders. "The police will get all this mess straight-ened out. Until they do, perhaps you and Gil could go on a nice vacation, do you think? Take your mind off of things?"

Cara returned a brief, but polite smile and said nothing.

Maura cleared her throat, opened the envelope, and pulled out what appeared to be a sketch. She turned it toward Leigh. "Does this man look familiar?" she asked.

Leigh surveyed the portrait critically, then nodded. "It looks like the kidnapper, but I would say his face was a bit fatter. Who gave this description?"

"The PI," Maura answered. "Now that we've got a name to put to the face, we can run it by the police departments around Boaz, Alabama, where the first call to Gil came from, and also around where Mason's been living the last few years. It's a long shot, but we could get lucky." She turned the sketch toward Frances. "Any chance this is your shooter?"

Frances shook her head quickly. "No, he had lots of black hair. Skinnier, too."

Maura held the picture towards Cara, whose eyes flickered over it hurriedly. "Don't know him," she said quietly. Then she rose. "Excuse me. I think Mathias needs changing." She scooped the toddler up from his post in the kitchen, where he was rearranging the cookware in Leigh's cabinets, and carried him off to the bedroom.

Leigh watched her cousin depart, then rose and lifted the forgotten diaper bag from where it hung on the back of Cara's chair. "I'll just go check on her," she explained, following.

She found her cousin sitting idly on a corner of the bed, with Mathias squirming unhappily in her lap. "Play, pan!" he protested, but his mother seemed not to notice.

"Here, sweetheart," Leigh offered, taking the tod-

dler from his mother and directing him to the shoe
tree in her closet. "Want to play with my shoes?"

Mathias's face gleamed with pleasure as he started
pulling shoes two at a time out of their neat plastic
pouches and dropping them in a heap on the floor.
Leigh returned to her cousin, who still sat numbly
on the bed. She was about to say something when
Cara straightened and cleared her throat.

"Thank you. I'll clean up the shoes in a minute."

"No problem," Leigh answered.

"I know you think this bothers me," Cara said
with sudden firmness. "But it doesn't."

Leigh knew better than to argue with her cousin
when she started talking nonsense. It was just an
exercise with her. A way of working through things.
"Oh?" she responded mildly. "It would certainly
bother me if I were you."

"Well, you're not," Cara said flatly. "You have a
father who loves you. A great father."

"He loves you, too."

"Yes. He does. And I don't need anyone else in
my life. Particularly a troublemaker."

"I understand completely."

They sat in silence a few moments before Cara's
real questions began.

"What did he look like?" she asked quietly. "I
don't mean hair and eye color. I mean, when you
looked in his eyes, what did you see?"

Leigh thought a moment. "Aside from his reac-
tions to the kidnapping and the blackmail? Humor.
Optimism. Enthusiasm for life. A certain restless-
ness." *Just like you.*

Cara drank in the response, but looked away as
she spoke again, her voice unsteady. "He didn't ask
you anything about me, did he?"

A stab of pain ran through Leigh's chest, and she

wished she could answer differently. "No," she said gently. Then she added, "But we haven't exactly chitchatted."

Cara's eyes remained calmly impassive as she nodded. After a moment she spoke again, barely above a whisper. "I don't understand why he would be upset about Mathias's birth announcement."

Leigh thought a moment. Truthfully, she didn't either. What exactly had he said? That Trudy had sent it to him, and that he hadn't liked "finding out that way." She frowned. What did he expect? Jerk was lucky to find out at all. He should have been happy about it, but instead it made him angry. Angry at who? Lydie? She was the one whose past sins he had supposedly bragged about exposing. Or maybe he resented Gil, a young upstart who had everything he himself had spent his whole life chasing after. Or maybe the whole story was one big whopping lie.

"I don't understand it, either," Leigh answered. "But maybe—I mean, I'm sure we haven't seen the last of him."

Cara rose from the bed, her sea-green eyes flashing. Leigh recognized the look—it was the same vague, festering animosity that used to appear whenever her father was mentioned, ever since the day of that fateful visit to Trudy Dublin. "I have to go now," she said, her voice stiffly pleasant. "Thanks for all you've done, Leigh."

The subject of Mason Dublin had been closed. Cara walked out of the bedroom and began to move wordlessly around the apartment, silently restoring the disaster zones her son had left in his wake. Frances eagerly jumped in to help her, no doubt thrilled with the opportunity to reorganize cookware. Maura rose to leave, and Leigh walked her outside.

"Cara OK?" Maura asked, tossing her head back in the direction of the apartment.

"I wish I knew," Leigh answered solemnly. Sometimes she wished her cousin was a little less strong-willed; stereotypical wounded-female blubbering would be much easier to deal with than Cara's torturous, gut-burning brand of denial. They had all hoped that growing up, marrying, and having a baby of her own had muted her childhood feelings of hurt and betrayal, at least a little. Now it was all back.

And there was no happy ending in sight.

"I don't suppose," Leigh began with a sudden feeling of desperation, "I mean, is there any chance Mason is telling the truth? About not being involved in the blackmail, at least?" Her heart beat quickly as she posed the question. All logic and rationality told her that Mason Dublin could not be trusted—and that only a fool would give him the benefit of the doubt. But she wasn't all that good with logic and rationality.

If the question sounded stupid, Maura gave no indication of it. "There's always a chance," she answered. "His being in Pittsburgh could be a coincidence, given his sister's hospitalization. I've talked to most of the people who work in Trudy Dublin's unit, and though none of them has seen anyone in her room, one nurse's aide did notice that someone has been leaving fresh lemon drops on her bedside table.

"But deciphering Mason's claims of how all this came about isn't our biggest concern right now," she continued heavily. "The person who just took a shot at him is."

Leigh nodded uncomfortably. "I know. I'm living proof that just being in Mason Dublin's company can be dangerous. But—" Her optimistic side reared its little-used head again. "He did try to warn me, didn't he? That's why he followed me home. He said that he was trying to protect the family."

Maura threw her a look that bordered on sympathy. "From what you told me, it sounds like what he did was ask you to drop the kidnapping and blackmail investigations."

Leigh frowned. "I suppose that wouldn't exactly hurt him, would it? Still, his concern about the family's safety *seemed* real." She paused, realizing how gullible she sounded. "Well, it did," she finished stubbornly.

"Koslow," Maura reprimanded. "Focus. I didn't want to get into this back there"—she nodded in the direction of Cara and Frances—"but you may have more to worry about than just being in the wrong place at the wrong time."

Leigh focused.

"Have you wondered how Mason knew that his sister had been assaulted in the first place?" the detective continued. "Trudy couldn't possibly have called him herself, and he wasn't contacted by either the police or the hospital, because no one knew where to reach him. He wasn't staying at his sister's place when it happened, either. In fact, none of the neighbors claim to have ever seen him—though Trudy had only been at that apartment a few months."

"Maybe he got worried when he couldn't reach her," Leigh said tentatively, skeptical of her own suggestion. "But then, I wouldn't think Trudy and Mason had one of those chat-every-Tuesday-at-four kinds of relationships."

"I doubt it," Maura responded. "But you're assuming that he had no idea his sister might be a target."

Leigh blinked, and her stomach churned violently.

"You're saying that his sister being beaten nearly to death—that it had something to do with him?"

"It was a break-in with assault and battery. Vandalism too: drawers opened, contents dumped. But no known valuables taken. Not even plainly visible cash." The detective's eyes bored into Leigh's. "What I'm saying is that it looks like Mason is telling the truth about at least one thing."

Leigh waited, her heart pounding.

"This is no time to be his relative."

Chapter 17

Leigh glanced over the morning paper and sipped her coffee glumly. It was election day. Warren probably had five or six different political breakfasts he could and should be attending, but instead he was standing over her stove, flipping chocolate-chip pancakes.

"I'll be fine," she said for the fortieth time.

"I'm not leaving you alone," he said for the forty-first.

"I'll go to the office. It'll be perfectly safe there."

He glared at her. "Yesterday I left you in the capable hands of the world's most overzealous mother—and you got shot at. I repeat, I'm not leaving you alone."

"I won't be alone," she argued. "I'll go to Cara's farm. They have security guards 24/7 now."

He brought a stack of pancakes to the table and served himself three. "Like that matters. Sending you to stay with Cara is like having Jessica Fletcher look after Miss Marple. You're not getting out of my sight."

Leigh groaned. Touched as she was by his concern, she hated ruining election day for him. She took a bite of pancake and ate it guiltily. "Then let me come with you—whatever you have to do," she suggested. "I'll just hang on your arm and smile. Promise."

He looked up at her brightly and started to reply, but was interrupted by the phone. Leigh jumped up to answer it, hoping fervently to hear Mason Dublin's smooth voice on the other end. Assuming he was still alive and kicking, she had plenty to say to him.

"Hello?" she said eagerly.

"It's me, Koslow," Maura answered.

Leigh's heart skipped a beat. It was the detective's official police voice, and it didn't sound happy. "What's up?" she asked nervously.

"I just got a call from West View—it seems there's been a break-in at your aunt Lydie's place. Your parents aren't home. Any idea where they might be?"

"No—I mean, yes," Leigh fumbled. "Dad's off Tuesday mornings, and Lydie and Bess are supposed to be flying in today. They're probably on their way to the airport to pick them up."

Maura paused a moment. "Right. I haven't been able to reach Cara either."

"She never answers at the farm," Leigh responded quickly. "You have to call her cell phone. Should I go over to Lydie's now? I can tell you if anything's missing."

The detective hesitated. "I suppose—"

"We'll be right down," Leigh said quickly, hanging up.

Her aunt's house had rated three police cars and Maura's unmarked, but the crowd was thinning as they arrived. She bounded up the porch steps and met Maura at the door.

"Was it Mason? Did they catch him?" she asked breathlessly.

The detective regarded her evenly. "Nobody's caught anybody, Koslow. Whoever it was was gone when the Ross Township police got here." She threw her arm across the door, preventing Leigh from entering. "Sorry—you can't come in until the photographer is through."

Warren came up behind them. "There wasn't any violence, was there?" he asked Maura worriedly. "Who reported the break-in?"

The detective shook her head. "Clean break-in, clean exit. The locals responded to a call from a neighbor saying that an unfamiliar man had forced open the front door of the house. By the time they got here, he was already gone."

Mrs. Snodgrass. Leigh whirled around and started back down off the porch. "I'm just going a few doors down," she said quickly to Warren, cutting off his forthcoming protest. "I'll be right back."

As expected, she found Dorothy Snodgrass lounging comfortably on her porch swing, the wrought-iron end table beside her set with a plate of cookies, a china tea pot, and four matching cups—three already used. "Figured I'd have company this morning." She smiled. "How are you doing, young'un? I hope your aunt didn't have nothing messed with."

"I don't really know yet," Leigh answered nervously. "Tea?"

Leigh nodded heartily. If there was ever a call for Mrs. Snodgrass's special—this was it. She wasn't driving, and her neurons could use a chill.

"Oh, not that one, dear," Mrs. Snodgrass said when Leigh picked up the delicate pot to help herself. "That's for the officers. The good stuff's inside." She shuffled into the house with a grin, emerging almost immediately with a Pitt Panthers thermos and an oversized plastic Penguins mug. She filled the latter to the brim, then handed it to her guest and returned to her seat with a plop.

Leigh thanked her and took a swig, smiling as the

warm liquid melted its way down her throat. It was surprisingly sweet and tasted a little of ginger. There was no telling what was actually in it, and it was probably better she didn't know. She took the M&M cookie Mrs. Snodgrass held out to her and alternated a few bites with a few sips, feeling a little better with each.

"The man you saw," she began finally, her voice nice and steady again. "Was he middle-aged, medium height, with red hair graying a little?"

Mrs. Snodgrass eyed her strangely. "Oh, no. He was real tall. Thin as a rail. Mess of black hair on his head. Pacing around nervous like. I'd never seen him before in my life. Know good and well Lydie wouldn't want him there. That's why I called the police. I tried your mother too, but she was out."

Leigh took another long swig of tea, hoping it would counteract the surge of adrenaline Mrs. Snodgrass's words had just produced. "How good a look at him did you get?"

"Pretty good," the older woman said proudly. "He drove by real slow at first—I think he was looking at the house numbers. Then he parked at Lydie's and knocked on the door. When it didn't open, he started walking around just looking it over. Then he went back to the door and started jiggling. Brazen son of a bitch, pardon my French. Didn't like the looks of him."

Leigh took a deep breath. She needed it. "Mrs. Snodgrass," she asked unsteadily, "do you know who Mick Jagger is?"

She snorted. "Doesn't everyone? What's some middle-aged rocker got to do with anything?"

"I was wondering if the man you saw looked like him at all."

Mrs. Snodgrass stared at her a moment, then at

the Penguins mug, as if wondering whether she'd overdone it . "You think Mick Jagger broke into your aunt's house?" she asked hesitantly.

Leigh laughed, spewing a mouthful of the glorious tea across her jacket. "Of course not," she chuckled. Then, thinking she was sounding a bit too happy awfully fast, she wiped her mouth and set down the mug. "Of course not. It's just that I thought they might have something in common."

Mrs. Snodgrass thought a moment, then looked at her. "Oh, I see. Yeah, I guess the guy did have big lips. Skinny face, big lips. Ugly as sin. That what you mean?"

Leigh nodded, feeling a sudden, overwhelming uneasiness. There was no point in denying that Lydie's intruder and Mason's would-be assassin were one and the same. He'd found Mason's sister; now he'd found his ex-wife. If Lydie had been home . . . Her blood chilled.

"What's wrong, dear?" Mrs. Snodgrass inquired gently. "Is this man dangerous? And why were you expecting a middle-aged redhead?"

Leigh swallowed. "The man who broke in could be very dangerous, yes," she admitted. "And I thought—I mean, I was hoping it wasn't him. I was hoping it was Mason Dubin."

Mrs. Snodgrass's eyes widened. "Cora's father? Oh, no, dear. I'd know him in a minute. This man looked nothing like him. Why is he dangerous? I don't mean to pry, but if there's some psycho prowling round the neighborhood we all need to be on guard, you know."

"It's kind of a long story," Leigh answered. "But if anyone sees that man again, they should definitely call the police. And they should stay away from him."

"Will do," Mrs. Snodgrass promised. "Now, I see that my future County Council representative is over there watching you like a hawk. Reckon he'd like some tea, too?"

Leigh rose, feeling a little wobbly. "No, thank you," she answered. "He's my designated driver."

"Cookie, then?"

She smiled and took another—peanut butter this time. "Sure. And thanks for keeping an eye on Lydie's place." Mrs. Snodgrass nodded, and Leigh started down her porch steps, having the odd feeling of unfinished business nagging in her mind. She was halfway through the next yard when she stopped and whirled around, jogging back to the porch and taking the steps up two by two.

"What did you mean about Mason Dublin?" she asked breathlessly. "How would you know him if you saw him? He never lived here. Did you know him when he was still married to Lydie?"

Mrs. Snodgrass simply sat and looked at her for a moment, then her face registered a certain sheepishness. "I never actually met him," she said quietly. "But I've seen him."

Leigh's heart pounded. "When? Recently?"

"No, dear." Mrs. Snodgrass looked distinctly uncomfortable. "I haven't seen him in years. But he used to come around—back when you girls were little."

Her pounding heart seemed to stop in mid-beat. *"What?"*

"Oh, dear." Mrs. Snodgrass buried her face in a napkin. "I'm sorry if I've spilled something I shouldn't have. I knew Lydie didn't want Mason near you kids. I would never have said a word to you, but—well, it's been so long. And you're all grown up now. I didn't think it mattered anymore. Aw, hell—the truth is, I just didn't think. I'm sorry."

"Don't be sorry," Leigh said quickly. "Are you telling me that—even years after the divorce—Mason used to come around to see Lydie?"

The older woman shook her head. "I wouldn't say that. I'd say he came to see Cara. He would watch you two play sometimes. Drove your aunt nuts. Mind you, Lydie never came right out and told anybody he was her ex-husband. She just asked me to let her know if I ever saw him skulking about, which I did. But I never doubted who he was. Cara looks just like him, you know."

Leigh was numb. How much was alcohol and how much was shock, she wasn't sure. "Thanks for telling me, Mrs. Snodgrass," she said mechanically. "It's—good to know. I guess."

She drifted off the porch again and was met at her aunt's yard by a concerned-looking Warren. "Special tea, eh?" he said warily, studying her. "Better stick with me. Mo says we can go in now."

Leigh nodded and handed him the cookie. She had thought she knew everything about her aunt's house—and her aunt.

How wrong she had been.

She walked slowly through the living room of the old house, careful not to step on any of the loose papers, books, and writing paraphernalia that had been dumped from the drawers of her aunt's secretary.

"The pattern is very similar to what the police found in Trudy Dublin's apartment—minus the violence," Maura explained grimly. "The intruder seemed to be looking for information that Lydie would have written down." She led them into the kitchen and pointed at the now-empty drawer underneath the counter where the telephone sat. "Most likely, Mason Dublin's latest address."

Leigh stepped forward and sorted through the pile of telephone books, church directories, and half-used note pads that littered the linoleum. "I'm not sure," she said sadly, "but I do think Lydie's address book is gone. It was green. About this big"—she held out her hands—"but I could be wrong. She could keep it somewhere else now."

"Maura," Warren broke in, "do you think we're dealing with the shooter?"

She threw them both a heavy look and nodded. " 'Fraid so. The neighbor's description matches Frances's. Probably came looking either for Mason Dublin or for info about where to find him. That means he didn't catch up with Mason after the shooting, if anyone cares, but it also means he isn't giving up easily. What I'm concerned about," the detective continued grimly, "is how he knew to come here."

Leigh didn't think her blood could get any colder, but she was wrong. First this man had tracked down Mason's sister, then his ex-wife. It was foolish to assume that Mason's daughter—or any other relative—was out of his reach. She swallowed anxiously. Had he hurt Trudy because she wouldn't give out information about her brother's whereabouts? Or, she thought with a shiver, was he just trying to send Mason a message?

"There's something else you should see," Maura said soberly, stepping into the dining room and motioning for them to follow. "Jagger-lips left a calling card."

Leigh moved anxiously through the door frame, and her eyes went immediately to the large oval mirror that hung over the buffet, its once shiny surface

now marred with scrawls from a black permanent
marker.

Mason—Funny Money line in 36—or they all lose.

Leigh stared at the jagged script, her heart beating
fast. She turned back to Maura and shook her head.
"It doesn't make any sense to me."

"It's likely a code to set up either a delivery or a
meeting," Maura explained. "The shooter's trying to
make contact with Mason without tipping off the police, and he's betting that Lydie can get in touch with
him—or vice versa."

"Funny Money as in counterfeiting, I suppose,"
Warren said thoughtfully, "and 'in 36' could mean in
36 hours—or days. But what does the 'line' mean?"

He looked at Maura, and she shook her head. "No
idea yet. But we're working on it."

"*Or they all lose,*" Leigh repeated grimly. "That's
the threat to make Mason show himself." She took
a deep breath. "I don't think I want to know who
loses what."

"Take it easy, Koslow," Maura said quietly. "We're
getting closer. Mason dropped some valuable information in your last conversation, and we've been
piecing some things together. That bar he worked at
in Alabama—it's a little dive called the Brindle Blur,
located right outside a big dog track. Seems it's a
famous watering hole for ex-cons. Mason started
working there not long after he got out of the Federal
pen on the counterfeiting charge, and that's where
he'd been up until about six months ago. Didn't
cause any trouble—record's clean. But I fed the blackmailer's names he gave you—and the sketch of the
one who did the kidnapping—to the local police
down there. I sent down a description of our shooter
too, since there's a good chance that's where he met

up with Mason." Her voice lifted confidently. "Odds are they'll know something."

"Mason could tell us all that himself," Warren growled, "if he had the guts to come forward."

"He tried to keep the gunman from finding his family," Leigh heard herself saying. "He warned me that we shouldn't have anything to do with him." She was defending him, and she didn't know why. This was his fault, after all—all of it.

"Oh, dear Lord," a soprano voice drawled. The threesome moved quickly to the living room, where Frances had just come through the doorway, wringing her hands. "Who on earth made this mess? Is everyone all right?"

Lydie Dublin pushed around her identical twin, her face pale. Leigh's aunt Bess, her modified beehive sagging down to more of a robin's nest, was right behind her. Randall Koslow brought up the rear. "We got the message you left with the airline," Lydie said breathlessly, addressing Maura. "A break-in! Was anyone hurt?"

"No," Maura answered quickly. "No one was here. The intruder just emptied a few drawers; there was no significant property damage. As far as what's missing, you'll have to tell us." She glanced up at Frances and Randall. "Have you filled these ladies in on the situation?"

Randall nodded. "As well as we could. Did Mason do this?"

The phone rang, and Lydie jumped as if she'd been stung. She walked into the kitchen and picked up. Two seconds after she'd said hello, her voice rose to a shriek. "Where have I been? What business is that of yours? Did you mess up my house?" she railed accusingly. The living room's occupants followed her en masse. "Somebody's been going through my

things!" she continued indignantly. "Of course I
don't know! I've been on the other side of the
world." There was a long pause while Lydie listened
with a frown on her face, her fingers nervously twist-
ing the phone cord. "You do whatever you have to
do," she said finally, her voice deathly grim. "If anybody gets hurt—" She stopped and looked at the
receiver, then slammed it down. Her body sank onto
a straight-backed kitchen chair, and her eyes closed.

Maura quickly grabbed for the phone and dialed
star 69.

"That was Mason, wasn't it?" Frances asked softly.

Lydie nodded, her eyes still closed.

"He knows who did this?"

She nodded again.

"Did he give you a name?" Maura asked, her ear
still to the phone.

"As a matter of fact, he did," Lydie said blandly,
opening her eyes. "He said that all this was happening because a man named Torr wanted something
from him, and that he would have to go and get it,
but that once it was delivered, we should all be out
of danger." She shook her head with disbelief.

Frances scowled. "That man—" she muttered.

"No answer," Maura announced, hanging up the
receiver. "Probably a pay phone." She jotted something in her notebook and began to explain the situation to Lydie and Bess. She hadn't gotten far before
Frances shrieked again.

"Oh, heavens!" she wailed from the dining room.
"What does this mean?"

As the others filed in to look at the mirror, Leigh
stood and stared at them through a numb sort of fog.
He used to come around, Mrs. Snodgrass had said. She
and Cara had been led to believe that no one had
heard from Mason since the day he left—now thirty

years before. And yet her aunt Lydie had just picked up her phone on a Tuesday morning to find her ex-husband at the other end of it.

And neither she nor Frances had seemed surprised.

Chapter 18

If anything could get a person's mind off her family being stalked by a madman with Mick Jagger lips, Leigh thought to herself, it was poll-hopping on election day. Suddenly desperate to put some space between her and her mother and aunts, she had insisted Warren take her along on his rounds to the district polls. He would have preferred to leave her under lock and key, but she had convinced him that bobbing and weaving through a plethora of very public locations was a reasonably safe alternative.

As he shook hands and schmoozed his way flawlessly through the day, Leigh stood beside him, Nancy Reagan style, trying to make her broad, plastic smile seem sincere.

It was an uphill battle. No amount of distraction could stop her from wondering whether Cara had found out about the break-in yet, or whether Lydie had decided to tell her anything else about Mason's actions in the last thirty years. As for the latter, she doubted it. No one realized Leigh knew about Mason's clandestine visits to see his daughter, so why confess to Cara now? Lydie would have enough grief facing up to why she'd lied about how he left in the first place.

They were on their way to Warren's next-to-last stop when his cell phone rang, and Leigh picked up anxiously. "It's Maura," she reported. "She wonders if we can drop by the county detectives' office." Warren nodded, and within a few minutes they were seated on uncomfortable chairs by the detective's cluttered desk, sipping bad coffee.

"Did you find out who this Torr guy is?" Leigh asked anxiously.

" 'Fraid not," Maura answered. "The name and description didn't ring a bell with any of the PDs in Alabama, and a nickname isn't enough to go on for the national databases. But we did come up with something on the kidnapper."

Leigh leaned forward.

"The PD in Tallassee, Alabama, think our man is William P. Gordon, a small-time crook they run in periodically. He's sixty-two, divorced twice. Priors are gambling, bookmaking, mail fraud. Nothing violent. He's been living in a mobile home outside Tallassee for the past twelve years—spends most of his time at the dog track."

"So did they pick him up?" Leigh asked. Maura looked at her heavily, and she braced for bad news. "Don't tell me they don't know where he is," she said anxiously.

"Oh, they know where he is. As of noon today, he's in the Tallapoosa County morgue."

Leigh sat for a moment without saying anything, and Maura went on. "They went out to his place to question him and found him roughed up bad. He died on the way to the hospital."

Roughed up. Just like Trudy Dublin, she thought miserably. "You think it was the same person who's after Mason?" she asked with alarm.

"Not likely, unless he could be in two places at one time," Maura answered. "But it could have been Mason himself."

Leigh jerked up her head, surprised. "No, it couldn't," she said firmly. "He isn't violent. And that guy was his friend—sort of."

Maura stared back at her incredulously. "Just yesterday, you told Mason that Gordon had tried to blackmail his son-in-law and kidnap his grandson—not to mention frame him for it. And he told you not to worry, that he would 'take care' of him. Remember all that?"

"He just meant he'd make sure Gordon left us alone," Leigh said confidently. "I know he wouldn't hurt anybody."

Warren threw her a hard glance. "No, you don't," he insisted. "How could you? You've barely spent five minutes with the man."

"It was a full five minutes," she debated, "on two occasions. I can tell if someone is capable of murder or not. Trust me, he's not."

Warren and Maura exchanged skeptical glances over the desk, but Leigh ignored them. She realized she was defending Cara's father yet again, and she could analyze her reasons for that later. But right now all she knew was that trying to finger Mason Dublin for a murder was a waste of time. And they needed all the time they had.

"Besides," she went on, "how could Mason get back down to Alabama so fast? He'd either have to fly or drive all night, and he's injured." She remembered the secret relief she had felt when Lydie announced that it had been Mason on the phone. At least he was still breathing. There had been a fair amount of blood on the pavement, and though no one else seemed to care, a part of her feared he would have the gall to check out on them before everything was resolved. And by everything, she meant Cara.

"It's not impossible, Koslow," Maura said placatingly. "But you do have a point. Gordon's death could have nothing to do with Mason or Torr. But I'll be plenty surprised if it doesn't have something to do with his sudden shift into violent crime."

"Mo," Warren said thoughtfully, his mind on a new track. "I've been thinking about the 'funny money' in Torr's message, and what Mason told Lydie about Torr wanting something. If that's true, do you think it could be—"

The detective nodded quickly. "I thought of that, too."

Leigh's eyes darted from her husband to her friend. "Could be what?" she asked eagerly.

"I've been doing a little research on Mason's counterfeit operation," he explained to Leigh. "The one that put him away."

She wasn't surprised. Virtually anything that had to do with money interested Warren. When since her concussion he had had the chance to do research, she couldn't imagine, but once he got a fiscally-related problem in his head, he was like a dog with a bone.

"It seems that all of Cara's artistic talent didn't come from her mother," he explained. "Mason created a set of metal plates—bill-stamping plates—that were exquisite. Photo-etched in very intricate detail. He and his partner produced fake fifties and hundreds that were very difficult to detect with the naked eye. It was certainly possible, but you'd almost have to be looking for them. By the time the authorities got wise, thousands were already in circulation. Even afterwards, the two continued for months without getting caught. The genius of the operation was that they never unloaded very many bills in one spot. They traveled constantly, plus they had a network of underlings funneling bills at different points all over the country."

"That was how they finally got caught," Maura interjected. "One of their worker bees got greedy."

Warren nodded. "One of the distributors unloaded too many hundreds at once, got picked up, cut an immunity deal, and sold out both Mason and his partner. The two were arrested and convicted, as you know," he said to Leigh. "But here's the kicker. The plates were never recovered."

Maura leaned forward. "There was quite a buzz about them for a while," she explained. "I bet the place Mason was living back then got picked over pretty good by people wanting to take up where he'd left off. Good plates used to be worth their weight in gold. But the authorities assumed no one ever found them, because no new counterfeit bills ever turned up."

"And then, of course," Warren interjected, "the method became obsolete."

"Because of the new bills?" Leigh asked.

"Right. The Federal Reserve started printing the revamped hundreds with counterfeit detection devices in 1996. The fifties followed the next year. Fakes made with Mason's plates wouldn't stand a chance today."

"Then why would Torr want them?" she asked. "I don't get it."

Maura and Warren exchanged glances again. "There could still be some use for them," Warren suggested. "Many of the old legitimate hundreds and fifties are still in circulation. Torr couldn't pass off new bills straight from the plates, but if he had some way to realistically age them, they might pass for old bills."

Maura nodded, but her face was frowning. "I can

see Torr having some use for Mason's plates. But I
can't see anybody killing over them. The attack on
Trudy, the shooting at your apartment—that's a lot
of violence just to pave the way for a white-collar
crime. And a tedious, time-consuming one at that."
She shook her head. "It doesn't fit."

"I see what you mean," Warren admitted.

"I wish it were as easy as Mason handing over a
set of plates and this Torr guy going away happy,"
Maura said quietly. "But my gut tells me there's a
lot more going on. And right now, Mason Dublin is
probably the only one who can clear it up." She
leaned back in her chair again, assuming a more casual stance. "You guys celebrating at home tonight?
Or are you having a victory party somewhere that
I'm not invited to?"

Leigh had to smile. "The world's most honest and
frugal politician, spend campaign money on a victory
party? Please. Team Harmon will be content to leech
off the general democratic levity at the gubernatorial
shindig in Station Square. But we *will* be celebrating,"
she said proudly. "The response at the polls has been
plenty encouraging."

Warren didn't smile. "It'll be close," he said distractedly. "Why do you ask, Mo? Do you think it's
safe for Leigh to be out in public?"

Maura's brow furrowed. "Her staying out of sight
as much as possible is definitely a good idea. But the
reason I'm asking is Mason. We know he has your
home phone number, and I'm hoping he'll use it. If
he does make contact, and you can get him to give
you Torr's full name and a translation of that message, we may be able to get somewhere. Better yet,
you might be able to convince him to talk to me in
person. He'll fight it, but you could try guilt-tripping
him about endangering his family. If he's not respon-

sible for any of this violence himself, he's got nothing
to worry about from Allegheny County. But he could
help us put this other guy away."

Leigh looked at Warren. "She's right. Maybe I
should stay home in case he calls, at least for part of
the night. I think I could talk sense into him. Really,
I do."

Warren frowned. "You're not staying at the apartment alone. I'll stay with you."

"Not a chance," Leigh protested. "You're going to
that party at the Sheraton and you're going to have
the time of your life, and that's an order."

"Children, children," Maura said mockingly.
"Let's not fight. Warren, I'm sure Leigh will be safe
enough with you at a crowded, ticketed political
rally. Leigh, just forward your calls to his cell
phone." The detective stood up and collected her
coat from the back of her chair. "When I filled in
your parents and your aunt on the news, I told them
they'd be wise to camp out at Cara's for a few days.
With all the guards Gil hired, that place is safer than
Fort Knox. As for your apartment building, the own-
ers have tightened security, and the Ross police are
going to keep an eye on it until further notice. Now,
if you'll excuse me, I have somewhere I have to be."

She whistled softly as she put on her coat, and
Warren and Leigh exchanged quizzical looks. Maura
wasn't somber as a rule, at least not when she wasn't
working. But the whistling thing was new. Despite
the seriousness of the last few days' events, the detective seemed pretty darned cheerful.

"What are you looking at?" she demanded playfully, giving Warren another hearty back clap.

He caught the desk just in time to avoid pitching
forward. "Nothing," he replied, eyeing her steadily,
"I was just wondering who you've been looking at."

Maura's eyes twinkled evilly. "Careful, wise guy," she warned. "I haven't voted yet."

The Sheraton on Pittsburgh's riverside Station Square was the place to be this election night—or so it would seem to those enamored of the glamour of politics. Leigh was not, but she was happy enough for her husband that she could fake it. The early returns showed him winning by an easy margin, and after a few hours and a glass of wine, she was able to convince him that he could safely bounce around the festivities without having to keep her in a four-foot radius. She was sipping her third glass of virgin punch (a truly excellent combination of 7-Up and raspberries) when she realized that the high-pitched hum in her ears was not due to the punch being spiked, but to the phone in her purse ringing.

She located the cellular and lifted it quickly to her ear. "Hello?"

A man's voice spoke on the other end, but the ambient noise was so loud she could barely hear it. "Wait a minute," she insisted, then hiked off to find a quieter spot. "Are you there?" she asked hopefully, pausing finally on a veranda with a view of the Monongahela River. "Mason?"

"What the hell's going on there?" The now-familiar voice sounded loud and clear. "You got half of Pittsburgh in your apartment?"

Leigh smiled, her heart beating at a good clip. "No," she answered briskly. I forwarded the call. The question is—where are you?"

"That's not important," Mason answered. "What's important is that I'm headed back to Pittsburgh now, and I'm going to set things right. Is everybody OK?"

She paused, trying to choose her words carefully.

"Everyone's fine. But we'll be a lot better off if you come in and talk to the police."

To her surprise, he chuckled. A good-natured chuckle, but one laced with tension. "Right, kid. Sure. And then maybe we can send Lassie for help, too."

Her eyes narrowed. "Don't patronize me. I happen to know the detective working on the kidnapping case. In fact, she's my best friend."

He didn't say anything for a moment. "Look, no offense, but I have this thing about people who incarcerate me. Not interested. Thanks anyway."

"Don't hang up!" she begged.

"Wasn't going to," he said calmly. "But if you're worried about keeping me talking long enough to run a phone tap, you've been watching too many *Dragnet* reruns. There's Caller ID now—much more efficient. Still, I'll spare the cops the effort—I'm at a pay phone on the turnpike. I won't be for long."

"*Cagney and Lacey*," Leigh said defensively. "And I know all about Caller ID. Why are you on the turnpike?"

"The truth? I've been visiting at our family farm, which now belongs to someone else. I thought I'd dig up a spot in the private pet cemetery. Any more questions?"

Several came to mind, but she decided she'd better stick to the program. "I'm serious about you talking to my detective friend," she continued. "She doesn't want you, she wants this Torr guy. And she can't go after him without more information."

"She can have all the information she wants, but it's not going to do her any good, and I'm not going to any police station."

Leigh ground her teeth in frustration. "Why not?

She said there aren't any warrants out for your arrest."

"Oh, really? That's good to know. I really should keep better track of that sort of thing."

Her face reddened. "Stop making jokes! I need to know more about this Torr. What's his real name?"

Mason was quiet a moment. "Look, Leigh," he said softly. "Nobody's taking all this more seriously than me. But I'm telling you, your policewoman friend, however upstanding she may be, cannot do squat about Torr. I have to handle this in my own way."

"Just tell me his name," she asked again, her tone turning a bit desperate. She wasn't sure why he had called her, but she was terrified that he would hang up before she got what she needed.

"Fine," he said placatingly. "I'll tell you whatever you want to know, and then you promise to do me a little favor, OK?" He didn't wait for an answer. "Got a paper and pen handy? The guy's name is Torrence Bagley. His enemies call him Torr, and he hasn't got any friends. He's an arms dealer and a smuggler and he operates out of the Florida panhandle. He's already got warrants out in every state south of the Mason-Dixon line, so your friend can just take a number."

Leigh scribbled on the back of her checkbook with one of her father's free Heartguard pens. "Keep talking."

"That'll get her all she needs to know," he answered. "Torr's record will speak for itself. Now for that favor you owe me."

She was silent.

"I don't mean to scare you any more than you're already scared, but this Torr is dangerous, real dangerous. Before he showed up at Lydie's I didn't think he knew anything about my ties to your family, but now I know otherwise. It was Gordy that sold me out—your kidnapper. You don't have to worry about him anymore by the way; he's back in Alabama."

Leigh's heart rate quickened further. "How do you know?"

"Called him last night and gave him hell. He's not a bad fellow, like I said, but he's running from his own demons right now."

She hesitated, but only a moment. "Well, according to my friend the detective," she began, "they caught up with him this morning. He's dead."

A long silence followed, ending with a string of muttered curses. When Mason spoke again, his tone was weary. "Look, Leigh, I don't really know how much Torr knows about the family. Gordy wouldn't admit selling me out at all; I just knew he was lying. So I don't want you guys to take any chances. You've all got to leave town, ASAP. You hear me?"

She had a mental flash of Trudy, lying broken and pale in her hospital bed, and felt queasy. "He beat up your sister, didn't he?" she asked quietly. She supposed that being shot at should produce more emotional horror than the memory of a stranger with a wired jaw—but it didn't. Taking potshots at an enemy was one thing. Beating an innocent woman nearly to death was another.

Mason didn't answer for a moment. "He was trying to find me," he said stiffly, betraying a sudden, strong mix of guilt and anger. "He knew I had a sister—she was part of the old counterfeit ring. But I didn't think he could find her." There was another pause. "She knew where I was, but she wouldn't tell him. I wish she had."

Leigh swallowed. "Why is he looking for you?"

There was no response.

"He's trying to kill you, isn't he?" she asked, her

voice rising. "He would have killed you at my apartment building, but you moved suddenly, and he missed. Oh, my God, I forgot to ask. Are you all right?"

There was a slight pause, and from the tone of his voice she imagined that he had cracked a smile. "Just grazed my shoulder; thanks for caring. And I doubt he was trying to kill me so much as slow me down. Sort of like pulling the wings off a fly."

Leigh shivered. "What does he want from you?"

Mason didn't answer, and she took a breath and plowed on. "He left you a message on Lydie's mirror. I want you to tell me what it means."

"What message?" he asked quickly.

"Will you tell me what it means?"

"Just give it to me."

Leigh groaned in frustration. "Mason, you have to help the police catch this guy!"

"I'm handling it," he said firmly. "Now give me the damn message."

She hesitated a moment, not sure whether she should use the message as a lure, or whether keeping it from him would serve only to put them all in more danger. In the end, she spilled it.

His voice, when he finally spoke again, was thin. "OK. No problem—I've got what he wants and I can get it there on time."

"Get what where?"

Mason Dublin was proving excellent at ignoring questions—yet another trait he had passed on in his genes. "Listen, kid. Forget about the police. No revolving prison door is going to end this thing. It's up to me and I'm going to take care of it once and for all. But in the meantime, you've got to get your family out of town."

"If you knew your daughter," Leigh said steadily,

"you would know she never runs from anything. None of us are going anywhere. We're going to stay put and work with our happy, friendly, *capable* police force."

Mason muttered something under his breath. "Then for God's sake, call that friend of yours and make sure she keeps a watch on . . . on everybody. It should all be over soon. That Gil guy have security out there?"

Leigh's heart warmed. He did care, damn him. "Yeah. And by the way, 'that Gil guy' would give his life for your daughter and grandson."

Mason didn't answer for a long time. "Good for him," he said finally.

The line went dead.

Chapter 19

Sixty-three percent, Leigh crafted carefully with the tip of the purple frosting dispenser. She made the numbers fill up the whole surface of the cake, which was actually Betty Crocker blueberry muffins. Having never owned a muffin pan, she had always baked them this way.

She toted the concoction into the bedroom on a tray, along with two glasses of orange juice, two mugs, and an entire pot of premium coffee. "How's the head, Mr. Councilman?" she asked with a smile.

Warren smiled back at her, only slightly bleary-eyed. "For the last time," he said mildly, "I did *not* have too much champagne last night, and I do *not* have a hangover. What you saw was pure adrenaline. My head is fine."

"Whatever you say, dear," Leigh agreed, her eyes twinkling evilly. "I'm sure you won't be needing these Tylenol then."

He looked at the two caplets as if they were an ice cream sundae with caramel sauce. "No, thanks," he insisted. Then he looked at the muffin-cake and smiled. "Looks great."

Leigh placed the two Tylenol on the edge of his plate, then dug in. After she had let him eat four servings, covertly down the Tylenol, and thoroughly reminisce about the victory, she decided it was time to come clean. "Mason called last night."

She should have waited until he had swallowed the coffee in his mouth, but her timing was poor. He sputtered the brown liquid out over his lap, drenching his next piece of muffin-cake. "I told you to tell me if he called, no matter what else was going on!"

"Yeah, I know," she said calmly. "But since when do I ever do what anyone tells me? You deserved a night of unfettered fun, and you got it. I called Maura right away and told her everything—there was nothing else you or I could do about the situation last night."

Warren exhaled with a growl. "What did he say?"

Leigh summarized the conversation. "I'm sure Maura's on top of things." She puzzled a moment. Something about her conversation with Maura had deserved further thought, but in the heat of the election returns, she had forgotten about it. "You know, I called her on her cell phone, and a man answered."

"Oh? Who?"

"I'm not sure. I thought the voice sounded familiar, but all he said was 'Polanski,' and then Maura took the phone."

"Well," Warren said matter-of-factly. "She did have a date last night, didn't she?"

"A what?"

He laughed. "Oh, come on. Surely Mo has been out before. I know she didn't date in college, but—"

"I've never known her to go out on a single date with anybody, ever," Leigh said firmly. "I thought—"

"You thought what?"

"Nothing."

The phone rang, and Leigh jumped to answer it. She was still trying to place the mystery man's stern, yet thin voice when her thoughts were interrupted by her mother's screechy one.

"Leigh, dear, you and Warren need to come out to the farm right away. Maura's coming over and we're having a family conference—well, not a full-blown family conference, under the circumstances. She feels it would be best not to involve the extended family; she didn't even want Bess to come because she isn't directly tied to Mason. Neither are your father and I, of course, but since our house is right next to Lydie's she thought it would be better if we stayed at the farm, too, and I figured—"

"Did something else happen?" Leigh interrupted, her heart pounding.

"No, dear, we're all fine. But Maura said that Mason had contacted you again, and that she had further information she wanted to deliver to all of us at one time. So can you—"

"We'll be there in ten minutes," Leigh declared hastily.

Maura had not yet arrived, and once everyone had given Warren their congratulations, the mood in the farmhouse quickly deteriorated. Cara fluttered about trying to serve drinks that no one wanted, Gil sat at the dining room table brooding over the PI's file, Lydie stood motionless looking out a kitchen window, and Frances was on all fours in the living room, wiping the baseboards with a napkin. Leigh's father, of course, had been at the animal clinic since dawn.

Warren politely took a cup of coffee from Cara, then accepted Mathias's tacit invitation to help throw cardboard blocks through the window of his plastic play castle. Leigh stayed in the living room. She hadn't yet confronted her aunt about the bombshell Mrs. Snodgrass had dropped the day before; she wanted answers, but since the jet-lagged Lydie had been hit with everything from blackmail to kidnapping to breaking and entering within an hour of her return to Pittsburgh, she was willing to cut her a break. Her mother was another matter.

"Aren't you supposed to be back at work today, dear?" The sound came from somewhere in the vicinity of Frances's rear end, which was bobbing up and down between the wall and the couch. "I called Hook first, but they told me they didn't expect you until tomorrow."

"I've been planning for months to take yesterday and today off," Leigh explained, "because of the election." That her daughter would be sacked from a job because of truancy was one of her mother's greatest fears in life—and though the advertising field had indeed proven good for several sackings, none, Leigh was proud to point out, had anything to do with not showing up for work. The fact that she was now her own boss and couldn't be fired in any event had done little to stem Frances's phobia. Neither did her mother's own stated view that a married woman should concentrate more on the house anyway.

"Mom," Leigh began quietly, looking over her shoulder to make sure no one else was in earshot. "How much did Lydie tell Cara?"

Frances's rump immediately disappeared, and her top half emerged. She eyed her daughter warily, lips pursed. "She told me that she explained about the bank robbery, and how she had asked Mason to leave. She tried to make Cara understand that it was for her own good. I think it went all right." Her torso vanished again.

Mrs. Snodgrass's words rang in Leigh's ears again, and she cleared her throat. "Lydie didn't seem too surprised when Mason called the house yesterday," she said suggestively.

The bobbing rump stilled. "You have to admire Cara for wanting to do her own cleaning, even though heaven knows they could afford the help, but still, just look at how much gunk I've got off this—"

"Mom," Leigh interrupted. "I know there's more to the story than you've told me. Mason didn't take off without a backward glance, did he? He's been back—more than once. He came to see Cara."

Frances's head reappeared. Her face was puckered into a defensive frown, but her eyes showed alarm. "Mason Dublin would say anything to get what he wants," she retorted quietly. "He's a shyster, a confidence man. What nonsense has he been telling you?"

Leigh surveyed her mother's face carefully. So it was true. "Mason didn't tell me much of anything," she said honestly. "Mrs. Snodgrass mentioned that she would recognize Mason if she saw him. She didn't know it was a secret that he used to come around the house—I suppose she thought that you and Lydie would level with us when we grew up."

Frances's face paled. She looked at her daughter regretfully for a moment, then shuffled around to the front of the couch and sat down with a plop. "Well, I always thought we should have," she said with a sigh. "Lydie planned on telling Cara the truth eventually, as soon as she became mature enough to handle it. But when she turned eighteen Mason was in jail, and what good would it do to tell her then? Of course, the years kept going by, and then Cara was married and happy, and seemed so settled that Lydie couldn't bear to rock the boat."

Leigh found herself biting her lip. She wanted to be furious, but she was determined not to personalize this whole mess. What mattered was Cara. She could understand Lydie's desire for her daughter not to grow up stigmatized as the child of a criminal. But what she grew up with instead was the pain of believing that her own father had turned his back on her. Forever. No visits, no calls, no birthday or Christmas presents, not even a postcard. No questions asked. Not a single thought in her direction. Which was worse?

"I'm not criticizing Lydie's decisions in the past," Leigh said stiffly. "But as of now, I do think Cara has a right to know the whole truth. And if Lydie wants to be the one to tell her, she'd better do it soon—before Maura gets any further on this investigation."

She looked again at the doors to the parlor, making certain they weren't being overheard, then sat down beside her mother. "So, what is the truth? How much contact has Lydie had with Mason over the years? Did he *want* a relationship with his daughter, or didn't he?"

Frances opened her mouth to answer, but before she got any words out, Lydie appeared in the kitchen doorway, her face drawn and pale.

"Leigh," she said unsteadily, coming into the room, "could I talk to you a minute?"

Leigh nodded and Frances scuttled off murmuring something about dusty window blinds. Lydie took over the spot her sister had left on the couch and began talking with one eye aimed warily toward the kitchen.

"I, um—I know you've already heard a lot of the story about how my marriage ended. But I just wanted to make sure you understand why I did what I did."

Leigh looked at the sweet, hard-working aunt she

had adored her whole life. She looked tired. Bone tired. "You don't owe me any explanation," she said softly.

"No," Lydie insisted, "but you're getting one anyway. You grew up being kept in the dark along with Cara, and there's a reason for that."

She took a deep breath. Leigh waited.

"Mason Dublin isn't an evil person," she began. Her voice was firm, but it was evident from the trembling in her lower jaw that speaking on the subject at all was akin to walking on hot coals. "But he's trouble. And he always will be. After the robbery, I finally accepted that. This whole business now just proves it." She paused a moment, then looked at her niece closely. "You've met him, you've talked to him; you know how he is."

Leigh wasn't sure she knew what her aunt meant.

"He's charming," Lydie explained, her face hard. "He's got that million-dollar smile, and he's always ready with the wisecracks. He has a way of making you want to trust him. You felt that, didn't you?"

Leigh shrugged, not sure what she should say.

Her aunt nodded. "You're a natural skeptic, Leigh, just like your mother. She never did trust Mason. He worked on her—hard—and eventually she did come to like him, though she still won't admit it. But back then I was too naïve, too trusting. I only wanted to see the good in him. And Cara's worse than I am. I knew when she was little that if he ever got to her, she would love and trust him immediately—and then he would hurt and disappoint her too. Over and over again." She paused a moment, and Leigh couldn't help but notice that her self-confident, capable aunt had aged at least a decade since her return from India.

"It's a powerful pain to be let down so much by

someone you love," she said quietly. "I never wanted Cara to go through that. That's why I told her that he had left with another woman before she was born. I didn't want her to feel that she'd been personally abandoned, but I didn't want her to fantasize about him being some kind of hero, either."

"She did," Leigh said automatically, wishing immediately that she hadn't. "We both did."

Lydie nodded. "I know. I was wrong to think that I could keep Cara from thinking about him at all. It was foolish. But I didn't know what else to do."

Leigh swallowed. "So you asked him to leave and never come back."

"Yes."

"But he did anyway."

Lydie looked up, her pupils wide, and Leigh explained quickly. "Mrs. Snodgrass mentioned it. It wasn't her fault—she thought we knew."

A deep sigh escaped Lydie's lips, and it was a moment before she spoke again. "That was the worst part," she began softly. "Letting Cara believe he'd never even laid eyes on her. He was there at the hospital when she was born. He came around all the time, for a while. You've never seen a prouder man." Her face smiled a little, then just as quickly clouded over. "But I yelled and I screamed. And finally I convinced him that the best thing he could do for her was to stay out of her life for good."

"He didn't, though, did he?" Leigh prompted. "He still came around to see her every once in a while— he just did it on the sly. He didn't let her see him, and he didn't want you to see him."

Lydie nodded. "If it weren't for Mrs. Snodgrass, I might never have known. But he came around at least a couple of times a year. And he called me to ask about her. Of course, he never admitted to the visits."

Leigh felt her blood begin to pool in her toes. Mason visited; Mason called. And all the time Cara was so desperate for information . . . she never even knew what he looked like. Now Leigh could understand why.

"Do you remember when Cara played Elizabeth in *The Homecoming?*" Lydie asked suddenly.

Leigh nodded. She remembered well that Christmas at the Red Barn Theater, when her aunt Bess had sprayed her beehive gray to serve "the recipe" as Mamie Baldwin. Leigh and Cara had both auditioned for children's parts, and though she had her heart set on the part of Erin, the casting director had stuck to redheads. Leigh still hadn't gotten over it.

"Mason was there," Lydie continued. "I saw him in the audience. I never knew how he found out about the play, but he did. I went to confront him after, but of course he took off before I could catch up to him." She paused again. "He's good at that."

Leigh still sat, disbelieving. How many times had Cara been in the same room with him? Had he ever tried to talk to her? Would she even remember?

"But when Cara was a teenager, he was convicted for the counterfeiting," Lydie continued somberly. "He went away for a long time then. He missed her high school graduation, and college too. I've no doubt he would have been there if he could, no matter what I said. When he finally did get out of prison, she was working in New York City. Whether he ever tried to visit her there, I don't know."

For a long moment, neither of them spoke. Finally Leigh asked another question, her voice more of a croak. "Did you worry that he would tell her who he was?"

Lydie shook her head. "No. He agreed with me
when she was a baby that she was better off without
him. He wasn't capable of staying out of trouble—
he still isn't. The reason I never wanted him anywhere around her was because I knew that if she
ever caught a glimpse of him, she would recognize
him. They look so much alike. But he promised me
he would never interfere with her, and as far as I
know, he kept his word."

Her eyes turned wistful. "At the beginning, I used
to think that maybe someday he would change. That
he'd be happy living like an ordinary man with a
little steady money and no big deals on the horizon.
But then I realized he was never going to change.
He was born to be discontented, always reaching for
that next star. He's not the type to hurt people, mind
you, but he's got no respect whatsoever for the law."
She sighed again. "He's a fool, plain and simple. And
I was a fool to marry him in the first place."

"No, you weren't," Leigh said quickly. She believed her own words, but at the moment she was
hard pressed to understand why, much less to de-
fend the statement. She looked away and suddenly
realized that the pieces of at least one of the puzzles
in her head were starting to fall into place.

"So you and Mason have been in contact on a
fairly regular basis all along," she began expectantly.

Her aunt nodded. "More or less. He always kept
up with what Cara was doing."

"But when she got married—you didn't tell him,
did you?"

Lydie's eyes turned guilty, but resolute. "No," she
admitted. "No, I didn't. It wasn't right of me, perhaps, but I didn't want him there. He would have
tried to stay out of sight, but even if Cara didn't
notice the resemblance, someone else certainly would

have. With all the family around—" She shook her head. "I just couldn't have him there. He could have ruined the wedding, everything."

Leigh had to admit her aunt had a point. "So you told him after the fact?"

"Yes."

"And when Mathias was born?"

Lydie squirmed a bit, but remained defensive. "How could I take a chance on his ruining the happiest days of Cara's life? No, I didn't tell him she was expecting. But I would have told him about Mathias eventually."

"But Trudy got to him first."

Lydie's lips pursed. "Yes, and as I suppose you already know, Mason was furious with me. He got even more furious when I refused to let him see the baby."

Leigh's eyebrows rose. "He wanted to see Mathias?"

"He would have been on the next bus, if I'd cooperated. He had this idea that he would sneak over while I was baby-sitting. But I couldn't do that—it just didn't seem right. It wasn't fair to Cara, and Mathias certainly wouldn't benefit."

Leigh took a deep breath. It was all making sense now. Mason's anger at Lydie, his imbibing a little too much and spouting off to his drinking buddies. His ex-wife thought she was so high and mighty, did she? Well, he happened to know that she had committed a crime, too. And he could get her put away for it—or at least get some money out of the slimeball who had stolen his only daughter. . . .

Frances jumped suddenly through the doorway, practically contorting herself to precede Cara into the room. "Well, look—they're both in here!" she said loudly.

Cara threw her aunt an odd sideways look and

floated into the room with Mathias on her hip. Her face was drained and tight, much like her mother's. But where Lydie's features showed anxiety, hers were laden with pain. She looked briefly at Leigh and her mother; then, perhaps recognizing the guilty looks on their faces, turned away. "Maura is here," she announced flatly. "Perhaps we should all move into the dining room."

Chapter 20

Detective Maura Polanski was all business when she took a seat at the Marches' dining room table, notebook and binder firmly in hand. She refused Cara's offer of hot spiced cider and simply started talking.

"First off," she began, "I'd like to assure everyone who doesn't already know that our kidnapping suspect, William Gordon, is now dead. I just got off the phone with a detective down in Alabama, and he's eighty-five percent sure that this Gordy fellow was taken out by loan sharks. Apparently he had overextended himself at the dog track one too many times. The blackmail scheme was probably his one last hope, and when Gil called his bluff, he got desperate. After the kidnapping went sour, he gave up and took a train back home. He should have gone someplace else."

"What about the second blackmailer?" Gil asked, his jaw tight. Perhaps someone else could feel bad about Gordy's untimely death, but it was clear no tears would be shed at the March table.

Maura gave a nod. "Good news there. The detective's got a tentative handwriting match for us—a young guy named Sammy Jones. He's a regular at the Brindle Blur, the bar where Mason worked, and a frequent visitor to the county lockup, mostly on possession and petty theft—nothing violent. The blackmail letter was probably more of a lark than anything. Main thing is, he's been behind bars all week, so he's got nothing to do with what's been happening here."

Gil nodded solemnly. He looked as if he was going to say something else, but then he stopped himself. Leigh felt a pang of sympathy. They all realized now that it was Cara's appearance on the *Movers and Shakers* show that had started the whole blackmail cascade in motion. Gordy and Sammy might have picked up the idea from Mason, but they could never have acted on it without knowing where the principals lived. Tracking down a Cara and a Lydie somewhere in the U. S. who might or might not still be named Dublin was hardly worth the effort, but with the information dumped right into their laps, the temptation had proved too great.

Leigh's eyes moved from Gil to Cara, who had been staring blankly at her own full cup of cider. There was certainly no point in berating her about it now.

"What we should concentrate on now," Maura continued heavily, "is the issue of Mason Dublin's reappearance in Pittsburgh, and all that's happened since. Nothing's for sure here, but I'll give you my take on it. After Mason had served his counterfeiting sentence at the Federal penitentiary, he settled down to an ordinary life, of sorts, with the bartending job in southern Alabama. Didn't commit a single other offense, as far as we know. Then, six months ago, he up and disappears, apparently to hide out from a career criminal named Torrence Bagley." She pulled a fax out of her binder and held it out toward Leigh's mother. "Mrs. Koslow, do you recognize this man?"

Frances leaned over the table and tilted up her head to see through her bifocals. "Oh, dear," she muttered. "I couldn't swear that was the shooter, but it certainly could be."

Maura turned the picture so that everyone could see it, and Leigh shrank back a little. The man didn't look in the least familiar, though he could have made an appearance in a nightmare or two. He was six-foot-three, according to the ticks on the wall behind him, with another inch in greasy, mussed black hair. His angry, dark eyes were set in a gaunt face with a large, thin nose and angular jaw. Large, full lips framed his mouth and then some. If he were trying to look like a criminal, he couldn't have done a better job. But then, Leigh supposed no one looked their best in a mug shot. Her own were certainly not scrapbook material.

"Take a good look," Maura encouraged, "because this man is someone to watch out for." She consulted her notebook. "He has a long history of arrests for receiving stolen goods and illegal sale of arms; he's also suspected to have been involved in weapons smuggling, but no convictions there. A few assault charges—again, no convictions. And he's under suspicion in at least one open murder investigation."

Leigh cast a glance around the table. Her relatives had gone pale en masse.

Maura took a deep breath before continuing. "According to Mason Dublin, 'Torr,' as he's called, knew he had a sister because she had been part of the counterfeit operation. This tells us that Torr knew about the counterfeit operation, which is probably what ties him to Mason in the first place. Torr would have been too young to have had anything to do with the original ring, but he might have had some interest in either Mason's expertise or the leftover paraphernalia." As Maura explained about the bill-stamping plates and Mason's widely revered artistic abilities, Leigh watched her cousin's face. It remained perfectly blank.

"One way or another," Maura continued, "Mason got on Torr's bad side and took off. But Torr didn't let it go. He went so far as to drive to Pennsylvania and track down Trudy Dublin in Pittsburgh. He wanted to know where Mason was hiding, and he might also have thought Trudy had something he wanted—like the plates. Either way, she resisted. You know the rest."

Leigh's stomach flip-flopped, and from the look of the table's other occupants, it wasn't the only one.

"Torr stayed in Pittsburgh after he put Trudy in the hospital, probably hoping her brother would show. He did. The fact that Mason was running around the hospital outside of visiting hours wearing scrubs tells us that he knew somebody might be watching. But he wasn't careful enough, because eventually Torr saw him. Unfortunately, that was the same day he ran into Leigh and followed her home."

Lydie uttered an exclamation and dropped her chin into her hands. She exchanged a tortured look with Frances, but said nothing more.

"Torr took a shot at Mason in the parking lot— whether it was just a warning or meant business, we don't know. Mason was injured, but nonetheless managed to give Torr the slip."

Maura paused a moment. "And if you want my take on the big picture, here it is. I don't think Torr's presence in Pittsburgh—or even Mason Dublin's— was directly related to the blackmail attempts. I think Mason's probably telling the truth that he heard about the kidnapping on the news and panicked because he thought Torr might be behind that too. He was worried about Torr taking a step beyond Trudy and terrorizing the rest of the family. That's what he wanted to warn Leigh about. But he screwed up—because in following Leigh home from the hospital, he led Torr right to her."

Leigh could see her mother's face going gray, and she piped up quickly. "But Torr has no reason to pester the rest of us now. He's just waiting for Mason to respond."

Six hopeful pairs of eyes turned toward the detective, but her answer was less than reassuring. "Torr can't know for sure that Mason ever got the message on the mirror. He may be looking for other ways to lure him back out in the open." She looked at the anxious faces around the table with sympathy before continuing.

"In the beginning, Torr probably went to the bar to seek out Mason's counterfeiting expertise and or equipment. After Mason double-crossed him and took off, he would have pressured some of the bar's regulars for information. My guess is they didn't have anything to give him, not at first. But after *Movers and Shakers* aired, one or the other of Mason's "buddies" decided the info on his family could be worth a buck. So as for whether Torr knows who and where all of you are—I'm afraid we have to assume the worst."

Dead silence descended. Mathias, who had been sitting happily in his honorary uncle's lap, suddenly started to squawk, and Warren took him quickly out of the room, tossing him in the air on the way. Mathias's discontent turned at once into squeals of pleasure, and his happy laughter cut through the tense air like a knife.

"We can assume that for safety's sake, sure," Leigh began, struggling to say something—anything—positive. "But this whole situation is only temporary. This Torr guy wants something Mason has, and

Mason plans on giving it to him as soon as possible. So once that's done, it'll all be over. Right?" She looked hard at Maura, willing her not to disagree. But either telepathy wasn't the detective's thing or, more likely, she didn't choose to lie.

Maura threw a sober glance back at her friend and exhaled. "It's possible this whole thing is about the counterfeiting plates. The message on the mirror certainly gives that impression. But I don't think that's all of it. Maybe Mason took Torr's money and never delivered the goods. But it's hard to believe the plates alone were worth this much trouble." She paused again, clearly not anxious to deliver the rest of her thoughts. "The traveling, the tracking . . . the unnecessary violence against Trudy. I'm afraid it all points toward something more personal."

"So what does that mean to us?" Gil asked harshly, jabbing an expensive fountain pen against the table. He looked more unnerved than ever, which Leigh didn't find surprising. He'd been dealing with the *Movers and Shakers* fallout for almost two weeks now, and despite his diligent efforts, things had only gone from bad to worse. Tough going for a man who existed to fix things.

"It means that a nice neat drop-off of the plates— if that's even what Mason went to get—isn't going to satisfy Torr," the detective answered.

"So he wants revenge," Gil responded, letting out a frustrated breath. "And he won't be happy til Mason suffers." He threw a hard glance at Maura. "One way or another."

Cara stood up from the table, her face flushed. For a moment her eyes flashed fire at her husband, and her mouth moved as if she were ready to say something. But then she simply turned and walked out of the room.

Gil's expression turned guilty, and after a moment he shoved his chair back from the table and followed her. Leigh, her mother, and her aunt remained at the table, staring helplessly at each other.

"Mason's a fool," Frances said solemnly. "If this Torr does have it in for him, he can't possibly confront the man and walk away."

"I have a feeling he knows that," the detective offered quietly. She looked at Lydie. "The only way Mason can end the threat to his family is to stop running. And if he won't work with the police, I'm afraid that leaves only two options. Either he's willing to commit murder himself—"

Lydie quickly shook her head, and Maura finished heavily.

"Or else it's a suicide mission."

Gil came back down the stairs looking miserable and angry at the same time. "See what you can do," he said to Leigh, tossing his head in the direction of his and Cara's bedroom. "She won't talk to me."

Leigh mounted the creaky stairs of the farmhouse with trepidation. She wasn't sure what had been going through Cara's mind lately, and she doubted she was likely to find out. When her cousin got in one of her stone-wall moods, she was virtually impossible to crack.

Yet it wasn't long after Leigh had settled herself on the edge of the bed that her cousin, who was standing at its foot, began talking. Loudly.

"He's going to get himself killed now, do you realize that?" She was looking not at Leigh but at her own reflection in the antique floor mirror. "He hides out for thirty years, shows up and gets to know *you*, then kicks the bucket. Isn't that just priceless?"

Wicked sarcasm was a tool Leigh wasn't above

using. She decided to take a risk. "Maybe you could kill him yourself."

Cara whirled around, her eyes flashing. Then, as Leigh had hoped, her composure finally broke. Tears welled up in her eyes, followed by great, racking sobs that shook her body as she slumped over the edge of the mattress. Leigh sat quietly next to her, and after five minutes, the worst was over.

Cara raised her swollen face, her eyes once again resolute. "He can't die, Leigh," she said firmly.

"He won't."

"It's not fair. I want to see him first. I want to see him so I can look in his eyes and tell him I never want to see him again."

Leigh cracked a smile. She hated herself for being such a sentimental schmuck, but she couldn't help it. If they ever had a chance to meet without the baggage, Mason and Cara would adore each other—she was sure of it. "Your mother told you why he really left?" she asked carefully.

Cara nodded, then shrugged. "It doesn't matter. Infidelity, bank robbery, what's the difference? He had a child and he didn't care. He could have come back after the statute of limitations ran out. He didn't."

Leigh took a deep breath. It was Lydie's place to tell the rest of the story, but when would she? There was no excuse for Cara being kept in the dark any longer. How could she possibly resolve all the convoluted feelings she had about her father when half of them were based on a falsehood?

"He did come back, Cara," she said before her mind had a chance to change. "He came back a lot." Thinking no more, she dove headfirst into the truth as she knew it—how Mason had agreed with Lydie that their baby daughter was better off without him, but that he hadn't been able to stay away. She relayed Mrs. Snodgrass's claims, the story about his attendance at *The Homecoming*, and Lydie's confessions about keeping the wedding and Mathias's birth a secret. Cara sat perfectly still through it all, listening with a blank expression on her face.

When Leigh had finished, she sat back and waited for her cousin's response. She expected a brief show of anger toward Lydie for keeping her in the dark—and perhaps just the smallest glimmer of happiness. Though it wasn't the happy ending of her childhood dreams, it had to mean something to know that her father—in his bizarre way—did care.

But neither emotion materialized. Her cousin stood stiffly, then began to repair the rumpled bed.

"Cara," Leigh asked, concerned. "Why aren't you saying anything?"

She turned around then, her tear-stained face as blank as it ever had been. "Because," she said matter-of-factly, "I have nothing to say."

Chapter 21

"I'm just really in the mood for it, that's all."

Warren stared at his wife as if she'd gone even more insane than she usually seemed to be. "Your family is living under armed guard here at this farm, the countdown to Mason's mystery rendezvous with a violent criminal is on, and you want to do a dinner dance on the Gateway Clipper?"

Leigh nodded sheepishly. "Come with me, please?"

He continued to stare at her. "How dumb do you think I am? Now tell me what's up. Because if you're planning on some clandestine rendezvous of your own—"

"It's nothing like that!" she insisted, getting desperate. "It has nothing to do with Mason, I swear. I just need a change of scenery, and we haven't had much time alone together lately. Don't you trust me?"

He surveyed her carefully with his gorgeous brown puppy-dog eyes. "No."

Leigh groaned. She had tried. She really had. But since she hated admitting defeat, she would give it one more shot. "Just get in the car, Harmon."

He didn't move. They stood in Cara's driveway, the Brittany spaniel, Maggie, reaching new heights of centrifugal force as she raced around their legs in a wide arc. "I'm not going anywhere until you tell me what's going on." He leaned back on his VW Bug, his arms crossed lazily across his chest. "There's no rush."

"Yes, there is," she argued, opening his car door. "I'll explain on the way. Get in."

He still didn't move.

"Warren!"

He cocked one eyebrow at her defiantly, then leaned down to pet Maggie, who had temporarily ceased her orbit. "Spill it, my dear," he said calmly. "The truth this time, please."

Leigh narrowed her eyes at him. "If it weren't for all this stuff going on with Mason, you'd go with me, wouldn't you?"

"Sure."

"OK," she said with relief. "Then it's not my fault. You can tell your volunteer campaigners that. Better yet, you can just test out those great acting skills you're always bragging about. Now get your butt behind the wheel and drive us to Station Square pronto, Councilman—or you're going to miss your own surprise party."

Once the cat was out of the bag, the rest of the family decided to head down to the party right behind Leigh and Warren, rather than following at a respectful distance as had been the original plan. All seemed eager to escape the confines of the farm—so much so that even traveling with a posse of private security guards seemed a reasonable price to pay.

To his credit, Warren did a wonderful acting job, and Leigh enjoyed garnering kudos from the loyal staff who had planned everything so carefully. The Gateway Clipper was in fine form, and as the old-fashioned riverboat sailed away from the dock, Leigh took in the twinkling downtown skyline with a sigh.

She had always loved dinner cruises, but she would enjoy this one a whole lot more if she knew Mason Dublin was not about to do something stupid.

A hand clapped her heavily on the shoulder blades, and she didn't need to look to know it was Maura. She also didn't need to look to know that her friend would be wearing that same bizarre, goofy smile that had started popping up whenever she wasn't talking business. "Councilman today—President tomorrow," she said proudly. "I always knew that kid would go far."

Leigh chortled. "As I recall, you used to say the only thing he'd ever be president of was the International Brown-Nosers Society."

Maura smirked. "Yeah, well, we were young. We both underestimated him. But now I'd say you're in serious danger of that First Lady thing."

"Tell me about it." Leigh made a face. "Highest-ranking unpaid job in the country, and I'd probably get fired."

"Be a trendsetter," Maura joked. "Make the White House business casual."

Leigh's eyebrows rose. "I like that."

"At least you wouldn't have to cook."

"True." Leigh noted the even-rosier-than-normal glow on her friend's plump cheeks and couldn't stand it anymore. "All right, Polanski. Fess up right now. Who is it that's making you so blasted happy all of a sudden?"

A flicker of self-consciousness crossed Maura's face, but it was replaced just as quickly with her policewoman demeanor. "Look, Koslow," she said stiffly, "I do need to talk shop for a minute. I just came from the hospital. Trudy Dublin's talking."

Leigh's eyes widened. "Really? Does she know

where Mason is? Does she know what 'Funny Money line in 36' means?"

Maura shook her head. "I'm not sure what she knows. All I'm sure of is that she doesn't trust police. I couldn't get anything out of her." She let out a breath. "That's why I was hoping Cara would be willing to take a shot at it. Any information Trudy could tell her about Mason might help us figure out where he and Torr were planning to meet. Without that—"

Her voiced trailed off, and Leigh looked at her intently. "You think Torr will kill him, don't you?" she asked quietly.

The detective answered without hesitation. "Yep."

Leigh looked away. It was a reality she wasn't prepared to deal with. Not now. Not when Cara had finally gotten so close to having all her questions answered. It wasn't right. "Maybe Torr does just want the plates," she reasoned out loud. "Maybe Mason can deliver them and still get away."

Maura threw her friend a heavy look. "I got a call back from an ATF agent this afternoon, one who's been on Torrence Bagley's trail for a while now. The perp is even worse news than I thought. He's an antisocial personality, and wily as they come. The agent thinks he's responsible for at least three homicides, but he doesn't have enough evidence to prosecute any of them. He's wanted on smuggling and weapons charges all along the Gulf Coast, but no one has managed to apprehend him. This case is big, Koslow. If we could just get hold of Mason, I'm sure we could work out some sort of immunity deal in exchange for his cooperation."

"You said Mason wasn't wanted."

"He's not, not that I know of. Yet. But something's

keeping him from coming forward. Maybe Torr knows something that could put him away, too."

Leigh's shoulders sagged. She wanted to believe that Mason was over his illegal proclivities, but she knew that was naïve. Hadn't Lydie been wanting to believe it for the past thirty years?

"So we have to reach Mason first, somehow," she thought out loud. Had she remembered to forward their home calls to Warren's cell phone? She had. But there had been no further word from Mason. Not even a hang-up when Warren answered.

The riverboat sailed slowly past "The Point," the picturesque downtown park that marked the junction of Pittsburgh's three rivers and the birth of the Ohio. Veering north, the boat glided smoothly upstream on the Allegheny, giving them an impressive view of the new Pirates stadium. It was a relatively balmy night for November, but the wind over the water— and the thoughts in her head—were making her shiver. "Maura," she asked thoughtfully. "What do you think Torr really has against Mason? What could he have done?"

The detective was quiet for a moment. "I have a theory," she said finally. "The ATF agent told me that he almost had Torr six months ago. It seems that he was peddling explosives and had found a primo clientele. Domestic terrorists—a band of messed-up rich kids with money to burn. They were set to make a purchase, but somebody tipped off the authorities in time to intercept it. They got the terrorists, they got the explosives, but they didn't get Torr."

Leigh swallowed, her heart lightening a bit. "You think Mason tipped them off?"

Maura shrugged. "It's possible. The timing's right. It would explain why Mason dropped out of sight, and why Torr's so hot to find him."

"But that means Mason did a good thing!" Leigh said brightly. She knew she needed to stop it—in a few days she'd gone from defending Mason without cause to thinking of him as some kind of sympathetic, unsung hero. It was idiotic, but somehow she couldn't help it.

Maura raised her eyebrows questioningly. "Yeah. It would also mean Torr is out for blood."

Before Leigh had a chance to dwell on the thought, their conversation was interrupted by a volunteer who whisked her off the deck and into the dining area. Dinner had begun. She picked nervously at her chicken breast, trying to smile as Warren's supporters treated him to an impromptu roast. She wished she could put Mason Dublin out of her mind long enough to enjoy her husband's big night, but it wasn't to be. She watched out the dining room windows as the boat sailed back down the Allegheny and along the Ohio toward Avalon, her mind returning always to Cara. Would she be willing to talk to Trudy? Would she go tonight?

As dinner wrapped up, Leigh made her way toward her cousin, who stood on the top deck pointing out to an uninterested Mathias the spot on the bluff where her beloved Victorian house had once stood. Cara saw her and turned immediately.

"I want to go see Trudy, as soon as we dock. Will you go with me?"

Leigh blinked. "Of course, if you think it will help."

Cara nodded. "I want Gil to take Mathias home right away, but I don't want to go to the hospital alone. And I think Trudy will be less intimidated by you than my mother, don't you?"

Leigh surveyed her cousin's eyes, which were sparkling again for the first time in days. "Maybe. You feeling . . . better?"

Cara turned away. "I'm managing," she said flatly. "Gil insisted we take not one, but two security guards with us, so we should be fine. Do you think Warren will mind?"

Probably. Leigh waited until the riverboat was almost at the dock before mentioning the field trip. Warren was in high spirits, and she wanted him to enjoy it as long as he could. After buttering him up with a brief necking session on the lower deck, she launched rapidly into the plan, careful to mention the one-to-one guard-to-woman ratio and the fact that the whole thing was Maura's idea.

He frowned throughout. "Two days ago I left you safely ensconced in our apartment under the capable care of Sergeant Frances Koslow, and you still managed to get shot at. And now you're taking off with the world's second strongest calamity magnet? I don't like it."

She smiled. "I love it when you're overprotective, really I do, but you know this is something we should do."

He frowned again. "Let me come too, then."

"No way," she argued. "I heard Joyce say everyone was heading out for drinks afterwards—and you need to be there, at least for a while. You've got your cell phone, Cara has hers. We'll go straight back to the farm and you can pick me up there later."

He ground his teeth, but said nothing.

"Great." She smiled. The gangplank was in place, and the passengers were starting to unload. She gave him another quick kiss and took off. "And by the way," she said over her shoulder, "Maura is definitely seeing someone. You need to find out who."

A devious smile flickered over his face, and she

stopped cold. "Warren Harmon!" she screeched. "You already know, don't you? Tell me! I know him, don't I?"

He had the nerve to laugh. "You'll find out when Maura's ready to tell you," he said slyly. "I see that Cara's down there waiting for you. Better get a move on."

She delivered one last, perturbed glare and went to join her cousin.

"This is Dan," Cara said pleasantly, "and this is Ed. They are under the strictest orders not to let us out of their sight, poor things."

Leigh greeted the mobile home-sized gentleman who had attached himself to her side. "Hi, Ed." He smiled back politely, rotating his head on a square device that was supposed to be a neck.

"Dan is Trent's brother," Cara continued. "You know, the PI? Dan and Ed played football together at Penn State." Leigh nodded at the solid young black man who towered over Cara, wondering how he could possibly share a gene pool with the skinny, intellectual fellow she'd bumped heads with at the bus station. "OK," she said with amusement. "I feel safe. Let's roll."

Dan insisted on doing the driving, and since Cara was the only person Leigh had ever known to have a worse driving reputation than herself, that was fine. In no time their escorts had delivered them to the high-security wing of Allegheny Central, where Maura had had Trudy moved to as soon as Torr was suspected of the attack. The guards then waited patiently in the corridor while Cara and Leigh slipped inside the small room.

Trudy Dublin didn't look much better, but as her alert eyes riveted immediately on her estranged niece, it was clear she was feeling better. The corners of her mouth wrinkled in an odd arrangement that, barring the metal in her jaw, might be a smile.

"Hello," Cara said amiably, sitting down on the foot of the bed. "It's good to see you again. I was sorry to hear you were in the hospital."

Leigh stood a few steps away, not wanting to interfere. Her cousin, who had always been skilled at making people feel at ease, launched easily into a rambling line of chitchat that bore no witness whatsoever to their first, rocky meeting. Trudy spoke only a few words, but her eyes spoke volumes. She seemed very pleased to see her niece again. And, Leigh was increasingly sure, she also wanted something.

After Cara had talked for a while, Trudy raised a hand and began—slowly—to ask a question. "Have. You—" Every word seemed painful. "Seen. Mason?"

Cara's back straightened. "No," she said calmly. "But I know he's here. He's talked to Leigh." She took a breath. "He's in trouble, Trudy. The man who beat you up is trying to kill him."

Leigh's heart beat fast. This whole conversation was costing Cara a lot, and she prayed it wouldn't be for nothing.

Trudy's eyes saddened, and she nodded her head.

"If you know where he might be," Cara said gently, "please tell us. I know you probably don't trust the police. But the detective on the case is a good friend of mine, and she told me that if Mason can help them catch Torr, he'll almost certainly get immunity—"

Trudy's face had darkened, and she began to shake her head. "No. Police," she said staunchly.

Leigh could see anger brimming in her cousin's eyes, but she covered it well. "I understand. No police. But we can't let Mason go to meet Torr alone.

Maura told you the message Torr left on the mirror. If you understand it, you've got to tell me. If 'in 36' means in thirty-six hours, they could be meeting tonight." She swallowed. "He could die, Trudy."

Cara's voice faltered slightly on the last words, and Leigh's heart felt like lead. The effect was not lost on Trudy, either. The older woman's eyes began to tear, and she wrested them away from Cara and out into space. Her gaze moved toward the partially open door, and as Leigh followed it, she saw Dan's head quickly duck away from the crack. Trudy's eyes hardened. "Don't trust," she said harshly. "Prison is death. To him."

Cara stared at her aunt a moment longer, then rose from the bed. She turned away from them both, and Leigh could see she was trying to collect herself. When she faced them again, her eyes were moist, but determined. "Trudy," she began, her voice strong as steel. "I've never even seen my father." She held her aunt's gaze firmly. "*And I don't want to see a corpse.*"

Trudy made a groaning noise, then turned her face firmly toward the far wall, jaw clenched.

Cara waited a moment, then dropped her shoulders. "We'll be going, then," she said, making an obvious effort to keep her voice kind. "If you need anything, here's my number." She dropped a business card on the bedside table and started toward the door. Leigh turned to leave as well, but Trudy's pained voice stopped them both in their tracks.

"His dog," she said intently.

Cara walked back to the bedside. "Mason has a dog?"

Trudy nodded. "I was. Keeping. Ruby Jo has. You take?"

"You want me to take care of Mason's dog until you're out of the hospital," Cara translated. Trudy nodded. "I can do that. Maggie loves company. Ruby Jo—is she a neighbor?"

Trudy nodded again and painfully delivered an address. Cara listened carefully, said good-bye, and hastened Leigh out the door. "We'll have to make a little side trip," she announced to the guards in the hall. "An apartment complex here on the North Side." She delivered the street and apartment numbers, and Dan wrote them down on a pad he removed from his pocket.

"I'll let your husband know," he said dutifully, pulling out his cell phone. Cara nodded, and the foursome started walking.

They were heading off in the car again when Leigh's mind flashed back to the day she'd met Mason in the hospital, and he'd asked for her phone number. It was a small thing, but it made her smile. Cara didn't need to write down numbers, either.

Ruby Jo, a stooped black woman who looked only slightly younger than God, opened her door to the two women and two gigantic men without a trace of apprehension. "Who the hell are you?" she said casually, her hand attached firmly to the studded collar of a silent pit bull.

Dan started to speak, but Cara interrupted him. "I'm Trudy Dublin's niece," she said as pleasantly as possible, her eyes darting nervously toward the pit bull. "She sent us to pick up her dog. Thank you so much for keeping it."

The woman's wrinkled face broke into a smile. "Well, why didn't you say so?" she said pleasantly. She released her hold on the dog, which slunk disinterestedly back into the apartment. "Killer's a pussycat," she said disdainfully, shaking her head.

"But I figure the harder I hold him, the scarier he looks, right?"

Cara gave a smile of relief. "Do you think he'll come with us?"

Ruby Jo looked confused. "Killer? Oh, no, child. Killer's mine. Had him since he was a pup. You're wanting the greyhound. Wait here. I'll get him."

Leigh offered her cousin a supportive grin. She should have suspected Mason for a greyhound owner. He did work next to a dog track, after all. He had probably dropped the dog off at Trudy's when he went underground.

In a moment Ruby Jo returned, pushing the reluctant retiree by the haunches. "He's the laziest sonuvabitch I ever saw," she said with exasperation. "Can't believe he was ever a racer. You're welcome to him. How's Trudy?"

"She's better," Cara answered. She reached down to pet the fawn-colored greyhound, which drank her in with liquid brown eyes and flicked its tail lethargically. "Was there," she asked a little hesitantly, "a collar? Or something?"

The old woman shook her head, and Cara's shoulders seemed to slump in disappointment. Leigh watched curiously. Had Cara expected the dog to be some sort of clue? Was that why she was so determined to get him tonight?

"No leash neither," Ruby Jo explained. "I dragged him out from under the bed while the hospital folks were working on Trudy. Helluva watchdog, eh?"

"I'm sure he'll follow us," Cara said confidently. The dog had indeed taken to her and was leaning against her legs as she talked. She moved a few steps away and clucked to him, and he bounced back to her like a spring.

"Give my love to Trudy if you see her," the

woman told them as they started to leave. "I'd go myself, but I don't get out anymore, you know."

Leigh looked into Cara's disappointed face with concern. Had she really thought this dog was the key to finding Mason?

"Oh, by the way," Ruby Jo called after them. "His name is Funny Money."

Chapter 22

Leigh's eyes locked with Cara's.

Funny Money?

"Funny Money line," Cara whispered. "Where's the nearest dog track?"

"Wheeling," Dan offered, and Ed nodded his massive head in agreement.

"No," Leigh interjected, the gears in her brain turning. "That's not what it means. 'Greyhound line.' They're meeting at the bus station!"

Cara stared at her, her lively eyes filled with sparks. "Well, let's go, then."

The bus station was only one river away from the North Side, and Dan covered the distance quickly, protesting all the while. "I'm not supposed to take you anywhere but the hospital and home," he said, his voice the closest thing to a whine that a 250-pound man was capable of.

"Just drive," Cara said authoritatively, punching on her cell phone. "I knew Trudy was giving us a clue," she exclaimed. "I knew it. She understood the message, but she was determined to keep the meeting place a secret from the police. She was hoping that if I figured it out later on my own, I would try to stop Mason myself."

Leigh studied her cousin anxiously. "But you wouldn't. Right?"

Cara threw her a defensive look. "Of course not! That would be idiotic. I'm calling Maura right now."

Leigh breathed a sigh of relief. Warren would kill her for this, but Maura would be there soon, and they *did* have bodyguards, after all. What could happen?

Cara hung up her phone just as Dan brought the car to a stop in a primo on-street slot. "I didn't talk to Maura directly, but they're notifying her. And the city police."

"So what do you think you're going to do now?" Dan asked nervously. Leigh shook her head in amazement. She'd never met a man yet—no matter how huge or domineering—that her petite, strawberry-blond cousin couldn't play like a harp.

"I'm not sure," Cara answered distractedly, tapping her fingers on the car door as she peered out the window. "Mason could show up here any time or not at all. As could Torr." She bit a fingernail. "Or they could be inside right now."

"We should wait for the police," Leigh said quickly. It was easy to be the voice of reason around Cara—she was probably the only person in the world with an even less well-developed sense of self-preservation than Leigh had.

"Yes, we should," Cara agreed, stepping out of the car.

Dan jumped immediately out after her, protesting.

"You two stay here and keep an eye out for the police," she said calmly, completely ignoring the hulking man at her elbow. "If nobody's inside, we'll be back in a jiff."

As Cara drifted fearlessly into the bus station with Dan at her heels, Leigh attempted to shift the weight of the antsy greyhound that had taken up residence in her lap. *It will be OK*, she told herself. *The police will be here any minute.*

"I think Dan's met his match." Ed chuckled.

Leigh grinned at the ex-football player, who hadn't said another word the entire trip. "And how," she agreed. Her eyes swept lazily over the entrance to the bus station, and her stomach churned nervously as she imagined Mason looking at the same view, wondering if he would ever come out alive.

She shifted her gaze to the side street, and it was then that she saw him—two second's worth of a silhouette, dodging behind the back corner of the building.

She sat up straight.

"Whuzzat?" Ed inquired, following her gaze.

"Mason," Leigh said in a whisper, pushing the greyhound onto the floor and opening the car door. "He's here."

"Stay in the car," Ed ordered.

"It's not Torr," Leigh argued, holding the whimpering dog back with one hand while she stepped out. "It's Cara's father. He's not dangerous."

"But the police will be here any second," Ed insisted, getting out behind her. "Just sit tight."

Leigh wanted to cooperate. Really, she did. But she knew the possible price tag. "If Mason sees a police car a mile away, he'll take off again," she reasoned. "Then as soon as it's gone, he'll come back and get himself killed. I've got to talk to him now."

Not wanting to wait any longer, and not sure that Ed wouldn't pick her up like a sack of potatoes and stuff her into the trunk, she walked briskly away from the car and toward where Mason had disappeared. To her relief, she realized the bodyguard was following her. He was muttering profanity, but he was following her.

She reached the spot where she thought she had seen the silhouette and took a deep breath. It wasn't an alley, exactly, but it was close enough, with a line of trash cans and bins to hide bodies—or parts thereof—behind. It was also as dark as sin, the street lamps failing to penetrate much farther than where she stood. Ed grabbed her behind the elbow and clamped down tight, but his zeal was unnecessary. Leigh had no intention of taking another step.

"Mason," she hissed. "If you're in here, speak up right now. It's just me, Leigh, and I've got a body-guard. The police aren't here yet, and I hope to God Torr isn't either."

A dark figure stepped out of the shadows and walked quickly toward her. "Are you crazy?" it said angrily. "Get out of here, now! Do you want to get yourself killed?"

"No," Leigh retorted, just as hotly. "But you seem to. And I won't let you. You've got to work with the police on this. They can handle Torr, I promise you."

Mason stepped into the light. "No, they can't," he said firmly. "Now I'm not going to tell you again. *Go away.*"

Leigh grunted as Ed pushed her roughly forward. She fell onto the hard concrete with a whomp, two-hundred-plus pounds of linebacker following her lead. After a moment Ed rolled off limply, and Leigh struggled to her hands and knees, both of which were in pain. "What the heck did you do that for?" she cried.

"Quiet!" Mason bent over the bodyguard, and Leigh realized that Ed hadn't rolled off her of his own volition. Her eyes widened in alarm as she noted his closed eyes and slack body.

"Oh, no," she murmured in horror.

Mason, who had been feeling around under Ed's

sweatshirt, pulled back a hand that, in the dim light, appeared to be covered with oil. Leigh felt her insides roll.

Mason let loose with a long string of four-letter words, pulled a handkerchief out of his pocket, and stuffed it back up under Ed's shirt. He then pulled off his own jacket and put it over the bodyguard's chest.

Leigh heard a footstep.

She could only presume that Mason heard it too, because before she realized what was happening, they were both up and running.

"Get in!" he yelled at her, releasing her arm and flinging her toward the passenger side of a dirty tan Tempo. She obeyed without hesitation and fell onto the dingy vinyl seat in a heap. No sooner had she sat upright than the car took off with a violent lurch, toppling her back onto her side again.

"You OK?" Mason asked anxiously as she fought her way toward vertical again. He was driving like a maniac. She grabbed the door with one hand and braced the other on the dashboard.

The front of the bus station whizzed by, and though Leigh had the impression of passing close by a big black man and a petite redhead on the way, she couldn't be certain. Downtown Pittsburgh was jerking around in front of her like trees in *The Blair Witch Project*, and her stomach was somewhere in the vicinity of her Adam's apple.

The car was moving forward, but as far as she could tell Mason was looking only backward, his eyes plastered on the rearview mirror. "I don't think he's following us," he said grimly. "Not yet."

Leigh struggled to get her breath. "What happened back there?" she asked, thinking as she said it that it was a pretty dumb question.

"Torr had me in his sights already," he replied angrily. "Making me sweat, no doubt. You two messed up his plans."

"But he can't just go around shooting people in public!" The words came out in a shriek, and she immediately shut her mouth. She was beginning to sound hysterical, and she hated sounding hysterical. Not unless death was imminent would she ever let herself sound hysterical. "How can he be that careless and never get caught?" she said more evenly.

"He's not usually careless," Mason answered dryly. He was still looking out the rearview mirror, but had suddenly slowed the car to a normal speed. A black-and-white police car, sirens blaring, passed them in the opposite direction. "He's just really, *really* pissed off."

Leigh stared at him. If anyone had a good reason to get frantic, it was him. Instead, he was now signaling politely to make a left.

"But why shoot at Ed?" she asked, the shrieky edge creeping back into her voice again. She would never forgive herself if the bodyguard . . . She couldn't even think about it. Paid professional or no, whatever happened to him would be entirely her fault.

"I'm no expert, but I don't think the bullet went into his chest," Mason said calmly, seeming to sense her guilt. "More likely the blood was coming from his shoulder, because he was breathing all right. Either way, he won't have to wait long for help."

"Where was Torr shooting from?" she asked, still feeling sick. "I didn't hear anything."

Mason shook his head. "He's fond of silencers, if you haven't noticed. He was probably staked out across the street in a car. The man changes cars like other people change underwear—I've never seen him drive the same set of wheels twice, and every one of them is a damned arsenal."

"But if he was aiming at you—"

"He wasn't aiming at me," Mason said matter-of-factly. "Sniper shot's too good for a snitch. He wants to look me in the eyes first."

If it was possible to feel sicker, Leigh did.

"Your bodyguard was just in the way. Torr's been after me for six months now and he thought he finally had me—he wasn't going to let some goon spoil things. He would have taken you out too, if he got the chance, then faced me in the alley."

She shivered. "So why didn't he follow us?"

It was another stupid question.

Mason scanned the streets around them in every direction, as he'd been doing every third second since they got in the car. "I'm not so sure he didn't."

The hysteria thing reared its ugly head again, and Leigh fought it back down with a deep breath.

"Don't worry," he said gently, "we're going to get you out of this. Just tell me where the nearest police station is."

A warm flood of relief swept through her chest. So. He was going to turn himself in after all. Thank God. "That way," she pointed with a smile, "about four blocks to the right and two over."

He turned the car, and she felt her blood pressure falling. Everything would be all right. For Cara, too. Because as rattled as she was, she hadn't missed what Mason had said about being a snitch.

"Torr's out to get you because of that terrorist bomb thing, right?" she asked.

Mason turned his head quickly, eyes wide. "How the—"

She smiled. "I told you my detective friend was good."

He looked back at her with an expression that was hard to read. Two parts relief, one part embarrassment?.

"I'm not a snitch," he said defensively, "in general. But those people were crazy. They were going to blow up an elementary school."

Leigh's eyes widened. "How did you find out?"

He shrugged. "Torr and I had some business. Well, I guess you already know about that too, don't you? He wanted to get into counterfeiting. I guess the weapons profession had an off year. Anyway, he had a buddy who'd developed this bill-aging process, and he'd heard my plates were the best ever made. So he tracked me down at the bar."

"The Brindle Blur," she said proudly, feeling better now that the police station was only a block away. "Cute name."

He raised his eyebrows, but went on. "I normally stay away from guys like him, but the money was good, and it was no skin off my nose. All I had to do was give him the plates, plus a little advice about distribution. After that we were through, neat and clean.

"But I was with him when he got a call on his cell—making plans to hand off the explosives. He didn't know I was close enough to overhear, much less listen, of course, but if you're smart you listen to everything, and I've got good ears. I got enough of it to know when and where—and why."

"But the ATF guys didn't get him."

He shook his head. "And I split. I knew it was only a matter of time before he found me. Guys like him can't afford to be generous." He leaned forward and caught sight of the zone station a half block ahead. "Call it the snitch deterrent program."

"Where were you all that time?" she asked, willing them to the safety of the station ASAP.

"I was setting up a place in Florida," he said soberly. "Trude and I have had some rocky times, but the last few years we've gotten back to where we used to be. She was moving too—we were going to make a fresh start." A look of pain shot across his face. "But I wasn't quick enough."

He pulled in front of the station and began to scan the streets around them in every direction. Like most Wednesday nights in Pittsburgh, however, both cars and pedestrians were few and far between. "OK," he said finally. "Get out. And take care."

Leigh's heart dropped down into her feet. "What?"

"Get out," he insisted. "Quickly, before he shows up after all."

She sat still. "But, I thought—"

He exhaled loudly. "You just don't get it, do you? I'm sure Pittsburgh's finest are very nice people, but I pick my own friends, and they're not it. I've been in prison and I'm not going back."

Her heart raced. "But you haven't done anything!"

A flicker of something like sympathy passed through his blue-green eyes, and he tossed his head in the direction of the backseat. "Try possession of counterfeit plates, with intent to sell same." He looked at her with a small, sad smile. "Don't try to make me out to be something I'm not, Leigh. It's been tried before."

She stared back at him, her insides tying themselves in knots. "If I get out," she said quietly, "what will you do?"

He gave her the same look again, the one that seemed like sympathy. "Leave town," he said simply.

Leigh's mind flashed back to when she was fifteen,

and a thirteen-year-old Cara had told her she was staying at school late for French Club. Leigh had doubled back just to make sure and found her heading off with friends to ghost-hunt in a condemned building. Cara had gone home, but one of her friends had put his foot through the floor and earned fourteen stitches.

And when Cara had told Leigh about French Club, her left eyelid had drooped, just as it always did when she was lying.

Just as Mason's was doing now.

Leigh crossed her arms over her chest. "No, you're not," she said firmly. "You're going back to confront Torr. And I'm not going to let you."

Chapter 23

Mason's expression turned aggravated. "Get out. Now."

"No."

"Leigh, I mean it. You have to get out."

"No. He'll kill you."

"No, he won't. Well, maybe. Probably not. What does it matter? Get out."

"I'm not going anywhere."

Mason exhaled in frustration and scanned the streets again. "I appreciate your concern, really I do," he said in a softer voice. "But we both know I'm not worth it. It's my fault any of you became targets in the first place, and you're going to stay targets as long as—"

"As long as you're alive," Leigh finished determinedly. "Or as long as Torr is free. You keep forgetting the second part."

He shook his head. "They're not going to get him, don't you understand? Torr's given the fuzz the slip so many times . . . And even if they do get him in custody, they'll never get a conviction on any of the big stuff. He's covered his tracks too well. He'll be out on the street again in no time."

"But he's getting sloppy," Leigh argued. "You said so yourself. We both just witnessed an attempted murder. That's no small potatoes."

"Did you see him shoot?"

She didn't answer.

"No, you didn't."

"My mother saw him shoot at you, though—at my apartment."

That stopped him, but only for a moment. "I can't risk it, Leigh. If he ever gets out again he might come after—" He broke off suddenly. "Are you getting out?"

Her arms remained folded defiantly across her chest. "I told you, no."

After looking around the area one more time, he peeled the car away from the curb. "Fine, then. I will."

They rode in silence for a block, while Leigh puzzled over what he planned to do—and something else. She studied his face, which had not broken a sweat since they'd reached the car, but was now starting to shine again.

"Why can't you say her name?"

His voice was thin. "Whose name?"

"Your daughter's."

He looked away and swallowed. "Who says I can't?"

"Then say it."

He was quiet a long time, his eyes glued to the road. When he finally answered, his voice was a hoarse whisper. "Cara was my idea. Lydie wanted to call her Susannah."

Leigh's tight mouth lifted into a smile. Nothing else might be going right at the moment, but the look in his eyes made her heart float right back into place. It was all she needed to know. "You should meet her," she said determinedly.

He shifted his eyes away and shook his head. "No. Never. Lydie told me from day one that our daughter would be better off if she never laid eyes on me, and she was right."

"And how do you know that?" Leigh protested.

"Well, look at her!" he answered. "She grew up without me, and she's perfect. It stands to reason I could only have messed things up. No kid needs a criminal for a father."

"Maybe not," Leigh said carefully. "But you're forgetting something."

"No, I'm not. I've had thirty years to think about what's best for my daughter, and I've done it. Now," he said, his tone changing abruptly. "I'm going to stop this car in a second, and I'm going to get out, and you're not. You're going to drive straight back to the police station. Understand?"

Leigh ignored the last part of the speech. "What you're forgetting is that Cara isn't a little girl anymore. She's a grown woman, and she can make her own decisions about who she does and doesn't want to be a part of her life."

"Well, she sure as hell doesn't want me," he answered firmly.

"You don't know that."

He was about to answer when his eyes, which were looking out the rearview mirror again, suddenly widened. Leigh's heartbeat raced as she turned to look over her shoulder at the street behind. They were being followed by a small blue Toyota whose driver's head seemed to touch the roof.

"Bloody hell." Mason leaned a hand over the back seat and pulled up a green backpack. "OK," he said seriously, "here's what we're going to do. I'm going to pull into that next alley there and get out of the car. You're going to slide over here and drive straight back to the police station. Got it? No arguments this time. I mean it, kid."

Leigh felt her core body temperature dropping, but her brain was still operational. Or at least she thought it was. She sat up straight and covertly took a firm hold on one the backpack straps. "Cara needs you," she said forcefully.

"Don't be ridiculous!" he bellowed in frustration. "Just get ready to slide over. I can't swear he won't shoot at the car before I get clear, so you've got to get out fast. Are you ready?"

Panic swelled in Leigh as she watched the blue Toyota closing in quick. What could she do? Could she simply drive away, leaving the lamb to the slaughter? Mason might not be much of a lamb—he was more of an old ram with an attitude. But slaughter was slaughter.

"You can't go!" she cried, clinging to the backpack. She realized she was touching dangerously on that hysteria thing again, but this was hard. "I can't go back to Cara and tell her I just let the father she never met get shot to death! I can't and I won't."

He looked at her heavily as he pulled the car into an alley. "You don't have any choice." His voice turned softer. "Look, kid. I appreciate what you're trying to do for my daughter, I do. But don't fool yourself. Good looks and charm aside, I'm not much account."

The car began to slow. Leigh's pulse quickened, but she kept her voice calm. "You're ethically challenged, granted. But don't you think Cara has the right to decide for herself whether or not she wants to get to know you?" The car came to a stop. "If nothing else," Leigh finished desperately. "Doesn't she at least deserve the chance to look you in the face and tell you to go to hell?"

A tiny flicker of amusement ran through Mason's

anxiety-filled eyes, but he remained resolute. "It's too late. Sorry, kid."

He jumped out of the car in one quick movement, wrenching the backpack out of Leigh's unsuspecting hands. She sat frozen, watching him move rapidly away from the car and toward the wall of the alley. She also noticed for the first time that his left arm was bound just above the elbow with what looked like strips of a T-shirt. So much for seeking medical attention. Evidently, he figured it didn't matter.

And maybe it didn't. The Toyota, which had followed them into the alley from a half block behind, was creeping steadily forward.

It could crush him against the wall, Leigh thought in horror. She stayed low in the seat, trying not to be too much of a target, but she couldn't drive away. Not yet. She just couldn't. There had to be something she could do.

The image of Mason being run down by the Toyota gave her inspiration, and she clutched the steering wheel tightly. Would Torr get out of his car? Could she run *him* down?

She watched without breathing as the Toyota halted with a jerk, its engine still running. The door opened, and a tall, lanky man unfolded his legs from the front seat. Big lips aside, there was no doubt as to his identity. He was skinny enough to be Ichabod Crane, with awkward limbs, a stooped gait, and unruly dark hair. He said something to Mason, but Leigh couldn't hear. She cracked the window open.

"—in the car?" Torr was asking, gesturing towards the Tempo. His voice was thin—and unnervingly casual.

"Just a girl I picked up," Mason answered humorlessly, not looking at her. "I told her to take off, that I had business with you and that I'd see her later."

"Uh-huh," Torr said lazily. Leigh was fairly certain he had a pistol tucked under his arm, but if he did, he didn't want her to see it. "I don't see her leaving."

"She's just frazzled," Mason said coolly, now giving her a look that could kill of its own accord. "Pimp's on her case."

Under different circumstances, Leigh would have laughed. But her face was as frozen as her hands were to the wheel.

"Now, Mason Dixon, my friend," Torr said calmly, "You're forgetting that I saw that same little piece at that fine apartment building up in the 'burbs. She's not a hooker, is she? Of course not. She's your daughter."

Drive away now. The command was pummeling Leigh from inside and out—screaming at her from the tiny part of her brain that was still rational, and drifting to her telepathically from where Mason stood sweating against the wall. Her plan to run over Torr was useless—she couldn't possibly hit him unless he stepped in between the two cars, which would be incredibly stupid. He was still standing safely to the side of his own car, which, she noted dismally, he could get back into at any moment. Just as soon as the deed was done.

Drive away now.

What she would have done next she could only guess at, and in truth didn't really want to know. Because before she could react to Torr's accusation, another car drifted quietly into the alley, stopping just behind the blue Toyota.

"And who the hell is that?" Torr demanded angrily.

"How should I know?" Mason replied in kind.

Leigh was in the minority, and it was a lousy place to be. She knew exactly who was in the car, and the mere thought was carving an ulcer into her stomach lining.

The driver door of the purple Saturn swung open, and Cara leapt out in one fluid motion. She stopped short where she was, looking from Mason to Torr in silence.

Even in the dim light, Leigh could see Mason's face drain instantly of color. Torr gave the newcomer an unabashed once-over, then dissolved into laughter.

"Well, well," he said finally. "My mistake, old boy. Here's the old chip, eh? Come to save her papa. Touching. Very touching. But she's an idiot, just like the other one. Now toss those plates over here. I haven't got much time." He pulled the pistol from its nest under his arm and aimed it straight at Mason's head.

Mason's eyes darted desperately from Cara to Leigh, and Leigh could guess what he was thinking. Torr was going to take the plates and shoot the despised informant dead, that much was for sure. But the Toyota was now boxed in. He would have to make one of them move—or take one of their cars himself.

Neither option was desirable. Yet as Cara continued to stand quietly, not saying a word, Leigh began to see a ray of hope. Perhaps Dan was still with her, hiding in the seat? Perhaps the plan was for him to sneak out and get behind Torr. In any event, the police had to be on their way; she did have her cell phone.

Leigh allowed herself a deep breath. Stalling, that's what they were doing. Stalling until the police caught up. Still, it was terribly risky for Cara to just stand there like that.

"She's not my daughter," Mason said loudly.

Torr chuckled again. "Right. Then you won't mind

when I kill her, too. Nice Saturn . . . I've been meaning to get me one of those. Now toss me the plates, dead man."

Mason hesitated. Once Torr had the plates in hand and his mark disposed of, he could easily take off in the Saturn just by flinging Cara to the side—or worse. "Come and get 'em," Mason growled, holding the backpack to his chest. His eyes darted out toward the street, and Leigh surmised his next move with horror. He was going to make a run for it, to draw Torr away from the two of them. But he wasn't going to get very far.

Torr seemed to read his mind as well. "Go ahead," he said calmly, now aiming the pistol with both hands. "It'd be fitting if you died with a hole in your back. *Snitch*."

The next second was an hour long, as Leigh jumped helplessly up and out of the car with no plan, hoping against hope that in the very same instant Dan would spring from behind the Tempo and tackle Torr on the fly. It didn't happen. What did stop Torr's trigger finger was an incredibly high-pitched, Carol-Burnett-style Tarzan call, which burst from Cara's mouth and reverberated through the alley like a fire alarm.

Torr flinched with annoyance, but his gun remained trained on Mason. "Shut up!" he snarled.

Cara appeared beyond hearing. The Tarzan call was followed by an ear-splitting stream of gibberish as she moved in a wild, zigzagging fashion toward the back of her car.

She's hysterical, Leigh thought with renewed alarm. And she was almost certainly about to get shot.

The gunman remained cool, but growled irritably as he swung his head a few degrees toward Cara.

It was all the distraction Mason needed. In a flash

of movement, he wound up his arm and heaved the backpack. Torr recovered almost instantly, pulling the trigger just as the heavy pack slammed against his arm. The exploding weapon fell out of Torr's hands, and as a diving Mason plowed into his knees, both men fell roughly to the ground.

Leigh jumped forward, her eyes focused on the pistol that lay only a yard from where Torr was struggling to his feet. She reached it in an instant and without a second's hesitation kicked it as hard as she could. The gunman watched and swore as his weapon skittered across the rough asphalt and disappeared under the Saturn.

"Run!" Mason commanded, still grappling with Torr's long legs.

Purple with rage, Torr turned his attention away from the gun and fell full force on Mason's chest, knocking them both almost underneath the still-running Toyota. He grabbed for the other man's neck and encircled it with his bony fingers. "Die," he growled.

Mason made one short, sharp choking sound, and then became quiet. Torr's white knuckles quivered with pressure as they clamped on his opponent's throat, and Leigh held her own breath as Mason's complexion turned blue. Cara instantly swooped in behind her father's head, pulling at the offending hands with all her might, but to no avail. Mason's struggles had began to weaken.

Leigh stepped forward and aimed a vicious kick at Torr's thigh, but the blow earned only a wince, and since he was on top of Mason, his more vulnerable targets were out of range. For a moment, Leigh thought she could hear sirens approaching, but the sound was quickly drowned out by an angry bellow from Torr, who had apparently just taken the full complement of Cara's teeth in his left wrist.

He reared his head against hers and knocked her aside with a resounding whack, and as Cara fell backwards in a daze, Leigh's eyes caught sight of the fallen backpack. It had stopped to rest just in front of the Saturn, and in an instant she had collected it, heavy plates in tow.

Whether Torr could hear the same sirens she did was unclear, but given the noise from the Toyota engine and his single-minded effort to strangle his victim to death, she doubted it. He showed no signs of letting go, and Mason was no longer moving.

She pulled the canvas taut over the metal plates inside, raised the pack over her head, and brought it down on Torr's.

His limp frame rolled off Mason and to one side.

All at once the police seemed to be everywhere, and for a moment Leigh found she couldn't move. Then a strong hand clamped down on her shoulder. "You all right?" Maura asked loudly, looking her over.

Leigh nodded. Uniformed officers were swarming over the two men, and as she stepped closer to where Mason lay, she was relieved to see Cara kneeling beside him, her forehead bruised, but her eyes alert. She looked up at Leigh uneasily.

Mason still wasn't moving.

Chapter 24

"Are you all right?" Leigh asked her cousin as a team of EMTs began to labor over Mason.

Cara seemed calm enough, but her voice was disturbingly ethereal. "Of course I am. Are you?"

Leigh nodded, wondering if Cara's serenity was merely the backside of her earlier hysteria. A gurgled sputtering noise issued from the ground, and they both returned their attention to Mason.

"He's breathing," a heavyset female EMT announced.

Leigh exhaled, her body crumpling in a rush of relief. Cara started to move forward, but the EMTs pushed her back. "Stand clear, ma'am. We need room to work."

A dull moaning sound escaped from inside the other circle of uniforms, and within seconds it had escalated into Torr's full voice, erupting with a venomous string of threats. As the police struggled to subdue their charge, Leigh took her motionless cousin by the shoulders and pulled her away from the fray. Now that she knew everyone was breathing, the big picture was coming back attached to a giant question mark. "Cara," she began disbelievingly. "What are you doing here? Where's Dan?"

It took a moment for Cara's eyes to focus back on Leigh, but when they did, she seemed coherent enough. "He's with Ed. We saw the car"—she inclined her head in the direction of the Tempo—"peel out, but I couldn't tell who was in it. Just when we noticed the two of you weren't in the Saturn, Ed came crawling down the sidewalk. Dan forced him to lie down on the ground and I called an ambulance—but then I saw the blue car taking off." She nodded at the Toyota. "I got a pretty good look that time, and I knew it was Torr. I also knew he had to be chasing you and Mason."

Leigh's eyebrows rose. "So you jumped in the Saturn and started following him? By yourself?"

Cara looked at her as though she weren't very bright. "Well, what else was I supposed to do? Somebody had to keep Ed from losing any more blood, and I certainly couldn't pin the man down. And the police couldn't possibly get there quick enough to follow Torr. So I figured I would just tail him and report where he was going, which I did."

Cara's eyes fixed once more on Mason as the EMS team swarmed over him, a stretcher now at the ready. "Should we have someone look at that bruise on your head?" Leigh probed, still worried about her cousin's mental state. It didn't seem right that she could have gone from hysteria to attack mode to normalcy in the space of a few minutes, particularly with a blow to the noggin. "I think it might be a good idea—I mean, with everything that's happened, considering how upset you got back there . . ."

Cara's gaze turned quickly back on her cousin, and she rolled her eyes in disbelief. "Oh, for heaven's sake, Leigh. I thought that raving female thing only worked on men." As she watched her cousin's startled look, she gave a small, but halfway merry laugh. "You never did give me any credit as an actress. Still ticked off about that *Homecoming* thing, aren't you?"

Leigh was spared a response as Maura Polanski pushed her way through the ring of EMS workers around Mason. After a few words, she backed up and approached the women, her face relatively upbeat. "Looks like he's coming around," she said evenly. "He'll need some attention for a while, but Ruth thinks he's going to make it just fine, and Ruth knows her stuff."

Leigh smiled with relief. She expected a similar reaction from her cousin, but Cara simply stood still, watching as the team loaded Mason onto the stretcher. As they lifted it up and toward the ambulance, a sudden high-pitched yowl cut through the air, followed quickly by the appearance of two skinny fawn-colored paws next to Mason on the edge of the stretcher. "Money?" a gravelly voice croaked. "That you, boy?"

Leigh jumped forward and pulled the greyhound down, securing him with an arm wrapped firmly about his muscular chest. "Yes, it's him," she answered, grinning at Mason's off-color face. "We'll take care of him. You're going to be fine, too."

Mason had no chance to answer. The EMS team moved briskly toward the ambulance, and in another instant, he was gone. Leigh returned to Cara and sank down on the ground, her arms still around the greyhound. She didn't think he would go anywhere, but the truth was that her legs had started wobbling.

"The dog was in the car the whole time?" Leigh asked incredulously.

"Cowering on the floor under the dashboard," Cara answered distractedly. "I tried to get him out, but he wouldn't budge."

"This dog belong to one of you?"

Leigh looked up to see a tall, pale man in plain clothes clutching a pocket notebook.

"I'm taking care of him," Cara replied.

He nodded and extended his hand. Cara shook it. "Gerry Frank, City Homicide."

Leigh remained rooted to the spot, the bottom half of her body feeling at one with the cold pavement as the man met her eyes and offered one of his familiar, lopsided, crocodile smiles. She sighed. As if fleeing from an assassin wasn't enough for one night.

"Leigh Koslow," he said with a nod. "Glad to see you made it through this one."

She tried to smile back. Really, she did. "Frank," she said flatly. She considered herself a forgiving person, but it was hard to forget someone who had once falsely arrested her for murder—even if he had apologized afterwards.

"OK, women," Maura broke in loudly. And, Leigh couldn't help but notice, a bit nervously. "I know you're probably anxious to follow the ambulance to the hospital, but we need to go over a few things first."

She and Frank took turns questioning Leigh and Cara, and when finally the detectives seemed satisfied, the cousins loaded the greyhound into the Saturn and prepared to take off. But where they were going, Leigh wasn't sure. Cara put the keys in the ignition; then she simply sat.

"You sure you're OK to drive?" Leigh asked hesitantly.

Cara didn't look at her. She maintained the same quiet coolness she had shown ever since the police arrived. "You know," she said suddenly. "When I stepped out of the car earlier, I didn't know how he would react. I didn't really know what I was going to do, either."

Leigh nodded, willing her cousin to continue. Where Cara's mind had been since she had learned the whole truth about her father, Leigh could only guess. She certainly had not shown the relieved happiness Leigh had expected upon finding out about his clandestine visits. But with Cara, one never knew. Perhaps it was all just taking a while to sink in. Hadn't she just risked her life for the man?

"But then I saw the look on his face," she continued. "He saw me, and he looked terrified. Mortified, actually. He seemed angry that I was there. He was acting like . . ."

Her voice drifted off, and Leigh cut in. "Like a father," she finished. "He was acting like a father who was afraid for his daughter. And mad at himself for putting her in danger in the first place."

Cara's eyes narrowed thoughtfully. "Perhaps . . ."

She was interrupted by the melodious beeping of her cell phone, which was stashed in her purse by Leigh's feet. Leaning over, Cara retrieved it. "Hello?" She listened a moment but didn't respond, her eyes still distant and distracted. "Here," she said finally, handing the phone to her cousin. "It's your husband. He wants to know where you've been all evening."

How much time had passed, Leigh wasn't sure. They had waited outside the emergency room at Allegheny Central for what seemed like hours, but probably wasn't. Time always seemed to drag when you were waiting for news, particularly when no one seemed to feel like talking.

Lydie and Frances sat stiffly and silently next to each other. They looked even more alike than usual, Leigh thought idly, because Lydie's eyes were for once every bit as anxious as Frances's always were. Randall was sitting by his wife's side, making a valiant effort to read an eight-month-old copy of *Better Homes and Gardens*, and Gil was rooted to the next chair by a sleeping Mathias, who had passed out half over his father's arm and half over the adjacent end table. Warren had gone to bring everyone something to eat, and Leigh sat fidgeting, by herself. Torr was in custody, true, and the initial information they had gotten seemed to indicate that Mason's near strangulation wouldn't cause any lasting effects. But somehow the worst didn't seem over. Not with Cara pacing back and forth like a specter.

The double doors of the waiting room suddenly swung open, admitting Maura Polanski's considerable form. She nodded at the assembled family members and made a beeline for Leigh. "Any news?" she asked, sitting down.

Leigh shook her head. "What's happening on your end?"

Maura's cheeks had that odd pink glow again. "Well, Torrence Bagley's not the talkative type. But it won't matter. We have two witnesses to his attempt to kill Mason. Then there's the shot he took at your bodyguard, not to mention the shooting at your apartment."

Leigh sat up. "How is Ed?" She had heard that his wound wasn't life-threatening, but she was swamped with guilt that he had gotten hurt at all. Sure, it was a job, but if she hadn't insisted on leaving the car . . .

"I just talked to him," Maura answered. "His girlfriend was with him, and he seemed pretty perky. He told me in confidence that he'd been hurt plenty worse playing football, but didn't get near the sympathy."

Leigh smiled in relief.

"Anyway," Maura continued, "add the shootings here to all the stuff the ATF guys have been working on, and our buddy Torr will be going away for a long, long time."

Leigh nodded. She could easily make it through the rest of her life without laying another eye on Jagger-lips. "And Mason? Is he in trouble?"

Maura tilted her head in a half shrug. "That's iffy. We suspect he was planning to sell the counterfeiting plates, but we don't know that money changed hands for that purpose. There's possession, but since ATF will need Mason to testify against Torr for the bomb sale, I don't think it'll be an issue."

"Polanski?" A voice called from the door. "Can I talk to you?"

Somewhere in the depths of Leigh's mind, a very tiny, but very loud, alarm began to sound. *Polanski.* It was the voice. The voice she had been trying so hard to identify. The voice that had picked up Maura's phone when she had called her on election night.

Gerald Frank.

"Yeah," Maura responded, rising. Then she looked at Leigh. "What's wrong? You look like you've seen a ghost."

Leigh rose slowly to her feet, staring at her friend in horror. *Maura . . .* and Detective Frank! He was forty years old if he was a day, half his hair was gone, and sure, he seemed honest and had that rapier sarcastic wit, but still—he had arrested her!

"Koslow?" Maura repeated, sounding a little anxious this time. "Something wrong?"

She was saved from answering by Warren, who had pushed past Detective Frank with a load of drinks and snacks. He took one look at Frank, Maura, and Leigh and immediately inserted himself between the two women. "Here are your Chee-tos," he said cheerfully, handing his wife a bag. "And Mo, don't have any BBQ chips, but how about a root beer? Your favorite, compliments of the house."

"No, thanks." Maura looked worriedly at Leigh for another moment, then turned toward the door. "I'll be around for a while yet if you need me." Frank held the door open, and they walked out together.

Warren delivered the remainder of the tray's contents to Frances and Lydie, then grabbed both his wife's hands and sat her down.

"Frank—" Leigh began weakly.

"Yes, I know," he interrupted. "He arrested you. We've heard. But he's not a bad guy, really. And Maura says he makes her laugh. So this is a good thing. Right?"

"But—"

"Have you noticed how happy she's been?"

"But—"

"Well, have you?"

"Yes, but—" Leigh stopped herself. Maura had seemed pretty darned happy.

"Dublin family?" A short, dark-complected man with a Middle-Eastern accent had entered the room from the other end, and all eyes fastened on him at once. "That's us," Lydie answered. Cara stopped pacing, but said nothing. Everyone but Gil rose.

"I am Dr. Paydar," the man said pleasantly. "Mr. Dublin is awake now. He is a very lucky man. If he had gone much longer without oxygen, I'm afraid we might be talking about brain damage—or worse. But so far there's no evidence of any permanent injury. Just some bruising of the throat and a mild concussion—evidently from his head striking the pavement." The doctor frowned slightly. "He had a previous bullet wound in his arm; we've treated that too, of course."

"Then he'll recover?" Lydie asked, her face still tight.

Dr. Paydar smiled patiently. "He'll be good as

new . . . as long as there are no more bullets. You can see him now, but only one at a time. He was asking for . . ."

It seemed as though they all leaned forward, waiting for him to remember the name. Would he ask to see Cara? And if he did, would she even go?

"Lee," the doctor finished triumphantly. "Is there a Lee here?"

Leigh stepped up hesitantly. She threw a glance at Cara, but her cousin wouldn't meet her eyes. "That's me."

The doctor waved her through the door, and she followed him to a partially open cubicle where Mason lay on a stretcher, his upper arm bandaged and his face pale and splotchy. His eyes, now disturbingly bloodshot, watched her approach with apprehension as he struggled to lift his head. "Are you two all right?" he asked.

His voice wasn't as weak as she had expected, but his lips were tight with pain. She motioned for him to relax. "Don't try to roll your head around. It hurts." She smiled. "I know these things."

"But are—"

"We're fine," she interrupted. "Cara's fine. Lydie and Frances and Randall are all out in the lobby with her—plus Gil and Mathias, of course. And you thought you weren't popular."

He smiled, but only a little. "Does she—Do you think she wants—"

"Does your daughter want to see you?" Leigh finished.

He nodded stiffly, then seemed to change his mind. "No, never mind. She wouldn't."

Leigh smiled. "Rule number one of Cara Dublin March: never try to guess what she's thinking," she chastised good-naturedly. "You'd be wrong, and it'd only tick her off anyway. She likes to be unpredictable."

He looked at her in confusion. "So you think—"

"I think you need to find out how she feels for yourself," Leigh said firmly. "You should have called her in here, not me."

He seemed to consider a moment. She watched various emotions flicker across his face, not the least of which was sheer panic, and a chuckle escaped her. "Mason Dublin," she taunted. "You mean to tell me you had no problem facing an armed assassin in a dark alley, but you're scared to death of a good, old-fashioned, female tongue-lashing?"

He looked at her in guilty misery, and she laughed out loud.

"You don't understand," he protested. "She's got to be furious at me for not being there—all those years. Even if she has been told why."

"I understand perfectly," Leigh retorted. "In fact, I'd say she's a veritable volcano of rage. But you know what?"

He looked at her questioningly.

"That's *tough.* Maybe giving you a good tongue-lashing is just what she needs."

After a moment, Mason's eyes warmed, and Leigh thought she saw a little of the twinkle come back. "She's a brilliant actress, isn't she?" he said proudly. "That screaming . . . it rattled Torr good."

Leigh's admiration was tinged with disgust. "You knew she was acting?"

He looked surprised. "Sure. Didn't you?" He paused a moment, his voice turning sober again. "She could have gotten herself killed, Leigh, and so could you. Trudy almost did die. All on account of a two-bit criminal like me." He swallowed. "I can never make that up to any of you."

"Well," she said brightly. "We'll let you try, anyway. I just snuck up to see Trudy a few minutes ago, and she's in much better spirits knowing you're safe. Maybe tomorrow you two can share some lemon drops. As for Cara, she's right outside. Now are you going to ask to see her, or not?"

He hesitated. "She's got to hate me," he said quietly.

"Maybe she does," Leigh said, smiling encouragement. "But I doubt she will forever."

Per request, Warren checked his watch again. "Forty-five minutes now. You think it's a good sign?"

Leigh's brow furrowed. "I wish I knew."

Now that Mason was out of the woods, there was no medical reason for the combined March, Koslow, and Harmon families to remain camped out in the waiting room. But after Mason had asked to see Cara, and after she had hesitated a full ten minutes before going in, and now that they had been alone together for a full forty-five minutes, no one could bear to leave until they knew the end of it.

"I'm sure it will work out all right," Warren said optimistically, giving Leigh's shoulders a squeeze with his long arm. "You want something else from the machine?"

She sat up. "Yes, but I'll get it. I need to stretch." She asked around for any requests, then headed out the door and down the hallway. The cafeteria was closed for the night, but her innate homing mechanism led her straight to a candy machine. She had just inserted her first quarter when a loud, merry sound drifted to her ears from around the corner. It was a laugh. Maura's laugh. Hearty, husky, uninhibited, and thoroughly mixed with the chuckles of one

Gerald Frank. Leigh turned around mechanically and walked back to where she had come from, forgetting the lost quarter, much less the Kit Kat.

Warren eyed her empty hands suspiciously as she sat back down. "No chocolate left?"

"You're right," she said, not listening. "He does make her laugh."

Her husband smiled. "So it's a good thing, right?"

She sighed, then looked back at him with a smirk. "I guess I can't very well hold a grudge against *every-one* who arrests me."

"Sweetheart!" Lydie exclaimed suddenly, jumping to her feet. They all watched as Cara strode back into the room, fifty-five minutes after she had left it.

"Is everything OK, honey?" her mother asked tentatively.

Cara smiled at her. "Of course." She walked over to where her husband sat and lifted Mathias gently from his arms. The toddler stirred, confusion blurring his sleepy blue-green eyes, but he didn't protest as his mother shifted him onto her hip.

"Come on, big guy," she said soothingly, giving him a little bounce. "Let's go meet your grandpa."